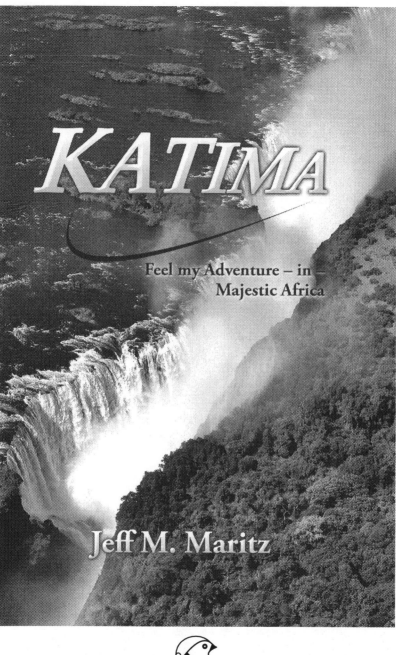

KATIMA

Feel my Adventure – in –
Majestic Africa

Jeff M. Maritz

PARTRIDGE
A Penguin Random House Company

Copyright © 2015 by Jeff M. Maritz.

Library of Congress Control Number:		2015941536
ISBN:	Hardcover	978-1-4828-3153-5
	Softcover	978-1-4828-3152-8
	eBook	978-1-4828-3154-2

Print information available on the last page.

To order additional copies of this book, contact
Toll Free 800 101 2657 (Singapore)
Toll Free 1 800 81 7340 (Malaysia)
orders.singapore@partridgepublishing.com

www.partridgepublishing.com/singapore

Introduction

My Weird Life

Before Katima

I am Mike. All the events that happened to me when I was a young boy are kind of branded in my head. In an instant, my life changed, and I experienced majestic Africa.

It was like a light was turned on, and I could see and remember everything in a clear image.

I was born in Northern Rhodesia (Zambia) in a small town called Mutulira. The area is known as the Copper Belt. We were living on the outskirts in one of the towns, Chingola. Nearby there were two other towns, Kitwe and Ndola. My folks were in the copper-trading business, and their job was making wall plaques and bangles and such. Times were good, and we lived a lavish lifestyle.

On many weekends, my folks would have *braai* (barbecue) parties at our large colonial-style house. At this time in my life, my dad, Daniel, discovered my mother, Mary, was having an affair. All hell broke loose, and like a sorry, sad hurricane wind blowing through our good lives, everything changed.

My brother, sister, and I were put in boarding school in Salisbury in Southern Rhodesia. We were there for around six months while my folks tried to sort out their messed-up lives.

They did stay together, but the boozing became an everyday event. One strange day in mid-November, we were taken out of the boarding school. My father said, "We are going back to South Africa," and that was that. Our dismal lives became even worse.

Like see-saw gypsies, we left Rhodesia. On the route to Durban in South Africa, we were put in another boarding school in a town called Stanger. I hated the place, and the kids at school and those sleeping in my dormitory

1

bullied me many times. This was a sad time in my life. I planned many times to run away, but I never did.

We stayed in Stanger until end-of-year holidays, and then, like a tornado touching down, our drunken folks took us back into their messed-up lives. They were living in Durban. We stayed nine months in this coastal city. We lived in a rundown flat that was one street from the main beach.

I learned how to surf the waves that crashed with force on the long, curved Durban beach. I was now a wild coastal boy, and using slang in my speech was the norm. My folks were consistently drinking, like two drowsy fish in a brandy bottle. Their drunken episodes were disgusting, and the fights and my mother's screams were horrific to hear.

Our lives were going down the toilet and at that time in our lives we were very poor and the future looked bleak.

One funny day, my dad was caught drunk driving and had to appear in court the following day. Instead, bags and boxes were packed, and we made a run for it. We left most of our belongings in the flat, only taking our clothes and a few items.

We departed Durban by stealing a hired car. We traveled nonstop toward Brakpan, near Johannesburg. The distance north was around 650 kilometers.

It was like a second tornado had touched down in Brakpan. Our sorry sad folks, who did not care much for their kids, left us stranded at our paternal grandma's. Her nick name was "the Battle-Ax" and her screeching voice would send shivers down my spine. The Battle-Ax was schizophrenic, and that bothered me.

During the year and a half that we lived at Grandma's house, I became very close friends with my good-looking cousin Zoé. We would go to the malls and have lots of fun.

We didn't see our folks for more than a year and a half, but my life seemed so happy—it suddenly changed from good to bad.

At the end of the second year, just before Christmas, my sorry, hopeless folks arrived and took us away from the Battle-Ax. We were going to live with them in Pretoria, the capital of South Africa. I was heartbroken and thought, *Why is all this shit happening to me?* For the next three years, we lived in Pretoria in the most horrific, poor conditions imaginable. We moved around from one suburb to the next, and I was in four different schools in three years.

At one time, we were two adults, three kids, and two small dogs, living and sleeping in a car. We were down and out, with no food to eat. We were close to death's door. I was so skinny that the kids at school called me "skeleton boy." My torn and tattered school clothes were a sight to see. All the kids kept their distance from me. I looked awful, like I had a disease. I was in such a state that death was not far away.

One strange day, our female dog had a litter of five pups. The following day after school, my father told us, "The two dogs went to the SPCA, and the five puppies went to heaven." Steve and Elise, my brother and sister, were crying and feeling sad. I could not cry, and my thoughts were that maybe some kind folks would adopt the two dogs. At least they would live and eat well. *Or maybe they would be put to sleep,* I thought. *Good-bye cruel world.*

After the dogs were gone, there were some days when we had no food to eat. Steve, Elise, and I ate the bag of leftover dog food.

My dad eventually sold the car for very little money. We moved into a rundown boarding house. It was the beginning of the worst time in my life. We were so poor that after school was out, Steve, Elise, and I would put on our torn and tattered clothes and go to the streets, begging for food or money.

Life can be so strange. In those years the black, Indian, and Chinese cultures were known as third-class citizens. Being a poor white boy and in the state that I was in, we were treated as "white trash."

I was in a confused state.

While begging for food or money at the white folks' restaurants, the owners or service personnel would come out and chase us away. The English fish-and-chips takeaway places were the worst. The English staff would chase after me while whacking me with a cane as I tried to get away. They would hatefully shout, "Bugger off!" It was only a fucking takeaway joint that smelled of bad fish and oily chips anyway, but at that time in my life, I hated the English.

Steve was always doing his own thing. Elise and I would beg for food wherever we could. Elise and I found a Chinese takeaway restaurant where they threw away all their leftover food. While we were begging for food, a big Chinese Sumo-sized chef felt pity for us. He put some of the leftover food in a large carton and saved it for us.

When the restaurant closed at around 11:00 p.m., he would come out of the back entrance of the Chinese restaurant and give us the leftover food carton for free. We would sit on the back step and gobble the Chinese food. The Sumo Chinese chef guy would look at Elise and me, shake his head, and laugh at us.

Life can be so strange. The Chinese folks were condemned to live in the same cities or towns as the white apartheid folk. And it was one of them who gave the poor, underprivileged white kids their leftover food to eat for free. Life can be a bitch.

It was in the middle of August when the shit hit the fan.

On this awful day, our lives changed forever. Elise and I came home from school and found my father all bashed up. He was knocked out cold, lying in his bloodied bed. My mother was not there; she was missing. Elise and I went looking for her.

At one door, we were told by an ugly, drunken, fat-slag cow of woman, who reeked of alcohol and tobacco, "Your mother, Mary, is in the front room with some biker dudes." She talked to us without her false teeth in her slithering mouth.

We made our way to that front room. The door was slightly ajar, and we saw my mother lying on the bed, passed out, with three biker dudes. There was a stench of boozing and pot smoking, and there were blood stains and spilled brandy on the floor.

It was so toxic that I almost threw up.

When you are a little kid and you witness such extreme events, everything seems to accelerate. We left that room and walked down the passageway, crying and not knowing what to do. Someone called the police. Our dismal lives suddenly hit rock bottom.

On that same afternoon, the police came by and took us away from our miserable parents. At the police station, a welfare lady signed some documents, and we were forcefully taken to a reform home known as "the Govie."

This place was cold and eerie-looking. It was known as the most notorious joint in South Africa; it was the bottom of the pit. This place became my hell on earth.

Before we ended up in this joint, we were free to do whatever we liked. Suddenly, we were locked up in this jaillike dormitory, with double burglar bars on all the windows. All the boys in this reform home were alien looking. They sized us up with their hollow ghostlike stares. Most of the young boys were druggies, and some were child rapists.

Steve and I were lucky; we were allowed to go to a normal school nearby while enduring the hell in the Govie joint.

From the first day in that awful place, there were daily fights. On every Friday night after lights out, there was a fight challenge. This happened in the seniors' room, and it was either boxing or wrestling. I was always picked on by a toothless, bad druggie boy named Tommy, and he consistently challenged me to a fight.

At school, my buddy Jerry showed me his karate moves, and each day, he would bring me an energy supplement drink in a flask.

I was a bit stronger than Tommy, so on every Friday challenge, I took him down. I was lucky to have my brother in the joint with me, and somehow God protected me. I was never raped.

Near the end-of-term holidays, I was in a panic, knowing that school was going to close for the year. During the first week of holidays in the Govie joint, I was living on the edge. Before I fell asleep at night, I pleaded with God, "Help me, please."

I was in a panic, and all that I could think of was, *I want to get out of here, and I want to die.*

Just before the end of term, my buddy Jerry had given me a shaving blade and a small vegetable knife. One night—and on the three nights that followed—I put the blade against my vein to cut my wrists. In the Govie joint, there were two girls in my life—Beatrix and my loving cousin Zoé'. These two girls saved me from ending my life.

I wondered why the welfare had put us in the Govie joint. On the last Saturday night in the joint, endless tears flowed down my cheeks. I was in a shocking condition and a dismal state of mind.

When the lights went out, I put the razor blade against my wrist. I could feel the pain and see the blood trickling from my arm. I wondered, *Should I kill myself now or wait until Sunday night?* Through my tears, I decided to wait until Sunday to end my life. I don't know why, but I gave myself one more day to endure all the pain in that shit-hole place. I could not sleep well on Saturday night. I woke up many times in a kind of panic.

On Sunday morning before breakfast, my whole body felt completely drained and tired. I heard thunder and saw that outside our dormitory, it was pouring rain. On this wet and rainy morning, everyone in the dormitory left me alone. No one talked to me.

After our crappy breakfast, I was lying on my bed, staring into space, thinking of death. Later on in the morning, an official summoned me to go to the superintendants office. I thought, *what have I done wrong now?*

As we walked down the shiny passage in the square building, toward the Sup's office, an ice-cold feeling went through my body. I felt agitated, and it bothered me.

We approached the two large wooden benches that were just outside of the superintendants large office. A lady was sitting on the bench to the right. As I walked closer to her, she stood up and said, "I am from the welfare." She took my hand, giving it a slight squeeze. I was confused. This was not the same lady from welfare that I knew. I sat down on the bench next to her. *What now?* I thought.

I remember feeling all hyped up and thinking, *this is the end of my life. I should have cut my wrists last night.* I wondered if she was going to take me to hell. *For sure they are going to throw me in the hot pit. I am a goner, and I am going to burn.*

I looked dreadful for I'd hardly had any sleep the night before. I was so weak, and my body was aching all over. I had huge ghastly black rings around my bloodshot eyes. There were bruises on my arms and a few cut marks on my face and lips from all the fights that I'd had over the past week. I had lost some weight because I wasn't eating well. I was in a shocking state from having worries all the time. I had an irritating cough, and every now and then my body would give a slight shiver, kind-of-a twitching motion all the time. My life was going farther down the toilet.

While I was sitting on the bench next to the welfare lady, I stared straight in front of me. My hands were shaking, and I was wondering what was going on. The welfare lady did not talk to me at all, but she glared at me as if I were a piece of shit.

I felt like I sat there for a long time, but I saw the Sup's office door open. Ben van-den Haas was standing in the doorway. He said in a very nice manner,

"Come inside, son." I looked up at him wondering why he was so nice and calling me son.

I thought, *he last time you saw me, you harshly scolded me. You … you … you are full of sh-sh-shit.* Thoughts continued to race through my head. *Why is this welfare lady here? Where is she going to take me? Is Steve coming too? Why am I here? What is going on?*

I stood there in front of Ben's office as if I was going to enter the gates of hell.

I must have stood there for about ten seconds; I was so scared. I stared at the open door that led into the office. I started to walk forward. As I slowly entered the room, a lady, all nicely dolled up, was standing next to one of the chairs. She had dark red hair and wore a stylish hat. I looked at her with my mouth open and asked, "Who are you?"

She looked at me with amazement. Shaking her head, she said, "I am your aunt Caroline, your mum's eldest sister. I have come to take you kids away from here." I stood there, staring into space. I could not believe what I had just heard. Endless tears flowed down my cheeks.

I began to sob loudly and could not stop. Aunty Carry grabbed me and held me to her. At that moment, Elise came in the office. A few minutes later, Steve walked in. Steve was also a little bashed up from all the fights that he'd had. He never did show any emotion, but I knew that he was glad we were leaving this place.

I so shocked that I wondered, *is one of my dreams, or is it true?*

From one hour to the next, documents were signed and our hair was cut. We were given the clothes we had been wearing when we first entered the gates of hell.

Like a wind blowing through our shitty lives, we were gone. I finally left the Govie joint. There were no good-byes, no handshakes, nothing. Aunty Caroline drove us away from Pretoria and toward a new adventure, to a place known as the Vaal-Triangle. One city and two towns made up the triangle over the Vaal River and were not far from one another.

I felt exhilarated and kept thinking one word: *Freedom.* I could not grasp the luck that had entered our lives.

My brother lived at Aunt Carry's house for one year; my sister and I lived there for two years. Aunt Carry was always complaining, and her screams were like a fire hydrant going ballistic. She was known as the "Carry Bitch." My life was free but boring.

There was something wrong with my cousin Tina. She was always in a sort of trance, rocking back and forth on a chair in the living room. My aunt and uncle worked during the week and on Saturdays. It was free time for me, though, and I always thought how lucky I was. Aunt Carry never knew about my almost ending my life. I always had a soft feeling in my heart for my aunt and uncle for taking us away from my hell of a life in the Govie.

My school time was approaching, and my sister and I were put in boarding school known as the Hostel. I was sent there on two separate occasions, and I was happy to be away from my weird family. The hostel was the best time in my school life.

In my entire school life, I was in nineteen different schools. My folks were the extreme having us live in so many city's and towns. The path that we were going on was thorny and sad.

Just before school ended for the year I was seventeen years old and drafted into the army in the Armored Devision. I was to report for duty in one month's time on 7th January 1974.

Like a wind dying down, school was over, and I was back with my weird family for a month.

In the December holidays, I started my mechanical engineering trade at a large iron and steel corporation known as Iscor.

January seemed to arrive in a flash, and I was on a Greyhound coach, traveling from Vanderbijlpark towards Johannesburg where the army headquarters is based.

This was the time in my life when I was on a path leading to where I would experience majestic Africa.

Someone in the heavens had given me a break.

Chapter One

My Time in Tempe

You Are in the Army Now

While I was traveling on the bus toward Johannesburg (Jo-burg), I felt lonely and strange. I had thousands of thoughts about my weird experiences in the Vaal Triangle towns.

It took around two hours to get to Jo-burg bus depot. I had to get on another bus to the army headquarters. When I arrived there, I was amazed at how large it was. After registration, I was told to gather out front with the other guys who were standing out there. We all looked weary and frightened. The army does not stop for anything. From one moment to the next, we were told to board the rows of Bedford trucks that would take us to the Jo-berg train station. We were over two hundred souls, leaving on a train to Bloemfontein. The journey was overnight, and we were scheduled to arrive there early the next morning.

It was my first trip on a train. I will never forget the rail track noise: *ke-tuc, ke-tuc, ke-tuc, ke-tuc*. All the sleeper compartments had six people in them. I was lucky to have the middle bunk. While traveling at night through the towns, I lay on my bunk, looking out of the compartment window. I could see all the sparkling lights flickering in the distance. My heart was beating fast and the grown-up feeling of being by myself felt weird.

All of us on the train felt wild and free. Some of the lads had beers with them; I bought two beers off one chap.

It was way past one o'clock in the morning when I finally crashed for the night. I could not sleep and could feel blood pumping though my veins. The excitement and adrenaline made me feel lightheaded. I must have had a few hours' nap and woke up feeling nervous. After another hour or so, we reached Bloemfontein.

It was just after five in the morning—still dark—when we arrived at the train station. The cool morning breeze sent shivers down my spine. My heart was pounding wildly, knowing that soon my life would change forever.

I saw many army personnel standing on the station platform, waiting for our arrival. I was one of the first souls to exit the train. It was a weird feeling when we left the train and assembled on the train station platform. We heard the sergeant major screaming at the top of his lungs. "You are in the army now! Stand straight, get in line, shut up, move, and stand in formation!"

This is it, I thought. *My life is now in control of whoever is telling me to do this or that.* I was well prepared because of my time in the Govie. I thought, *Here we go again. Why is there always all this screaming and shouting in my weird life?*

Everyone was in a panic—except me. I don't know why, but I felt calm and normal. It was like I was moving in slow motion while everyone else was speeding up and running around me like jackrabbits.

We were shuffled into a four-abreast formation. Within minutes, we marched down the platform and out of the train station. We were loaded like cattle into army Bedford troop-carrier vehicles, which were parked one street away from the train station.

I was in a strange city where everything looked different. I was lucky to be the last man on the bench seat near the flap of the open-back Bedford. I had a good view and could see where we were traveling, which was to a section of Bloemfontein called Tempe. This was where all the army barracks were located.

When we entered the suburb of Tempe, I noticed that all the camps were huge, and it seemed like a town in itself. All the guys on the train that came from Jo-burg were in the armored division. On one side of our camp was the South African Infantry (SAI) Division, known as "Free Troopers." They wore green berets. The paratroopers were on the other side of us; they were known as the "Para-Bats." They wore blue berets. The armored division was known as the "Panzer." We wore black berets. The armored division camp had two battalions. I was part of the Two Special Service Battalion, known as the 2-SSB.

The Bedford in which I was riding stopped at the main boom gate and proceeded to park behind the mess hall, canteen and officers' quarters.

We all dismounted and formed a line. The sergeant major called out our names and our assigned sleeping bungalow number. I was lucky because my bungalow was halfway up the row of buildings and in the center position of the camp. The SSB camp was huge, and I discovered that twenty-two of us would sleep in each bungalow.

From the main-door entrance, my metal frame bed was the third bed from the back wall on the right. This was a good position because the bungalow corporal would always come in through the front entrance. The showers and toilets were directly behind our bungalow. A hard gravel road was between the rows of bungalows. From the main mess hall, canteen, and officers' quarters, there were nine bungalows leading backward, seven wide. If all the bungalows were full of guys, there would be close to 1,400 armored division guys here. In those years, women did not sign up for the army.

It seemed as if I was in luck for our 2-SSB corporal and sergeant seemed to be okay. It was crew-cut-time, shaving all our hair off, number-one baldy style. It was strange seeing the lads with long hair and seeing them afterward with a bald-style haircut.

We received our brown army gear and our R-1 (7.62mm) rifles, with cleaning kit, webbing, and eight extra empty magazines.

After lunch we had to do some aptitude tests to find out which individual training was best for us. This army stuff happened fast. We never had time to think of what would happen next.

In the afternoon, after tea-break at four o'clock, we had to hand in our civilian clothes. We tagged our suitcases with our addresses and handed them to a sergeant to store for us in a warehouse. We were now all dressed in our "browns." It was then that we knew, as the song goes, "You're in the army now."

I was sectioned with twenty-one other guys in bungalow 33. The bungalow floors were super-shiny, and a dark green metal cupboard stood next to each bed. There was hanging space on one side of the cupboard and drawers on the other, as well as a space for boots.

On the first night, the bungalow lights automatically went out at nine forty-five. I was feeling strange and nervous as hell. I lay on a very hard mattress bed and thought of how extreme my life had been. When the room was dark and quiet, I lay in bed, preparing myself to handle whatever the army threw at me. Some of the young lads were quietly crying.

It took me a while to fall asleep, but my strange first day in the army had come to an end.

On Sunday morning, the lights came on at exactly six o'clock. I always have been an early riser and was first to make my way out the back door to have my shower. The shower area was huge with space for around twenty guys to shower in one open area.

Breakfast started at seven o'clock, after which, we formed a line and proceeded to a large lecture room. This was in the front section of the camp, where the officers' quarters were located. I was impressed with how organized the army operated. Everything worked in a systematic way. We did more written tests until lunch. We also had some top-brass guys give us a speech and inform us on what was expected from us in the army's Special Service Battalion.

After lunch we had to assemble behind the large mess hall. We were marched out the front gate to the large sports fields opposite our camp. The area was at least two kilometers long and around half a kilometer wide.

We were sectioned as two bungalows together in a forty-four man marching troop formation. Our group was bungalows 32 and 33 together.

We were positioned next to each other in the different height category, the tallest at both ends and the shortest in the middle. I had a good position, third from the front and the far left side. All through the afternoon, we were trained to take a certain length step and to march together in sequence. At first it seemed as if we were a bunch of idiots, and it seemed to be "mission impossible."

We were all exhausted from the heat and the continuous three-hour March training. A few lads passed out and were seated to one side to have water and recuperate. The rest of us had to carry on until the marching time was up. We all felt like dead ducks from the hot summer sun beating down on us and the consistent marching up and down—we marched until five o'clock in the afternoon, and that first day's marching took its toll on all of us.

After dinner, we had more lectures until eight o'clock. We had our showers and time to recuperate after the first day's events. This army stuff was tough on a young boy coming from "Civilian Street."

On the Monday morning, our basic training officially started. At four thirty, the lights came on. I was in a daze when I heard our bungalow corporal shouting at us, "Get up, and get up. You're in the army now." All the blankets were pulled off our bodies, and we were told inspection would be at five fifteen and we were to be ready. We all had a fast shower and got dressed in our army gear.

The beds had to be made up in a specific box style. Our brown towel was to be open and at the bottom portion of the bed. Our army utensils, Dixies (Rectagular aluminium cooking pots), knife, spoon, fork, toothpaste and brush, and comb were all laid out on the towel. Everyone had to be in the same form position and style.

Our rifle and webbing was hanging off end of the bed. Our magazines were propped out of the webbing. Oh gosh, everything had to be super-clean and in a certain position.

When our sergeant came in for the first morning's inspection at exactly five fifteen, it was pitiful. From the third bed onward, beds were not in good order. The sergeant ripped up the beds that did not look satisfactory to him, until he went through all of us. I was lucky for my bed seemed to be okay and was not ripped up. When he was done, he shouted in a loud, screeching voice, "Thirteen beds not done properly! obstacle course, for all of you after PT. In the army, we all work together."

At 5:45 a.m., we all had to gather into formation in our PT (physical training) gear in front of our bungalows. We were marched to the main gate, crossed the road, and gathered on the sports field. Our first day's physical training was around half an hour long. Little did we know that it was only a warm-up exercise for what was going to follow. It was push-ups, sit-ups, arm and leg stretching, jack-knives, and so on.

We had to gather at the main gate for a fifteen-kilometer run. *Oh shit*, I thought. *What are they doing to us? Fifteen kilometers on the first day's run? They are killing us.*

The route was around all the army camps and over a large hill. I was pretty fit for I had done a lot of sports activities while I was at school. The guys who smoked were the worst off.

The route was exactly fifteen kilometers long and was marked off with white paint on oval stones placed on the side of the road. Half of the distance was on the tar road, and the other half was on gravel on a hilly terrain. There were many up-hills and down-hill areas on this running route.

When the order was given to run, I looked at my wristwatch—it was six thirty in the morning, and we were running! I started off around the middle of the pack, but I passed the sergeant at the painted line across the road. He was standing with his stopwatch in hand as we crossed the white line.

While running, I figured out that the white stones along the path were spaced evenly. I knew that they were a hundred meters apart—I had counted the white stones, but I was smart and kept the information to myself.

I paced my running strides at a reasonable speed. After the first five clicks, I was at the top of the middle bunch. We ran up a hill and entered the gravel-and-bush terrain. We had gone around one-third of the distance.

I suddenly got a stitch on my side; and my gut had a cramp in it. Damn, it hurt. It was weird, because as I slowed down to a fast walk, I farted, and suddenly my cramp was less. I thought, *I just needed to release the morning breakfast's bad-eggs fart that was churning my stomach.*

Around that time I looked at my watch and figured out that I was around sixty seconds ahead of the time given for the trail run. I felt better and got my second wind. I started to speed up my strides and passed many guys who were walking.

Every now and then pain on my side returned. I released more air from my gut, and the fart smell was bad. It must have been old eggs.

During the uphill and downhill terrain, I lost a bit of time. My legs felt the pain, and I knew that I was not in good shape. Still, I was keeping up with this ten-man group of guys, running together.

On the last four kilometers, the tar-road section, I got my third breath and started to overtake a lot of guys who were walking and out of breath.

I kept the pace with five others in a group. In the distance at our main gate, the sergeant was looking at his watch as the guys passed him. It was a bit nerve-racking, and my feeling was that I must make it before the time allotted. I didn't want to go through the obstacle course for being late.

Our group ran faster as we approached the end line painted across the road. As I crossed the line, the sergeant looked at his watch. I looked at my watch and saw we were around ninety seconds ahead of the time allowed. I was out of breath but knew that most of the guys were slower than the time allowed.

We were sectioned to one side to rest on the grass field. I sat on the grass with around 40 percent of the camp's guys. I was totally out of breath but my body was hyped up, full of adrenaline. I felt the heat releasing from my exhausted body, and the blood gushing through my heart, which gave me a slight pain in my chest.

We saw the slower runners being sectioned off to a different area on the sports field. Their names were logged in a book, and they were immediately marched to the basic obstacle course behind the bungalows.

There were two obstacles courses, and the basic course was the easier one. A more extreme course was in the woods behind our camp—that would separate the boys from the men.

All was good. I seemed to fit in the army like a round peg.

We had our showers, rested, and had breakfast. After breakfast, it was lectures and rifle-assembly training. After lunch, daily marching was the norm until four thirty. Dinner was at five and more lecture training until eight. After the lectures were over, our bungalow was put through the basic obstacle course at night because of our dismal inspection that morning.

On that first week of extreme basic training, we were all exhausted every day from the nonstop training. Some of the boys were crying and saying, "I can't take this anymore." I also felt the pain, and my legs hurt from the morning PT running exercise, the obstacle course, and three hours of marching that afternoon. My body was sore as hell, and I was extremely hungry from expending so much energy.

From the first day in the army, I made friends with Jack, who was in the bed next to mine. He came from Cape Town and was a cool dude. He talked in a weird slang and used the word "bro" all the time.

He had an elder brother who had been drafted into the army two years back, as an infantryman. Jack mentioned that his brother had given him many tips on how to get things done quickly and how to save time to rest.

Before the lights went out, we would clean all our gear for the morning inspections. We would place our brown army trousers and shirts between the bed board and mattress so they would be pressed flat while we slept—it was just like ironing them.

Our brown boot tips had to shine like a bottle. We would put the polish on the tip and burn the polish with a lighter until it melted and turned a blackish color. With a cloth and spit, we smeared it evenly and used the shoe brush to shine it like a bottle.

I was learning all the army tricks, and I made sure that I was in the better group of guys. The lazy ones always got detention, and they were bullied by the stronger full-of-shit guys.

In the first three weeks of our six-week basic training, it was a struggle to keep all our guys in check. My fitness level was in the upper 30 percent of the guys in my bungalow. There always seemed to be some guys who didn't fit in the army and did not pull their weight. Many times we had to go through the basic obstacle course because of the lazy ones.

After the first three weeks in the army, we were given a more strenuous level of training. It was on a Monday morning that we were told that all the bungalows had to compete against each other. All sixteen bungalows in 2-SSB had to do certain trial times as a group. The whole unit was put through the extreme obstacle course at least three times a week.

Our running in the mornings was now a different route that was twenty kilometers long. Everything was on time trials—we had to finish schedules within a certain time.

I was in the right frame of mind. Every night before showering, Jack and I did fifty push-ups and a hundred sit-ups in one go. We started a trend, and many others joined in our personal exercise.

At this stage of our army training, we were extremely focused on being the best. If one person lacked in your bungalow, all were punished. In the morning, the slower-running guys were helped by the faster guys. It was weird to see two faster guys running on either side of a slower guy, with them half picking him up during the run.

I was extremely fit and in the top third of the faster-running guys in the camp. Jack and I were of the same ability, and our training was equal.

The most extreme training was when we had to jump off the back end of our moving troop carrier. It was high, and it moved at a reasonable speed. On my first jump, I landed a bit wrong, crashed to the ground, and hurt my arm.

After that first scary jump, it became easier, and it became a thrill. We always had to jump two at a time off the back end of the moving Bedford troop truck. Jack and I would always shout out "oh shit" as we jumped off the open Bedford truck. We would land with our legs together in a bent position in a backward roll.

When jumping off the back end of a Bedford truck it was with full webbing and rifles. We started a trend; eventually everyone was shouting "oh shit" as they jumped off onto the gravel road.

It is amazing how much faster we all did our training and how fit we were all getting. Even the lazy ones started to keep up with the rest of us.

I was eating like a pig, taking twelve slices of bread with my breakfast. At lunch and dinner, I took eight slices. The army food was always bad, but bread and jam with coffee was good.

From the third week until the end of our six weeks of basic training, we started off as the tenth best bungalow and ended up third best. Our opposite bungalow guys started eleventh and ended up sixth. Our corporal was in a good frame of mind and was pleased with our performance.

After our six weeks of basic training, we did combat training for the final six weeks. We were consistently doing maneuvers, rifle target shooting, and running twelve kilometers while wearing full army gear.

During the six- to twelve-week basic training, we had a lot of lectures, and we did many tests. We were all guided in the certain skills that we needed, in the direction that the army wanted us to be.

Basic training was tough for all of us. Many times at night or in the early morning, we were awakened for a "piss parade." It always happened in the early hours of the morning. I was a light sleeper and had no problem with it. I would always drink a bit of water before I went to sleep, so that I could have my piss and go back to bed. Some of the guys could not piss and had to stand there until they did.

In our bungalow there were three boys who were always below the fitness average. There was a farm boy called *Oere* ("Ears"). He had massive ears on his small head, which made him look weird. He was a lazy sod and sometime pissed in his bed. The stronger guys often beat him up.

Many times during the early evening, we put on full gear and went through the basic obstacle course. By the time our training was done for the day, it was always dark. Every night I did my push-ups and sit-ups before shower time and cleaned my gear for inspections before bed.

During our full basic training, many of the guys could not handle the pressure and the stress. Sometimes fights broke out and detention was given. The army never tolerated anyone causing uneasiness among the guys. The punishment was severe. When the trouble started, I always backed off and did my thing.

I was not the skinny boy anymore. I'd put on about fifteen pounds since my school days. I noticed it had become easier to run twelve kilometers in full battle gear with my rifle, and I did not get out of breath. I became very good at shooting my rifle on the shooting range. I was always in the top five shooters out of all the guys in 2-SSB camp.

My corporal mentioned to me a few times, "I will select the top twenty shooters out of all the basic training guys. They will be selected as snipers or gunners in the Panzers." It was so natural for me to be a sharp-shooter. My catlike eyesight was good and my combat shooting was above 95 percent.

In the eleventh week of basic training, we did a five-day maneuver in a mountainous area called Mazelspoort. It was about fifteen kilometers from our camp and in a destitute environment northeast of Bloemfontein.

We were next to the Modder (Mud) River, and it was in full flow with strong currents. Our campsite was huge, and we had to do a river-crossing exercise. A long thick rope extended from one large tree to another, and the same rope was suspended over the narrow section of the Modder River.

From the tree-to-tree position, we first had to learn how to slide down the rope while suspended below it. It was difficult at first, trying to hook our legs over the rope and pull ourselves on the tight rope. In some ways, however, the rope exercise was fun. On the first day, about half our bungalow could do it for around thirty meters before letting go and falling to the ground.

It was on a volunteer basses to cross over the fast-flowing Modder River on the suspended higher rope stretching about fifty meters over the river.

Below our campsite was another loose rope pulled across the river at a more shallow section, where the river flowed with less force. Guys were in the water to catch us if we fell from the rope. I was brave and was in the first bunch of guys who attempted the rope river crossing. Our corporal mentioned to us, "Don't look down, and just concentrate on your footwork and the sliding motion by pulling with your arms at a steady pace. Do not stop. Go all the way sliding until you can see the tree where the rope is tied on the opposite side. Look down, and you should be past the river and on dry ground."

I felt great, and on my first attempt, I proceeded at a smooth pace as I looked upside down at the tree on the opposite side. I could hear the gushing water below me, but I concentrated on the tree opposite the river. When I was about three meters from it, I looked down, and I had cleared about ten meters past the river's edge. I let my feet loose on the rope and dangled for a few seconds and let go to drop to the ground.

It was a great feeling, and everyone that made it over was cheered and applauded. On that day, only half of the unit attempted the river crossing and more than thirty guys fell in the Mud River. On the fifth morning we were all up at five o'clock for our usual roll call, dressed in full combat training gear with rifles, webbing, and full kit.

It was cold; the temperature was way below freezing, and we were shivering. I remember standing in the troop formation with ice on my eyebrows. My rifle was stuck to my frozen bare hand.

After breakfast, we all experienced the worst day of our army training. During the roll call, our sergeant major gave the orders that we would run back to camp. We noticed open Magirus army trucks with many long wooden poles on them. We were told that we needed to carry the poles and run, three guys to a pole, all the way back to Tempe base camp.

We all stood there in dismay, knowing that we were fifteen kilometers away from camp, and the power poles were heavy.

After breakfast roll call, we gathered three abreast in formation. Three at a time, we had to get a pole off the Magirus trucks. As we lined up with the pole on our shoulders, we were told, "You all need to be back at the Panzer camp for lunchtime." I was in luck; I was positioned with two stronger guys in our unit when we collected our pole.

The road out of Mazelspoort camp was gravel for around three kilometers. The tar-road section followed until we would reach our camp at Tempe.

We worked together as a team, although I was the weakest one in our formation. We got in a rhythm as we ran with that pole on our shoulders, and we all developed the same stride, gradually passing many groups who were walking beside the road with their poles. At the halfway point there was a water truck for all to have a short break. We rested for about ten minutes, and proceeded on to the second half of the exercise.

Our large marching field was in the last two kilometers toward our main gate. We knew we were close, and there were not many guys in front of us. We saw the Magirus army trucks parked on the side of the road. When we reached them, we had to load the pole on the open bed before we could rest.

I looked at the time and could see that it was about forty minutes before lunch. I knew that the other two guys were happy as well. It was a weird feeling, putting that pole on the Magirus truck and knowing that we did well. After that, we lay on our backs on the grass, totally exhausted and out of breath. Our shoulders and arms were sore.

Our names and times were marked on a sheet. We were told that we could go back to our bungalows and rest until lunch. Only six guys in our bungalow did well on the pole-running time. Just before lunch, there were twelve guys back out of twenty-two.

I knew that the other ten guys would have to do the extreme obstacle course when they finally got back to camp. The pole exercise really separated the boys from the men. I knew that I was in good shape. I was also lucky to have two strong guys running with me.

Just after lunch the earlier group was summoned to the main building lecture room. All the top brass in our camp were sitting on chairs on the lecture room stage. We were asked if some of us wanted to join the Armored Reconnaissance Force Troopers. We were told that the training would be severe, and only 40 percent of the listed group would be accepted.

I knew I was of a middle weight and that it would be almost impossible for me to make it. I decided to opt out. My vision in life was to be in the Panzer and become an armored gunner.

The two guys who were running with me with the pole joined the ARC Force. They were known as the "Armor Reckies" (ARC Force, or Armored Reconnaissance Corporation Force).

During the afternoon we attended more lectures. After dinner, the guys who were late with the pole-running exercise, had to go through the extreme obstacle course. The pole-running exercise had been a test of endurance and working together as a team. We were always encouraged to help our buddies next to you.

We had one more week left in our twelve-week basic training. We were all very fit, and went through the extreme obstacle course a lot faster time than before.

Chapter Two

Majestic Africa

Our Five-Day Survival Experience and the School of Armor

During the twelfth week of our basic training, our 2-SSB unit heard that we were going on an exercise. We were taken by Bedford trucks from Bloemfontein to Maseru. We had our full battle kit and knew only that we were going on a training exercise.

We were separated from the rest of the camp guys. On this trip it was only our corporal and sergeant with the twenty-two guys in bungalow 33.

Maseru is the capital city of Lesotho, South Africa. This is where the Drakensberg Mountains stretch as far as the eye can see. Near Maseru, the high peaks are close to 3,300 meters above sea level.

The distance to Maseru was around 160 kilometers from our Tempe 2-SSB camp in Bloemfontein. Just before we reached Maseru, the Bedford went down a path for about three kilometers. We stopped at a deserted campsite next to the Caledon River. The temperature was around ten degrees colder than in our camp at the Tempe base.

It was around nine o'clock that morning when we dismounted and formed a large circle around the sergeant, corporal, and driver. Only then did we learn what training we were about to experience—a five-day survival course. We were split up into four groups, two five-man and two six-man group sections.

I was in a group with Jack. The sergeant handed us one compass, one map, and a small book that described the types of food we could eat from the land. We each were issued a pack of twelve water-purifying tablets, ten fire-starting tablets (EZ-bits), and a pack of ten large round biscuits. Our group was also issued two flares and two yellow-powder smoke grenades. We were given one flashlight and told to use it wisely and to look at the compass and map when finding our bearings at night. We also were given a snake- and spider-bite kit and a list of the deadly snakes and spiders in this part of the country and small binoculars to get our bearings in the countryside. We received our orders on where to proceed on our first day's survival course.

Each group had a different beacon location to proceed to by foot, which was ten to twenty kilometers, away from each other. When we reached the beacon, we could make camp, rest, and sleep. Some were far away from the river and some were at the river's edge. On two maneuvers, it was a difficult terrain and proceeded into the night. On the difficult routes, it was estimated we would reach the beacons by about 10:00 p.m.

During our basic training, we learned to find and locate the North Star and the Southern Cross in the night sky. I was in the first group of five guys that was separated from the other groups. We had less than half an hour to study the map and find our location. On the first trail, we knew that we were going in a northwesterly direction. Our fifth day end point was close to the Welbedacht Dam wall. On this adventure we covered around seventy to eighty clicks. We were mostly on the right side of the river and crossed over it two times.

We figured out that the river section must be at a lower rocky section at these cross-over points. Our group was in a good frame of mind, and we felt happy about our distance routes. Our corporal said, "If you guys get lost, do not panic. Sit tight and shoot your flare gun at night before midnight. If we have not located you, sleep and release the smoke grenade at 6:00 a.m. or at noon. At the beacons you will find a red-painted wooden pole about eight feet tall with a big yellow smiley-face on the top part of the pole."

We were given five nails, a small hammer, and five two-inch round tokens with our group letter on it—we were Group A. These were to be nailed on the red wooden pole when we located the smiley-face beacon. We also received a red marker to write the time when we reached the smiley-face.

Group A was to start the trail mission first. We estimated that we should reach our first smiley-face before 6:00 p.m. We had no solid food with us, other than the ten biscuits that normally are issued in a patrol ration pack. We knew that we needed to reach our first smiley-face beacon before it got dark. We each carried the items given to us. By chance, I was in charge of the map and the compass. Jack had the tokens, hammer, marker, and bush-food booklet.

We figured out that all the beacon locations were close to the secondary dirt roads in the area. We knew that the sergeant, corporal, and driver would be traveling on the secondary roads to where the beacon locations were. We were not allowed to use the secondary vehicle roads; if we did, we would receive punishment.

We were trained to locate a faraway compass point, mountain cliff face or hilltop, or a large tree in the distance. We would mark it on our terrain map and make our way towards it. When we reached the located point, we would find another faraway compass point and do the same again. At all the compass-point locations, we needed to check the sun's movement so we would know the compass direction.

It was time to start our survival course route.

We knew the first beacon would be directly west and away from the Caledon River. It was an awesome feeling for me; I was excited on this adventure survival trail. The bush was thick, and it was a bit of an incline when we started on our first walking trail.

Jack and I were mostly in control; the other guys would just follow us and agree with us on our compass bearings. The first few hours were good; we were all in good spirits. We crossed over the gravel road and went over a gradual hill and down into a valley below.

When we came to the road section, we were happy and knew that we were only about five clicks from the smiley face. We were lucky, as just off the road we found red berry bushes that were good to eat. Jack checked the book and said they were edible, so we sat there next to the bush, resting and eating these red berries.

We rested for about half an hour. Some of the guys fell asleep. We scheduled our rest stops between noon and one o'clock for our lunch break. We were doing well, and I figured out that we should locate the smiley face between four and five o'clock.

I woke the guys at one o'clock, and we set off on our next direction. It was not too difficult. Jack and I observed the terrain height lines on the map. The narrow ones were steep terrains or sharp declines, and the wide ones were the flat gradual terrains.

On the map, Jack and I could see that the smiley red dot and circle was in a valley—the lines were closer together. It seemed to go slightly left and swerve to an incline and proceed normally again.

It took us a while to descend to the valley below. I figured out that we were within a kilometer or so from our smiley-face beacon. We worked as a group and knew that we needed to stay together at all times. We discussed whether we should go left or right. Based on our observations of the map, it seemed that we needed to proceed left in the valley. We all agreed and continued slowly through the dense bush. It was about forty minutes before we saw the cliff section in front of us. Next to a tree higher up on the ridge was the red pole and smiley face.

We all did the hand pat and shoulder bump, saying, "Yeah, we are good."

It was 4:30 p.m. Jack wrote down the time. I mentioned to the guys that we should make camp before we rested. We all agreed to make our sleeping camp on the higher ground in case it rained at night. Not far from the smiley-face pole was a flat section next to some trees. Our first night's camp was set.

We took all our webbing off and placed it by the trees. The other three guys were exhausted from walking on the mountain terrain, but Jack and I searched around the area for twigs and dried branches to make a fire later on.

At five thirty we saw the sergeant and corporal walk toward us through the dense bush. They looked at our time and said, "So far, the best time. You guys did well." They told us that Group C had made it to the smiley-face at five ten; Groups B and D were still in pursuit of their first smiley-face beacons.

We chatted jovially for ten minutes. The corporal whispered to me, "Boil your water and put two biscuits in it. It will become a good porridge and will fill you up for the night." Damn, we seemed favored by a grand corporal.

He also mentioned that we should sleep close to the log fire. The animals and creepy-crawly insects didn't like to be too close to fires. Just before leaving, they mentioned that the next three days' beacons would be more difficult to find. The fifth day was easy because the dam wall could be seen from far away. The corporal again whispered in my ear, saying, "There are some cactus plants with fruit on them not too far from your camp position. Scout the area in the morning." He did not say where they were, but damn, he was good guy.

Before the sun set, we did an analysis on the second day's survival route. We got all our ducks in a row and were in a good planning mode to be better than the other three groups in our bungalow. Our legs were hurting a bit; we were not used to climbing the bush terrain in these mountain areas.

On day two, we all woke up just as it was getting light. I told the guys, "Stay here because Jack and I are going to find breakfast."

Jack looked at me with a skewed smile. As we walked off, I told Jack about the cactus plants. We walked about a hundred meters and saw a bunch of the cactus plants on the top side of a small cliff. In our webbing we had army knives. We were lucky for there were exactly ten red cactus fruits that were ripe. They were full of thorns, but we cut them off and let them fall on my hard plastic rain jacket. We carried them between us. The guys were happy when we returned, and we had two sweet, juicy cactus fruits each for breakfast. What a treat it was.

It was just after 6:30 a.m. when I took our first morning compass reading. This route was directly south to southwest. We would cross over the vehicle road and make our way to the Caledon River. At this river crossing, we would track ten kilometers directly south. The red dot and circle seemed to be high up on a mountain. The map showed a mountain fortress called Moshoeshoe's. This mountain fortress was located about five kilometers from our next smiley-face beacon.

We found the gravel road and crossed it. The stretch toward the Caledon River took us another three hours. I had a feeling that we were a bit higher up than our location on the map. We decided to walk southwest for a few clicks, following the river. Damn, we were in luck again and reached the gorge. It was so grand, with the Drakensberg Peak Mountains not far away.

We decided to look for food around the gorge area. In one flat area we saw hundreds of white mushrooms. Jack had the book out, and we were in luck—we could eat them; they were not poisonous.

I cut loads of the mushrooms and wrapped them in my rain jacket and tied them to my waist. It was food for tonight, with my biscuit-porridge meal.

We sat on the rocks in the middle of the Caledon River, eating raw mushrooms for lunch. They had a kind of tingly taste, and I could feel that they were making me lightheaded. At that time, we did not know that they were "magic mushrooms" that would make us drunk if we ate too many of them.

We looked at the majestic surroundings and knew that we were in luck, walking through this gorge area. It was so grand to view this place. In my heart, I knew that on this mountain survival trip, we would experience majestic Africa.

We stayed there a bit longer than we should have. We left the gorge at around one thirty. We did not know that straight ahead of us were steep cliffs and a higher mountains incline.

The map showed that we were going in the right direction, up these higher elevated cliffs, but we all panicked a bit. By the time we climbed over the cliffs, the sun was setting behind the mountain. Damn, we were tired, and our legs were in pain from the continuous walking over rocks, cliffs, and thick bush terrain.

Our next red dot on the map was on a higher mountain slope, and the valley dropped to a fork shape behind it. Directly behind the valley was a large peak of the Drakensberg Mountains. Jack and I encouraged the other guys to keep up with us. We told them, "The faster we can reach the next smiley-face post, the sooner we can rest our sore legs."

We were all in a slow walking pace, and it was just after nine at night when we reached the top mountain slope. We were in a kind of a panic because it was dark, and the animal night noises were making us afraid. We decided to walk for around ten minutes more to see if we could find the smiley-face.

We were in luck—it was only five minutes before we saw the smiley-face post in an open flat spot on the edge of the mountain. We were so happy that tears ran down our faces. At the post, we collapsed. We were all out of breath, and our hard breathing sounds echoed through the night.

Jack nailed our token to the post and wrote down the time—9:10 p.m. I told the guys we did good for the sergeant had given us until 10:00 p.m. to reach our second smiley-face post.

It was cold in this part of the mountain. We were in luck for the three-quarter moon was rising over the mountain and shining ever so brightly. There were endless twigs and broken branches around the site, so we gathered them up and made a good bonfire.

It was coffee time and mushrooms and biscuit-porridge supper. I was hungry like a beast, and my body was aching all over from walking in the extreme incline in this mountainous region.

After supper, I lay on my sleeping bag, looking at the billions of stars in the clear black sky. We all spoke softly—or maybe we were just too tired to talk loudly.

I told the guys, "Tomorrow should be easier, going back down the mountain to the Caledon River." Jack and I had the same good fitness level. The other three guys were slower and complained all the time. Jack and I had taken control during the trip up the mountain. We had told the slower bunch, "If you do not keep up, we will leave you guys behind." After that, they did try with more effort to keep up with Jack and me.

That night we all fell asleep like dead rocks. I woke up first, just after 6:00 a.m. The sun was rising in the east, behind the mountain. It was foggy, but we could see that we were very high up on the mountain. We took a compass reading toward our next beacon on the map. We drew a straight line across and marked a section on the river where the river bent in an S. We just needed to follow the river downstream until we reach the S-curve in the river.

Every morning, we always changed our socks. We also washed and clean up. Jack mentioned, "We should go down the mountain faster, and we can relax longer at the Caledon River."

The third day's route seemed to backtrack, and we decided to make it back to the gorge area. We did well, and by 11:00 a.m., we were at the gorge. We had mushrooms for lunch. At the same time, we washed our feet and faces and brushed our teeth.

Jack and I studied the map. We knew we were about three clicks back on the river's gorge edge from our original compass route. Our distance down the river was good, and we reached the S-bend around 12:30 p.m. We took a compass reading and marked our next beacon in the far distance.

The terrain here was flat, and we could walk at a better pace. In half an hour, we crossed the road again. It was just after 5:00 p.m. when we reached the section of land where the bush was very dense. We knew that smiley-face post had to be somewhere close by. We searched for hour and suddenly, next to a huge rock, the red post and smiley-face was gawking at us. My heart was leaping out of my chest from happiness. What a relief it was to find the smiley-face. My feet were sore from the constant walking, and we all had blisters on our heels.

Jack marked down our time, 5:55 p.m. We rested for around half an hour and made camp. There was no time to put things off. Jack and I looked at the map for the fourth day's survival location, while the remaining lazy lot lay on their sleeping bags in a kind of daze. We knew that the fourth day's trail would be a mission. There were two smaller streams that flowed into the Caledon River. We saw that we could take two routes. The first was before the first stream; the second one looked a shorter distance but the terrain looked like cliff formations.

While the guys were resting, we decided to take the long route for it was gradual elevation and would follow the Caledon River. We worked out that the overall distance would be an extra three clicks. It would be a lot less dangerous and a shorter time getting there.

We decided not to tell the lazy lot. We drew pencil lines on the map, one toward the first stream that was due south and a little east from our existing smiley-face location. It was easier to follow a straight route down the Caledon River. We also needed to find a shallow area to cross the river and then find the fourth smiley-face that was on that side and close to the second stream that flowed into the Caledon River.

That night we had our porridge-biscuit dinner. I was feeling a bit weak. I needed to have a good hearty dinner—I missed the army food. The only good thing about this survival course was that there was always water while crossing the Caledon River. I knew that this was not really the extreme course. In a more daring survival situation, it would be much different. This was just a test to see if we could find our bearings in harsh valley and mountain regions.

The third night, we crashed early, around eight-o-clock and had a good night's rest. In the morning when I woke up, I heard Johan, one of the boys with in our group; say in a scared voice, "There is something heavy on my sleeping bag."

It was a foggy morning, and it was just starting to get light, but I could see that a snake had coiled up behind his legs. We were the only ones awake. I told him not to move. I slowly slid out of my sleeping bag. I could hear Johan crying softly. I moved toward the other guys who still were sleeping, but my eyes were glued on the coiled-up snake. It was a large green mamba, a poisonous snake. I gently woke up the others and told them to be quiet.

In silence, they slid out of their sleeping bags and slowly retreated away from Johan and the snake. Jack observed any information about snakes in his survival book, but there was nothing in the book on what we could do in this situation.

Johan had to lie still until the snake decided to move on. The book said that snakes always look for warmth, and it is common for them to curl up against someone sleeping on the ground.

We were in luck for the sun was now shining on our camp, and the sun rays were directly on the snake. Within a few minutes, it slowly slid away into the bushes.

Poor Johan—he was still in his sleeping bag. We moved toward him and saw that he was asleep. I guess he was so frightened that he just fell asleep. Ben woke up Johan by shaking him on the shoulder. Johan jerked and shouted, "Where's the snake?" We calmed him down, but some of the boys could not stop laughing. I felt bad for Johan and said loudly, "Come on, guys. It could have happened to any one of us."

We had our morning coffee and biscuit-style porridge. It was just after seven o'clock when I took a compass reading. We proceeded toward the Caledon River, and when we crossed the gravel road, it was only a five-minute walk to the river's edge.

Jack and I knew that our next route was to follow the river downstream until we found the stream leading into the Caledon River. The bush was thicker, and we had to walk away from the river while keeping in sight of it. The trek was slow, and I knew we would not reach our next smiley-face until night.

After two hours of struggling next to the river, we saw the stream leading into it. We were tired and decided to look for something to eat. We found nothing, and we all felt tense. We rested, and some of the lads had the remainder of their biscuits. Jack and I decided to skip lunch and have our biscuits for dinner. We would try to find some berries on the way to our next smiley-face point.

It was just after two o'clock when we slowly made our way down to the river. We were in luck for there were rocks and gravel walking sections next to the river. We must have walked around three clicks when we came to a rocky section; it was a shallow area with rapids from one side of the river to the other. It was our crossing point.

I was on a mission to proceed to the next stream. The bush was thick, and we sometimes had to walk away from the river. I was taking a lot of compass readings, knowing that the Caledon River was flowing in a twist-and-turn movement and going southwest.

At one point we found a grassy section and made up time. On this trip, we walked for an hour and rested ten minutes, and another hour, and rest.

We were progressing slowly and reached the last resting point at 6:10 p.m., before it got dark. I worked out on the map that we had around five more clicks to go. While walking in the dark, we struggled to keep on track. The moon was in our favor, shining very brightly above our heads. While walking in the moonlight and staying close to the river, we could see the Southern Cross stars ahead of us in the dark sky.

We struggled to walk, as we were tired and hungry. If given the chance, we could have eaten an ox. It was coming on nine o'clock when we reached the area where the stream flowed in from the opposite side of the Caledon River. I looked on the map and knew that we should be close to smiley-face post. We walked another fifty meters down a sandy bank and by golly gosh, the smiley-face post was on the side of the river in an open area for all to see. My heart exploded, and the tears ran down my cheeks.

I looked at the boys, and they all had tears in their eyes. We were so tired and walked toward smiley-face dragging our feet, seeming like zombies from *The Walking Dead*. We all crashed on the side of the riverbank, exhausted from this extreme survival course. Jack nailed our token to the post, and we were all surprised that it was only 9:10 p.m.

We were all hungry and exhausted from four days of consistent walking in the bush. Jack and I found some dried twigs and tree branches nearby and made a good bonfire next to the river. This was on a dry sandy level, away from the water's edge.

The location looked grand, and the full moon reflected on the surroundings.

For dinner, Jack and I had coffee and our biscuit porridge. The other guys went to bed without food. They all complained that this was the extreme and asked, "What is the army doing to us?"

My buddy Jack and I were in good shape. We looked at the survival course as an adventure trip.

In the morning, just before we departed at six o'clock, Jack and I studied the map. We decided that it was stupid to follow the river's edge. We needed to find the flat terrain areas not too far from the river. We knew the dam wall was only twelve clicks away from our river location. We took a compass reading exactly southwest. I was getting more comfortable with our compass readings. I worked out we should reach the Welbedacht Dam wall by lunchtime.

It was now the fifth day and all our food was used up. We all knew that we needed to get to smiley-face number five in a hurry. I encouraged the guys, saying, "Hey, guys, we are almost home, and the route is only another twelve clicks directly southwest. If we hustle, we should make it by lunchtime. I am sure that the sergeant and corporal will be there waiting for us. I have a feeling they will have food when we arrive."

The guys' eyes lit up. I showed them on the map that the terrain on our left looked like flatlands with no high slopes at all. Like a group of army boy's ready for battle, we walked at a reasonable pace away from the river's edge. I took my compass bearings, and we were all in a happy mood, knowing that soon this extreme survival course would end, and we could go home.

It was amazing how fast we walked—it was just after eleven o'clock when we saw the catchment Welbedacht Dam wall in the distance. We all smiled and were in a happy mood. In the next hour and forty minutes, we crossed over a gravel road and a train track. Not far from the train track, we could see a second road through the shrubs and trees. We looked right and could see the Bedford truck parked about two hundred meters from our location. It was next to a small bridge that crossed over the Caledon River.

Excitedly, we walked faster toward the Bedford. It was not long before our sergeant noticed us walking toward him. He was sitting on the hood of the Bedford, looking through his binoculars. He waved at us with both his hands. Within minutes we were there next to the Bedford, shaking hands. The corporal said, "You guys did well and are the second group to find us." I saw the big smiley-face on a red pole, tied on the rail in the center of the bridge. Jack and I walked over to it, and he nailed our last a token on it and wrote the time: 12:40 p.m.

We noticed that Group C had reached the pole at 12:25 p.m., and we asked where they were. At that moment, the sergeant came from the rear of the Bedford with a pack of freshly baked buns and sandwiches. He also gave us three beers each. Our faces lit up like a lighthouse. We all had tears in our eyes when he said, "You guys make your way down the edge of the bridge to the river, where the Group C guys are resting under the trees." We removed our webbing and R-1 rifles and staged them at the back of the Bedford truck. We made our way to the river's edge.

It was grand to see the other guys in our bungalow. We opened our beers, and the talk was of the extreme events that we had endured. We ended up resting for around two hours before we heard the Group B guys coming from the bridge toward the water's edge. Where the hell was Group D? At 4:00 p.m. The sergeant came down and told us that they were going to search for the last group. We all needed to stay put until they returned.

It was just before 6:00 p.m. when we heard the Bedford return to the bridge. We all walked up to the bridge and saw the weary lot at the back of the Bedford truck. The sergeant told us that they had been lost and were lucky to have been found. We all needed to hustle and get inside the Bedford. Where to now? We knew that it would be another two hours back to our 2-SSB camp in Tempe. We traveled for around five clicks to a town called Jammersdrift. We turned right and went down a dirt road to a resort called Caledon Resort Lodge.

We were all excited; we were going to sleep in a resort on our fifth night in the majestic Drakensberg Mountains. We walked to the parking lot area in front of the lodge entrance. We were shaking our heads in amazement and saying, "This is great." Our rifles were tagged and taken from us. We handed our map charts to the corporal for analysis of our route markings.

The sergeant gave us our six lodge keys. We were told to have a fast shower and to meet at the dining hall at 7:30 p.m. Group A hustled to find our lodge next to the river. Damn, we had a high spot with a good view looking down at the river's rapidly flowing waters.

We all had our showers and went to the main wooden log-style building, which had a safari feel to it. We found the dining hall outdoor area and made our way to the sergeant and corporal. We sat down at one of the two large dinner tables. Within ten minutes, all the guys were seated.

The sergeant sat at the head of our table. He stood up and said, "You all did well on your first five-day survival course. Groups A and C did very good, and for sure I would gladly be in a survival situation with them. They both figured out how to read the terrain and to mark their positions on the terrain map. I was also impressed that both groups took the longer route but had shorter times on day four. Group A should have moved away from the river route, and they could have saved an hour's trek. Groups A and C did all their trail treks faster than the time given.

"Group B started out reasonably good, but you guys lost it on the second day. And now Group D—you guys are not following orders on what you were trained to do. We had to bail you out three times on your trail trek routes. In a survival situation, you would die in the mountains." The sergeant was harsh, but this was not only an exercise. When the conditions happened in the real world, it could be a life-or-death situation on what to do when you were stranded.

The corporal stood up and showed everyone our Group A map, where Jack and I had written all our information. The corporal told everyone, "In the real world when you are stranded in the wilderness, this is what you guys need to do—write down everything on your map like the Group A guys did. They did the best map logging, and I would be stranded with them any time." Jack and I felt great, knowing our group did all the compass bearings and logging information on the map.

It was a grand night of good food and chatting with our bungalow sergeant and corporal. After dinner, we walked around the resort. We felt different, as if we were in Civilian Street. The following morning, after a sunrise breakfast, we were on route back to Tempe and our 2-SSB camp. We arrived at nine o'clock and were back to reality. We had to assemble at ten o'clock; we had officially completed our twelve-week basic training. We were marched to the lecture room, where we had to wait for our sergeant major to arrive. We were presented with a small 2-SSB army dish token. The best feeling for us was when we were issued the Best Rifle Range tokens. These badges looked bad-ass. Our names were read out, and we each went to the front and shook hands with the sergeant major and received our token and Best Shooter badges.

When my name was read, I heard that my combined average score was 233, and I was the fifth highest shooter of everyone in our camp. If the highest score was over 228 (out of 240 points), the token was a pure silver imprint rifle badge. The bronze badge was issued for a highest score of 212 to 227 points.

The rifle range was from 100 meters up to 600 meters. We had to lie on our stomachs in a sharp-shooter position and fire at a one-meter circular target. Hitting the bull's-eye was ten points, and the rings around it were eight, six, four, two, and one points. The field sporadic sign-board shooting range was great—we had to do a fast time-trial running pace and shoot at the target boards hidden in the shrubs and trees. The rifleman picture board head and heart display were the highest points.

It was a strange time for me. I felt all grown up and not the skinny school boy I had been. From one day to the next, everything changed. After basic training was over, we had time off. On the weekends, we could get a pass out of the camp. There was an army mall not far from camp that had a large movie theater.

At this time in the army, we met the other two camp infantry and "Para-Bats" guys. We could feel the tension between the different camps. On the second Saturday, the action was full on. Our group of armored division guys had just come out of the movies when we saw many guys having a brawl in the parking lot. Within a few minutes, the MP Jeeps came screeching to a halt, and the MPs, with their batons, stopped the fighting. I noticed most of the guys who were arrested were in the Para-Bats, along with some armored and

SAI guys. They were all loaded into a Bedford truck and taken away. When we got back to camp, we heard that the guys were sent to the military prison camp for five days.

In the second week that followed our first pass, we heard a loud commotion going on late one night. The noise was where the bungalows were closest to the Para-Bats camp's barbed wire fence. Some of the guys in our bungalow went to see what the commotion was all about. I decided to stay; I did not want to get involved. Jack also kept out of the fighting action.

The following morning we heard that the group of Para-Bats had cut a hole in the fence that bordered the two camps. While the armored division guys were sleeping, the Para-Bats whacked the guys in their beds with hard solid items in a sleeping bag. They disappeared back through the hole cut in the fence. Somehow, the armored guys had over powered and caught four Para-Bat guys. They whacked them real good.

During the morning line-up before breakfast, our sergeant major gave a harsh speech. We were told that three of our guys were in hospital and that the one guy was in a critical condition. He said that the army would deal with the matter and that the Panzer unit would not tolerate this shit. We were also warned not to enter their camp and to be vigilant when we went to the mall on our time off.

It was on the following Monday when, like a happy wind blowing in my direction, I got orders to report to headquarters.

Along with me, four guys from our bungalow, including Jack, were told to get all our gear together. We would be moved out of the main camp. Late in the afternoon, the Bedford trucks were lined up to take us away.

I was now stationed in a camp called the School of Armor. When we arrived, we had dinner in a nice mess hall canteen. After dinner we were sectioned to find a bed for the night in the empty bungalows behind the mess hall.

The army does not stop for anything.

The following morning, we all did more aptitude tests, and I was recruited as a 90mm gunner in the Panzer. We handed in our R-1 rifles, and we were issued a 9mm Star pistol and an army stiletto webbing knife. Life was treating me good, and I felt like "Bad Boy Mike" with my holstered gun at my side. I felt like Rambo and was extremely happy with where I had landed in the army.

I was now sleeping in a bungalow with all the gunners—there were four bungalows with gunners in them. I worked out that two were 1-SSB and the other two were our guys, 2-SSB. Everything was always based on performance and your ability to be better than the guy next to you. The SSB School of Armor looked more like an officer's camp. It felt as if I had moved up to a higher level.

The following morning we were issued our Panzers. We all started a six-week practical and theory course on the armored vehicles. It was a very exciting time for me, and we were all in a good army frame of mind. There was no time to think of anything else. Jack was recruited as a driver, and I was happy for him.

In a Panzer, there was a crew commander, a gunner, and a driver.

Every day wakeup call was at 5:00 a.m., and lights out was at 10:30 p.m. We were drilled on all the armored Panzer equipment. The crew commander and gunner operated three different radios. There were two different four-wheel Panzers. One would shoot a 60mm mortar and the other a 90mm mortar. The mortar turret barrel was a 50mm Browning belt-driven machine gun. The gun was fixed with the rotating barrel head.

On the top of the Panzer, in front of the gunner hatch, was a 7.62mm Browning belt-driven machine gun. This gun could rotate in a 270-degree angle. On the inside of the two armor-plated doors was a 9mm submachine-gun that could clip off with one yank.

The headset had a sun-protection slide visor. (In today's world, it would be UV protective lenses.) When the slide visor was down, it would enhance images and block out the sun's reflection. At night, it would block of most of the reflective shining lights.

After the first week of intense Panzer training, everything stepped up a level. We traveled at least eight hours a day in the Panzer. In the morning before breakfast, we did our physical training and a fifteen-click run. After breakfast, we mounted the Panzers and traveled two hours toward a mortar shooting range. This was out in the countryside in an area called De-brug. When we reached this destitute area, we did four hours of maneuvers and combat training. Every time it seemed to be in a different mountainous region. After the day's action, it was another two hours of traveling back to camp. After dinner, it was lectures until 9:00 p.m.

On every occasion on the mortar shooting range, I performed really well. It was weird shooting the 60mm mortars. The barrel was set almost vertical when firing the mortar and it would go high in the sky and fall back down and explode around a hundred meters in front of you. It was frightening to see it falling back down and exploding not far from the Panzer.

This was "big boys" training. I was a natural at firing the mortars. After a few weeks, we were trained with high-explosive, or "H-E," mortars. This was a different ballgame. The Panzer would thrust and rock backwards when firing one of these bad-boy mortars. The thrust motion always kicked up the dust around the vehicle. It was a great feeling, pressing my helmet against a padded rest above the glass viewing sight. I would set my coordinate degree settings and engage the mortar trigger mechanism to fire the H-E. My head would jerk backward for a millisecond, and I would see the mortar hit the target. It would explode with force—an awesome feeling. It was a total rush when I heard the mortar-sliding mechanism jerking back and forward. I could hear a loud "twahhh" echoing sound. My heart would race like a speeding bullet.

After three weeks of intense training, we were put into a formation troop of twelve guys. Each troop had one lieutenant, a sergeant, and two full corporals. At this time, the crew commanders had done there corporal training and got their two stripes. The gunners got a certificate and a badge to sew on their browns jackets or shirts. The drivers received their pass certificates. Every time these advanced training sessions happened, it felt awesome, knowing that we had been trained for any action to protect South Africa against the bad guys.

After our intense three-week training and written tests, the formation went like this: I was now sectioned in Troop One and in the front 90mm Panzer vehicle. I don't know why but in the army, I always seemed to get preference on troop selection and being in the front Panzer.

My commander was the best full corporal in our troop. I was the second best gunner, and we had the second best driver. In the second 60mm Panzer was a corporal with a gunner and driver. The third vehicle was a 90mm Panzer with the lieutenant and the best gunner and driver. The fourth vehicle was a 90mm with a sergeant, gunner, and driver.

Of course, the lieutenant had the best-scoring gunner and the best pass driver. The front Panzer had all the action and would need to lead the way on the patrols or maneuvers. That is why the second best-scoring gunner and driver needed to be in the leading Panzer.

In the fourth week of training, our bungalows were reshuffled. I was now sleeping in a bungalow with Troops One and Two together. The lieutenants slept separately in the officers' quarters. At this time in my crazy life, I felt different—all grown up and having no fear. Our training was more professional, and everything was done in a way that we don't have to think about what to do next; we did it automatically.

Somehow, my life had changed, and it seemed as if luck had come my way. My life was now in full throttle and nothing could change the direction that the army had chosen for me.

During my time at the School of Armor, I wrote letters to my teacher Loraine. She was my Afrikaans teacher during my last year at high school. We were close and our relationship happened suddenly, and we had a sexual relationship. I wrote at least three letters a week. Loraine was now teaching in an Afrikaans school called Pretoria North High. I really did miss the time we'd shared together and her warm body and all the exciting sexual times we shared.

In the sixth week at the School of Armor training, I got a strange letter from Loraine. After reading it, I knew that long-distance relationships are hard and they almost never last. Many tears ran down my cheeks, and my heart was sad. I knew that my life was changing by the minute. Loraine was twenty-six, and I was eighteen years old. She was at the age of getting married and having kids, and I was young and daring and exploring life. While reading her last letter, the tears could not be stopped. I felt lightheaded and emotional.

Loraine's last letter posted to me

Hey, Mike,

This will be my last letter to you. I have met a great guy, and I think it is best that we separate before one of us gets hurt. Thank you for showing me that life is exciting. Your letters from the army tell me that you are enjoying the army training and now are becoming an Armor Division vehicle gunner. I have to find what I want in life. I need to have stability, get married, and have children. Thank you for the awesome experience we shared together.

You will always be in my heart. I love you.

Take care of yourself.

Loraine

Why does it always happen that when a guy joins the army, the girl ditches him? From that day forward, all my attention was on being the best at what I could do. I had many thoughts of how my life had changed. Many nights, I would l would lay in bed and think of how close I had come to ending my life. I wondered why God spared me, preventing me from slitting my wrists and ending it all.

I felt different and not scared anymore, like I felt when I was in the-Govie reform-joint. I kept all my sad childhood experiences to myself. No one in the army knew that I had been in the Govie, the most notorious reform joint in South Africa. I always kept everything in my heart. I knew that somehow God had given me a break and put me with the best bunch of army guys that I could ever wish for.

Our 2-SSB Armored Division was great. The five troops' emblem names were awesome.

I was in Troop One, called the Scorpions troop. There was a black scorpion painted on the side doors of the camouflaged Panzer. Troop Two was called the Tarantula, Troop Three was Black Widow, Troop Four was Cobra, and Troop Five was Corral. In our five-unit troop and section division, we were known as the Venom Division.

The armored support trooper section had a full corporal section leader and a lance corporal with a tripod machine gunner. The section also had a rifleman radio operator and nine R-1 riflemen. The support section had twelve men in it, who were in a Bedford truck that followed the troop's Panzers. In the second Bedford troop carrier we had a driver, medic, two mechanics, and a land mine expert.

During the sixth week of our advanced training at the School of Armor, we did maneuvers with the 2-SSB support rifle troopers. They were the same bunch from our basic training camp. Life was blast while practicing a full battle exercise. It made us all realize just how much we had learned in such a short time. We did these maneuvers every second week. I was now friends with the guys in our Panzer. Greg was our full corporal crew commander, and Brian was our driver. We were great together, and we worked well as a team.

They were happy with me being their gunner. My combat shooting accuracy was getting better by the week. During our exercises, I many times was the gunner with the highest accuracy. That made my heart jump for joy.

It is strange how the army would keep information from us. It was sometime in late May 1974 when we heard that our 2-SSB was going to be stationed in South West Africa (Namibia). We heard that this desert and fishing-port location belonged to South Africa.

Greg, Brian, and I had a map of Africa with us, and we knew we would be stationed in the desert at a camp called Rooikop. Going to Namibia would be an experience and a blast.

Chapter Three

Rooikop in the Desert

Namibia Was a Blast in the Past

We were told to gear up and be ready to board a train for Namibia, South West Africa. It was early June, and we were on route to Walvis Bay in Namibia. It was a five-day journey that gave us time to relax.

In the mornings on the floor of our six-sleeper cabin, I did my regular fifty push-ups and a hundred sit-ups. This I would do before showering and breakfast. During most of the travel time we played card games—I was a hustler and made a bit of money on the side. My lucky streak in poker was good. It was also a good time to talk about our civilian lives and our families.

When the train crossed the border into Namibia, we could see that it was a semi-desert country. During the day it was hot as hell, but it was freezing cold at night. It took two days to travel through Namibia before reaching Windhoek (Wind Corner).

We were in luck for the train stopped in Windhoek for around five hours. We had time off while the diesel locomotives were fueled up and the train had an inspection. We ventured into the city before the train continued to Walvisbaai/ Walvis Bay (Whale Fish Bay). It was great; our troop did the walkabout, and we noticed buildings in the German-style architecture. Only then did I realize that Namibia was a German colony before it became independent. I was feeling adventurous and felt privileged to be in a different country.

We found a nice German pub called Edelweiss. We sat outside having some beers and snacks. It was also great to see all the good-looking girls walking past and sitting outside the pub. We could not stop staring at them. There were some really daring babes dressed up to make a guy's heart burn with sexual desire. Our talk was kind-of sexual all the time, joking and saying, "Oooh, I would like to give her one." We were young, and our hormones were taking over our bodies. We would smile at all the pretty girls. They knew we were hungry wolves wanting to eat them up.

It was around 3:00 p.m. when the train left Windhoek train station. The trip felt different. We traveled through a more extreme semi-desert terrain, and there were sand dunes everywhere. It was night when we reached Swakopmund beside the Atlantic Ocean. We traveled through the station at almost a walking speed. We heard that Walvis Bay was another thirty-five clicks going south, and the train should take around fifty minutes to get there.

When we arrived at Walvis Bay train station, it was late at night. There were many Bedford troop carriers waiting for us. The tar road leading up to the Rooikop camp was in reasonably good condition. There were no street lights going there, so it was pitch black dark.

Our camp at Rooikop (Red Hill) was thirteen kilometers inland and at a ninety-degree angle away from Walvis Bay. It was situated in the desert beside a large red rock—I guess it had a lot of iron in it. There was a small army airport next to our camp.

The area was known as Rooikop Valley. In the desert there was a large red rock hill that was shaped like an orange section that was buried three-quarters in the sand. It was about thirty meters high, two hundred meters long, and thirty meters wide. The desert was flat, and we could see Rooikop from miles away.

When we arrived at the camp, we found the sleeping quarters in a huge metal corrugated hangar. In the hangar was netting suspended between the support beams. The beds and steel cupboards were in rows on the concrete floors. It was a weird feeling, knowing that our armored vehicles were in the one-half of the same hangar. We were separated from the vehicles by a corrugated metal partition.

The first comment was, "We don't have to polish the floors." Our army gear was now khaki and blended in with the desert sand. I thought we all looked cool and dusted in our faded dessert gear.

We were told that after being six months in the army, we were now called *ou-manne*—old men. From the first day at Rooikop, life was so different. It was weird to wake up at 6:30 a.m. as it was getting light and have breakfast at seven thirty.

The food in the camp was great, and we had a small convenience store situated next to the main gate. We spent many hours cleaning our armored vehicles. It was strange to do maneuvers in the desert. The attack formations were different. Everything seemed to be in a relaxed mood, and our training was at a slower pace.

The officers all lived in Walvis Bay. During the week they would arrive around 9:00 a.m. and leave between 4:00 and 5:00 p.m.

After dinner, the camp was quiet, and we only had guard duty to attend to, twenty-four/seven. It was our troop's turn once a week to stand beat. We were off on every second weekend from Friday at 5:00 p.m. until Monday at 7:15 a.m. roll call before breakfast. Every Friday at five, a few Bedford trucks went to Walvis Bay. We could hitch a ride into town.

On our troop's first weekend off, Greg, Brian, and I decided to stay in Walvis Bay for the weekend. We rented some rooms in a boarding house in the center of town. We discovered that the boarding house was not far from the town's only movie theater.

It was just after 7:00 p.m. when we entered the movie theater. It was more like a theater hall, with a wide screen that pulled down. Behind the last row of chairs was a large projector on a table. It was great movie house. All the chairs were elevated and the seats were arranged in semicircle looking down at the stage area. It was a treat to sit in the theater and watch a movie.

We saw a lot of girls there. We would stare at them with their short skirts and dresses. We were hungry wolves, ready to pounce on them. Our African hearts were wild and beating fast. Next to the theater building was a roadhouse with a large area to sit and eat. After watching the movie, we went to the roadhouse for burgers and Cokes. The place was huge and always packed. There were many girls sitting at the classic American sixties-era booths.

We felt excited and strange at the same time. We noticed all the girls staring at us army boys. They'd giggle and laugh. Greg, our crew commander, was a good-looking blond boy, and he was always a front runner. After eating our burgers, Greg said; let's go chat with the group of girls at the table next to ours." The girls were around seventeen or so and all were pretty. Greg got up, and Brian and I followed him. He was smooth, doing his casual stance next to the four girls' table. He pushed his hair back with his fingers and said, "Hi. I have noticed that you girls are staring at us. By the way, I am Greg, and this is Mike and Brian."

I stood beside Greg and put out my hand. I shook their hands one by one, saying, "Hi, I am Mike," and so did my buddies. Greg said, "This is our first time here in Walvis Bay. Is there a bar anywhere, so we can buy you girls a drink?"

A pretty black-haired girl said, "Yeah, there are a few closer to the dockside area. We are not eighteen yet and are not allowed to go in." She smiled and said, "We're underage."

Greg stood there frowning. I butted in and said, "That's okay. There must be an alternative." I said, "Is there a store nearby where we can buy some beers?" It was around ten o'clock at night.

A pretty blonde German girl said, "You are out of luck. They all close at nine o'clock. Sorry."

I said, "You have a German accent. What is your name?"

She looked like a casual girl with whom I could easily talk with. She said, "*Ja*. I am Heidi, and you are Mike"

I replied, "*Ja*. You are right on, so where can we all have some fun?"

The dark-haired girl said, "Hi, I am Jessie, and this is Joslyn and Greta."

"Ah, another German girl," I said with a smile. "Is there anywhere in Walvis Bay where we can find some beers and have some fun?" I noticed that Heidi was looking at me and sizing me up.

"We can all go to Jessie's house," Heidi said. "That's just around the corner. Her father and mother are working the night shift and are not at home."

They all finished their soft drinks, and we went outside. We were in our army gear and looked cool with our bush hats on. As I walked through the doorway, I noticed that Greg had slipped his hand in Jessie's hand. Heidi was walking in front of me. I called out, "Hey, wait up, Heidi." I slid my hand in hers as I came up from behind her.

Brian seemed to be the slow one, and I guess he had two girls to choose from. He was a shy boy and did not know which one to hold hands with. We all walked to Jessie's house, only five minutes from the roadhouse. Here we were on our first night in Walvis Bay, and I was holding hands with a pretty German girl. We entered the garden and walked toward the house.

Jessie softly said, "We can sit on the veranda because my younger brother and sister are sleeping in the house."

We sat and chatted for a while, and I had a brainstorm. I asked Jessie if her dad had beer in the house. She hesitantly said, "Yeah, he has a lot in the pantry." I suggested that the other guys and I buy the beers from her dad.

I said to Jessie, "We will give you enough money for twenty-four beers. We can replace it in the morning while your folks are asleep."

We all chipped in and gave the cash to Jessie. Greg followed her in the house and came out with a crate of Windhoek lager beer. We all sat on the veranda at the large table and chairs. I was still holding Heidi's hand, sitting next to her at the table.

In the bright veranda light, I saw how good-looking she was. Jessie, though, was the perfect-looking girl, and Greg was all over her. Brian sat next to Greta, and I guess he was also fascinated with her German accent. After we finished our first round of beers, the girls were more relaxed, and the conversation was about kissing and sex and so on.

Greg did not waste any time. While we were on our second beers, he kissed Jessie. I saw Heidi looking at them having a full-on French kiss, tongues down their throats. I put my arm around Heidi's shoulders and pulled her chair closer next to mine, where our legs were touching each other. I asked her politely, "Can I kiss you?" She had amazing watery blue eyes and said, "Yeah, why are you so slow?" my-gosh, she was weird, and I did her a favor--I French-kissed her. After the third round of beers, the girls were getting tipsy and seemed to be getting looser.

It was now around midnight, and the girls mentioned that they needed to get home. We left Jessie's house, but Greg stayed back. Brian and I walked with the other girls home.

All of them lived close to Jessie's home. We went to Heidi's home last. I gave Brian the key to our rooms, and I stayed with Heidi for a while on her front veranda. I could see she was a bit nervous because her folks were home, even though they were asleep.

We chatted softly, and I kissed her many times. I asked her if I we could meet up in two weeks when I had my leave pass.

She asked me to wait and she would be back shortly. Heidi entered the house and returned a few minutes with a note. We had a fast kiss and she said, "We can meet up in Swakopmund (Black Hill Plane) in the next town nearby in two weeks, on the Friday night."

In the note was an address she had written down. She spun around and was gone, closing the door behind her.

It was a funny night. I knew that my time in Walvis Bay would be a blast. I stood there thinking, *Damn, I didn't ask her if we could meet up tomorrow.*

I walked back to the boarding house, feeling strange and excited at the same time.

I woke up early the next morning and knocked on Greg's door to see if he was up. It took a while for him to open the door. He looked in a daze from the lack of sleep. We chatted about the previous night's events.

Brian joined us in Greg's room about an hour later. After breakfast we ventured around the town center and the shipping dock area. After lunch we went to one of the bars. We had to show our IDs to get in. We were all over eighteen years old and had no problem getting in the Shipwreck Pub and Grill.

Being young, we had about six beers within a few hours. We had "pub grub"—cottage pie, gravy and chips, and veggies for a late lunch. Brian and I stayed behind and played pool while Greg left to meet Jessie at the dinner roadhouse, where we had met the girls the night before.

When he returned, Jessie, Heidi, and Greta were with him. All that was needed for the underage girls to come in to the pub was for someone over eighteen to sign them in.

That night we drank many beers, and we had a few shooters.

Heidi was wearing a short mini-dress with leg warmers underneath. She was slightly overweight and had wide hips. Her face was pretty with freckles on it. Her long straight hair gave her a wild, daring look.

Jessie was very good looking and her body was awesome. Greta was short and plump, but her smile would light up a room.

Brian looked so much in love with her. He would follow her around like a puppy dog. I had a feeling that he was a virgin. I noticed that Jessie fancied me and was mostly talking to me. I could feel the excitement between us.

We had a few more shooters with the girls and many more beers. I walked Heidi back to her parents' house. Heidi said, "We will see each other in two weeks on Friday at the address I gave you." I gave her a kiss and a hug, but the feeling was a little different, as if she had to keep a distance from me.

On Saturday night when I fell asleep, I was like a rock. In the morning, Greg, Brian, and I got together around eleven o'clock. We walked around Walvis Bay and to the shipping dock area. We had our lunch at the boarding house. After lunch we went back to the Shipwreck Pub and played pool and had many beers. We had arranged for the army Bedford to pick us up at 6:30 p.m., before it got dark, because the road back to camp was scary at night. There were no streetlights and when the wind blew, the desert sand covered the road. The headlamps on the Bedford were terrible, so the view would be blurry in front of the truck.

We were in luck on that Sunday night for the wind was calm, and we made it back to camp just as it was getting dark. My first weekend pass in Walvis Bay had been awesome. Our Scorpion armored vehicle guys had an awesome time with the hot chicks in town. Greg, Brian, and I were closer, and our friendship was great. While stationed in the desert, the mood was always kind of relaxed. We were now doing a lot of shooting exercises. The hot desert heat was becoming too much for us.

During the weeks that followed, we ventured many times up the Rooikop rock. It was a great view, standing on the highest section of the red rock. We'd get a six-pack of beer for each of us and climb up that red rock and sit there until the sun set. The semi-desert was very white and when the moon shone brightly, it illuminated the desert. At night, we could clearly see for miles away.

Time passed by and it was Friday our weekend off. Greg, Brian, and I, along with eight other troop guys, went to Swakopmund. Swakopmund was a small seaside fishing village of about five thousand people.

It was way past six when we got to a cheap hotel that Jessie had told us about. Greg Brian and I decided not to tell the guys about the party house that the girls had mentioned. After checking in, we had our showers and arranged to meet up in the lounge area at 8:00 p.m.

The guys went to the bar for some drinks and shooting pool. We told them that we were going for a walk about the village, to see how it looked at night. It was sort of a small lie, but we knew that we would have a better time alone. I had a map with me and knew that we had to walk away from the train station toward the dockside. After a fifteen-minute walk, we came to the edge of the town. I saw a large house near the railway track, and we could hear the music playing. We knew we had found the party house.

When we got closer, we noticed a few bikes parked on the side of the house. A few guys and many dolls were dancing on the front lawn. Brian seemed to be wary and said, "This place looks dangerous. Do you think it is safe?" I said, "Yeah, of course it is.

At that moment we saw Jessie, Heidi, and Greta walking toward us with a bunch of girls. I heard Jessie call out, "You guys made it!" Heidi came up to me and gave me a kiss on my mouth. Two of the other German girls did the same, saying hi and kissing me.

Heidi kissed Greg and Brian as well. Jessie did the same and French-kissed me. I was feeling funny but kept my cool and followed the girls into the house.

In the living room there was a large stereo system against the one wall. There were five sofas and two chairs against the walls. The living room was huge, the biggest I had ever seen.

We walked through the dining room and into the large kitchen at the rear of the house. I saw five old-style fridges against one wall. There was a long eating table with twelve chairs in the center of the floor.

Jessie introduced us to the five guys who stayed in this party house. They were all in their twenties. The biker dudes had long hair, beards, and tattoos everywhere. They all looked down-to-earth. I noticed Greg was frowning as he observed what was going on here. There seemed to be about five girls for every guy, and my mind went "boom." I saw Heidi open the first fridge, and it was full of beers. She passed us each a beer and said, "All the fridges are full of beers and the party is on."

A metal letter box was mounted against the wall next to a beer fridge. Painted on the side with red paint was "Beer money donation; only ten-buck notes."

I nudged Greg and Brian, and we all put a tenner through the opening of the letter box. That was it; we paid our cover charge and could party until we dropped.

I figured out what was going on here. Many girls asked us where we were from back home. They wanted to know how long we'd be here in the army. I knew they were all small-town hot chicks who were bored.

It was funny, for Heidi, Jessie, and Greta was in the mix of all the girls. In the conversations, we learned that most of the town's guys were away with work in other parts of Namibia. This small town had not much industry, and Walvis Bay was a low-paid fishing port.

While sitting outside, talking, with many girls around us, a biker dude came over to us. He spoke with a strange German accent. "The three of you army guys are welcome here, but I do not want to see the others who are in town. Most of the army guys only want to get drunk and fight with us."

"What do you guys do in these small towns?" Greg asked.

"There is nothing else to do in this small town but party and get drunk," he said. "Me and my guys are looking after all the girls in town. When it is time to rotate, we go to work and they stay behind."

The beers were flowing extremely fast, and it seemed like every fifteen minutes or so, one of the girls would bring another round of Windhoek or Hansa. I found out that the town had a brewery and some of the girls worked there. They would get the cases of beer, dirt cheap.

Jessie was hanging on my arm, and I knew that she wanted to be my girl. Greg looked at me strangely. I shrugged, as if to say, "What do you want me to do?" I noticed two girls look at us, as if they could see the tension.

They walked over to Greg, and they both put their hands around him. I saw them whispering something in his ear, and they walked off. The tension was broken and the party was full on.

Greg, Brian, and I were too drunk to make our way back to the hotel and crashed at the party house. We were young and enjoying life.

In the morning, I was up first at around seven o'clock, and I made some coffee. I was starving and found some bread in the bread bin.

I made my way to the front veranda and sat on a chair to look out at the sea. Small waves were crashing on the beach.

I was alone, as everyone else was still sleeping. About ten minutes later, I had the strangest experience. While I was having my mug of coffee and bread, Heidi came out of the front door and sat next to me. We were quiet for a while.

Heidi said, "It is a casual way of life here." She described the different way of life in these small fishing towns.

After our talk, I had a shower and waited for Greg and Brian to surface. It was around nine o'clock when Greg, Brian, and I were ready to venture to the town. Jessie, Heidi, and Greta asked if they could join us. They said they would buy breakfast for us at Hauser House Pub and Restaurant. Jessie hooked her arm in mine as we walked to town. Heidi grabbed Greg's hand. Brian had his flame, Greta, and it seemed as if he was building true love with her. His smile was so wide, and he seemed to be in heaven.

We spent the day with the girls, going to three pubs. The third pub was where the rest of the army guys were hanging out. They were all surprised at how smooth we were to pick up girls in this small town. We did not mention the party house.

When we got back to the party house with the girls, the party was full on. We stayed the night and got steaming drunk. On Sunday after lunch, we had a few drinks in the Station Hotel Pub and left Swakopmund at around four o'clock to return to camp.

Before we left Swakopmund, we made arrangements to meet up with the girls in two weeks, on our next weekend pass. It was weird—we had checked in the hotel but never spent any time in our rooms.

Each month that followed seemed to be the same as the next. The only good thing was that the South African Army had new, smaller Mercedes Benz Unimorg troop carrier vehicles. They replaced the old-style Bedford trucks. They had large tires on a short wheel base. It had all the trimmings, with eight gears. It also had four-wheel drive and a diff-lock lever that let all the tires rotate at the same time.

We were told that we would be stationed up on the Higher Caprivi Strip area, protecting Namibia where it borders Angola and Zambia. We were told that we would be up there for three months, from early October until early January 1975.

It was now the third week in July and we had to prepare all our maneuvers and formations regularly for bush warfare. We were stationed in the desert but preparing being in thick jungle.

We still had our second weekends off each month, and we would join the girls and party in the Swakopmund house.

Jessie was changing, and I had a feeling that she was building true love with me.

The months went by fast and my time was up. We were going to the Caprivi Strip. We got orders that we would be based in Katima Mulilo and stationed in a large base called Camp Katima.

On that last Sunday together, Jessie and I made a pact that we would get together after I was back in South Africa. She was going to write me a letter every day while I was up on the border camp. When we finally departed, I looked at her waving to me. She had many tears running down her face. In my heart I knew that this was it, and my Namibia exciting times were over. In the four months and a week in the Rooikop camp, Jessie and I had had nine weekends together.

My memories of the Namibia girls were that they were all laid-back and casual. When they partied and drank, the action continued solidly for days. Greg, Brian, and I always talked and laughed about our experiences with the girls. We would say, "Shit, these Namibia girls can party until I am man-down. I am so exhausted and tired that I have to leopard-crawl to the bathroom."

It was one more week to go before we would leave the Rooikop camp for the border. It was on this Tuesday when the wind picked up, and we had a full-on sandstorm, it happened around four-o'clock in the morning. The wind was so severe that we could not move or dare to get out of our beds. The storm was so noisy that it sounded as if the corrugated metal sheets were sandblasted from the wind. Next to my bed was a fire bucket with a loose plastic cover over it to keep out the dirt. I was smart and wet my face cloth in it and put it over my mouth. I put my army towel over my face and the fire bucket cover over my towel. I was breathing in the clean, wet moisture of the face cloth and not breathing in the dust that was choking us in that hangar building.

The storm carried on for around four hours before it started to settle down. During those four hours, many of the young boys were panicking. I could hear some of them crying. While the sandstorm was going full on, I fell asleep for around an hour. When I woke up it was starting to get light. I peeped through and opening of my towel over my face but could not see a thing. There was a cloud of dust hanging like fog in the hangar.

I also felt as if someone had emptied a ton of sand on my bed. I tried to move my legs. The blanket on my bed was heavy with all the sand on it. I pushed my legs straight until I could feel that they were a little loose. I slowly moved my arms until the sand gradually fell off my bed. Eventually, my arms were free under the blanket. I moved my legs and arms together until I had most of the sand off my bed. This storm was the worst that we had experienced. I was glad it happened while we were all sleeping in the hangar. If we'd been out in the desert somewhere, I am sure that there would have been many deaths. By eight o'clock, the wind died down, and we could get out of our beds.

We opened the hangar doors and saw how much desert sand had blown into our sleeping quarters. The morning's breakfast could not be prepared, so we all ate bread and jam with coffee. After breakfast it was roll call to see if we were okay. About fifteen guys had to see the medic with eye infections. We had to clean and remove all the sand from the inside of the hangar and clean our Panzers. It was after lunch when we saw a few officers come by. They were concerned if we were okay.

In the remaining days at Rooikop, we had a day off. The officers took us to a place south of Walvis Bay. It was a treat to see the rust-colored sand dunes there. They were not far from the white sand dunes, but we were told that during a sandstorm, the sand of the dunes never mixed.

We were told that the red sand dunes were the most dangerous dunes on earth. If you get lost in them, it is a death trap. The dunes consistently moved when the wind blew over them, and a compass would go around in circles.

All the Bedfords and some Unimorgs were parked on the harder desert next to the red dunes. We sat there beside the army troop carrier truck on some dried tree trunks for around four hours, chatting and observing the red dunes from a distance. We observed a high peak disappear and another two smaller dunes were formed. It was kind of hypnotic, seeing the red sand dunes come alive.

After lunch we made our way to some white dunes not far from our Rooikop camp. We had a lot of fun climbing up the dunes to the top peak. We would slide down on pieces of cardboard with the front bent up to form a ski. It was amazing how fast we could accelerate down the high dunes. The only issue was climbing back up again, but it was good exercise.

We knew that our army experience in the desert were over. On Tuesday we handed in our desert gear. We were back to wearing our army browns, our bush clothes.

Late in the afternoon we saw three Hercules camouflaged twin-prop planes land at the airport next to our Rooikop camp. On Wednesday before sunrise, we were taken in the Bedford trucks to the airport. While waiting to board the plane, the prop engines were started up. The noise was exhilarating, and the propeller wind was awesome to feel. In formation and with all our duffel bags, rifles, and full gear, we started to board the plane.

Our troop and support-section guys were first to board. We were in the front section of the first plane. My heart was in my throat—this would be my first flight on a plane, and it was a beast, a Hercules plane.

The latch back opening flap was opened to the concrete platform. It was so wide that a tank could be driven in and loaded in the belly of the plane. The seating was in harnesses suspended on the sides. My harness was next to a small window hatch and close to the open cockpit seating area.

Two guys were sitting in the open cockpit, flying the Hercules. The center section had four army Jeeps strapped to the floor. They were being transported to the border area.

While I strapped myself in the harness seat, my heart was beating like a Zulu warrior's attack drumbeat. Within minutes, the back hatch was hoisted up, and we could hear the whine of the hydraulics closing it. This happened while the plane was moving forward to the end of the runway. I remember the vibration and the brute-force feeling as this huge plane moved over the runway.

At the end of the short runway, the Hercules did a sharp U-turn. We could feel the plane jerk to a halt. The pilot started to rev up the four propeller engines. My heart was pounding. It felt more exhilarating than a roller-coaster ride.

The huge Hercules jerked slightly forward as the pilot held the breaks. This huge beast of a plane shuddered, as vibrations ran through the metal framework. I almost died from excitement.

It happened: the pilot released the breaks—and my heart seemed to leave my body. We were accelerating down the runway toward the desert ahead. The thrust and noise was like no other that I have ever experienced. The G-force pushed my shoulders against Greg, sitting next to me on my right. Brian, to my left, was forced against me.

The engines made a loud, whining, ballistic noise. The fat-bad-cat Hercules plane was hurtling on a path of no return, toward the desert at the end of the runway. The vibrations and shudder suddenly ended in a strange lift motion, and I heard a loud snap—and we were airborne.

The Hercules banked sharply left as it started to climb higher away from the airport. I looked out the small window and could see the Rooikop camp and the amazing red rock protruding from the flat desert landscape. It was a treat and a moment of joy.

The Hercules straightened out. While we climbed to the flying altitude, the propellers made a deep drumming sound. It was awesome to feel this heavy plane gliding through the open skies and clouds. The props went into a softer humming sound, and I knew that we had reached our flying altitude. Every now and then, the Hercules would free-fall a bit as it hit air pockets in the sky. I looked down the inside of the plane and saw some guys had throw-up bags over their mouths from their first flying experience.

My buddies and I could not stop chatting about this awesome adventure. We were in the right army frame of mind. We knew that where we were going, it would be a whole lot more extreme than what we had ever experienced.

Many hours passed before we heard the engine prop noise slow down, and the plane did a rapid descent.

While going through the clouds, I could hear that it was raining, and the loud plane noise was more like a muffled sound. My ears were also blocked from the difference in altitude and the fast descent of the plane.

When I looked out of the little window, I could see the heavy rain droplets streaking across the window. I knew that we were going to land in a thunderstorm.

All the big-brass officers were sitting opposite us. Our major spoke over the intercom, saying, "Don't be afraid. We are going to fly below the radar detection height, so we will be flying close to the tree-top level. We will be landing in a thunderstorm, and we are twenty minutes away from Mpatcha Army Air Base in the Caprivi Strip."

The major instructed, "I want you all to make sure that you are tightly strapped in your harness seats. The plane landing will be bumpy and more severe with the heavy rain that we are experiencing."

Coming from the desert and the endless sunny days, it felt as if we were entering hell. The Hercules plane was shuddering and swaying from side to side. We experienced many slight free-fall jerks as we flew low toward Mpatcha.

I thought, *I am sure this good pilot has done this route hundreds of times. It is just another normal day for him.*

It was like telepathy for the pilot said over the intercom, "Hey, dudes, buckle up. We are coming in for a crash landing." I heard the prop engines slow down, and the plane suddenly dropped like a falcon in the sky.

Brian was always afraid of heights and cried, "What the fuck! A crash landing?" Greg was a hoot and said; "Yeah, ma bro'er, with all this rain, the Hercules is going to go slip-slide skiing down the runway." I cracked up laughing and told Brian, "Hey, bro, the pilot's only joking. Hold on tight."

The Hercules plane landed hard with a loud thud as the many wheels made a forceful landing on the tarmac below. The pilot hit the plane's brakes with force. We could hear a screeching sound, and the huge Hercules plane shuddered forcefully for around ten seconds. We felt it slow down drastically.

My heart was pounding, and my body was trembling. At that moment, we heard the crazy-dude pilot say, "Yeah, we have survived. This is one of my better landings." Yep, he was crazy and maybe the best that we had, landing the heavy plane in those crazy conditions.

Chapter Four

Katima

The First Few Weeks in the Caprivi Heartlands

The pilot positioned the plane between the trees on the large concrete slab. The propellers were still spinning, and the noise was exhilarating. It was early in the afternoon, and the thunderstorm was in full force.

Within seconds the back hatch slowly opened up until it came to rest on the concrete slab. I knew we were going to be based in a tropical location, so I had my army raincoat tucked in my side webbing pouch. I unbuckled my safety harness and quickly put on my raincoat.

Most of the guys had not realized that we were going to a tropical area where it rained a lot. We heard a lightning bolt strike, sending lightning flashes in the dark clouds. The bolt hit the earth with an angry force.

We received orders to depart through the open rear hatch and to proceed in a slow run toward the large mess tent. While departing through the hatch, the wind from the props sprayed us with water. We covered our faces with our left hands while running in a fast trot. I gazed around at all the large trees and knew that we were now in the thick jungle, where the action was.

My heart was pounding out of control and the fear in me was electrifying. The experience of the noise of the Hercules plane and the sudden entry into this large tent made me feel as if we were dropped into a war zone. I knew from this moment onward, we were army-trained men.

In the large circus-style mess tent, everything happened fast. We were told to keep together with our troops and support sections and wait for orders.

Our 2-SSB major shouted through a loudspeaker. "Quiet!" He informed us that we would be sleeping in tents at the air base. We all needed to crunch up, sleeping twelve men in a five-by-five-meter tent.

Our armored troops had a fold-up style army beds. When opened up, it was about one foot off the ground. The armored support troops all had to sleep on the hard ground in rainproof sleeping bags.

It seemed as if our Troop One, "the Scorpions," always had preference. We were in the first tents, and Troops Two, Three, and so on. Our Lieutenant Trevor was a cool-cat dude and always made us sleep in a position that was practical for all. The rear formation armored-vehicle guys would sleep at the rear end of the tent. Greg, Brian, and I were vehicle-one guys and were sleeping near the front open flap. Trevor always told us, "If the shit hits the fan, it is easier to run out of the tent in your vehicle formation positions toward our armored vehicles."

After we had our dinner in the mess tent, we got confirmed orders that we would be leaving early the next morning for Katima Mulilo. We would travel in Bedfords in a convoy towards the Zambezi River. This was where our main base camp, Katima, was located. We would be based there for around three months on border-defense duty.

We all were excited. The talk was about how extreme the Caprivi border area looked and comparing it to the desert and the Rooikop army camp. When we left Walvis Bay, it was a blue sky and a hell-hot day. We landed in the jungle, experiencing a cold-wind tropical storm. Damn, it was the extreme.

After our cold showers, a few of us walked around the base camp. Mpatcha air strip looked more like a temporary landing strip base, with all the tents and vehicles scattered in the bush. I guess it was sort of camouflaged from the air.

Once back in our tent, I lay on my sleeping bag. My life was exciting in every way possible. I knew that Katima Mulilo was going to be an awesome experience.

Most of the guys in our Scorpion troop were tough and ready for action. We all looked at the situation as an adventure. My army buddies Greg and Brian were also in a good frame of mind. I felt secure, and I was happy and lucky to be with them.

I always experienced premonitions when I found myself in new countries. Namibia and the Caprivi Strip location had good karma. I was happy to be there. When the tent lights went out, I fell asleep, like a rock.

We woke up just before dawn. There was no time for showers. It was only brushing teeth and a fast splash of water on our faces. After breakfast, we got ready for our road trip to Katima Mulilo. The heavy rain had stopped but it was drizzling slightly. The low gray clouds made the morning feel gloomy. The mist and fog was hovering between the tents and trees. The air was damp in the thick African bush.

Roll call was taken, and immediately we had to mount the Bedfords parked on the muddy road leading out of Mpatcha Air Base.

Just before setting off, we noticed a strange-looking vehicle positioned in the front of the Bedford vehicles. Our lieutenant told us that it was a Hottentot god—a black tribal god. It was the back end of a tractor with a bulldozer scraper frame attached to the front of it. There were twenty-four wheels in the steering column mechanism. The tire frame was wide, covering the width of the road. The tractor-steering contraption had a thick armor, coned-shaped plate that could take the impact force of a land mine. The Hottentot-god contraption would drive up front, with the convoy of army vehicles following behind it.

Our troop and support section guys were in the third Bedford truck behind this land-mine sweeper.

It was just after seven in the morning when we left Mpatcha airfield base camp. The road was muddy from the previous day's rain. We could travel at only ten kilometers per hour. While traveling on these muddy roads, Greg sat beside the open back hatch and me and Brian and the rest of the bunch. We had a good view of the road and the thick bushland. At some really bad sections of road, the Bedford would whine in low gear and the tires would spin. On route to Katima Mulilo, we stopped two times. This was where the convoy had to go through the road sections that were washed away from the previous day's thunderstorm.

When the Bedford stopped, we had to dismount and get in a fighting formation on the sides of the road. It was a good time to stretch our legs. On the second dismount, five Bedfords were stuck in the mud, and it took hours to get them out.

The light drizzle continued, and we finally made it to Katima Mulilo at around three o'clock. The huge Katima army camp was on the right side of the road; to the left was the Zambezi River. I gazed at the awesome landscape with a hypnotic stare. My heart was pounding in my chest, and I thought, *Katima looks great.* The trees were very high and there were many of them next to the riverbank.

At the main gate there was a large sign that read "Camp Katima."

As we drove through the main gate, I noticed three layers of fencing around the camp. The center fence was electrified. I also saw endless rows of tents in different locations. They were in straight rows with wide paths between them.

The Bedford vehicles stopped one by one. We all dismounted and formed a drilling parade formation. We were the third Bedford to enter the camp and form a line in the front row section. It was great to be in the front line, facing the stage in front of us.

We saw the army guys that we were relieving. They all seemed happy going back to Civilian Street. They all looked rough; most of the guys had mustaches and beards and fairly long hair. We all had crew-cuts; it looked like a lawnmower had a field day with our hair.

While standing in formation the *ou-manne* (old men) mounted the Bedfords and called out, "*Tjords*" ("Cheers"). They had beers in their hands and said, "We outta here!"

Greg frowned at me, but I had a huge smile on my face and told him, "Yep, life is going to be a blast here in Camp Katima."

We stood in formation for around twenty minutes; while all the other army guys dismounted the Bedfords and formed a roll-call position. It was not long before we saw the big-brass guys walking toward the stage.

All the army brass sat on the wooden stage that was about three feet off the ground. There was podium in the center of the stage with a microphone resting on it.

The big cheese, General Botha stood behind the podium. It was the first time I had seen an army general. He was dressed in his army bush clothes, army cap, and all the castles on his army shirt. General Botha gave us a welcome speech. He congratulated us on completing our national service training and told us, "You are now in the real world, supporting Southwest Africa (Namibia) and fighting against the regime."

He assured us that we were the best at bush warfare and that we would eliminate all who dared try to attack the South African Special Service Battalion forces. He continued, "You will be exposed to many extreme elements in these harsh border conditions here in the Caprivi heartland and Caprivi Strip. Daily the Zam-boons [Zambian baboons; actually Zambian terrorist men] cross the Zambezi River and kill and rape the black Caprivi Strip women, men, and children. They will steal all their belongings and cross back over the river."

General Botha said, "The Zambian town Sesheke is just to the right of Katima Mulilo. That is where most of the Zam-boon Terks hide out." He raised his voice and told us, "We will not tolerate their killing and raping the Southwest Africa people who live peacefully here in the Caprivi."

We were told that we were more than twenty thousand South African armed forces protecting the Southwest Africa people. This was from the Skeleton Coast up to Victoria Falls.

This general was a hard case. He said there were about five hundred new arrivals. "I will take no shit from anyone who dares fight our South African boys. You are all trained to fight and to protect one another and the people of this land. Make us proud and be on your guard. We are strong, and they are weak. We are trained to kill these bastards, and they are brainwashed to rape the women and young girls and to take whatever they can find." he said; "May God be with you. We have an outstanding performance in this region, and sadly, we have lost twenty-seven men this year. We have killed thousands of these Zam-boons and Ango-lie soldiers (Angolan soldiers). You will be stationed here for three months. I want all of you to go back home safely and to be proud to have saved the people of this land." He sat down, and we all cheered and shouted, "Hoorah, General!"

Our Major Briggs got up and told us, "The army does not stop for anything." He informed us on the size of our camp and what our firepower was. He said, "Our main objective is to differentiate between the local black people and the terrorist black regime." It was mostly what clothes people were warring and the different attitudes when confronting them. Their Zambian languish was different, and their skin color was darker black.

In a flash, our troops' and support sections' names were called out. Our tent numbers were given to us. It worked out well for the Panzer unit had the best location, closer to the mess and large canteen building.

It sounded so great when the first troop names were mentioned. We heard "Troop One, Scorpions, will be in tents one to eight. Troop Two, Tarantulas, will be in tents nine to sixteen …" And he went on and on. When our tent numbers were called out, we had to hustle with our gear and find our tents.

My bed was first on the left, with Greg's on the right. Brian was in the right back bed. It was great for we were the only three in a reasonable-sized tent. We had a large steel Trommel next to our beds where we keep all our army gear in. The floor was covered with a thick hard canvas that kept the dampness out. The beds were army metal frames with a reasonably thick sponge mattress.

Our lieutenant was sleeping in the tent two up from ours. After about fifteen minutes of settling in, he was summoned to report at headquarters immediately. The rest of us were joking about this grand camp. We unpacked our duffel bags and waited for orders.

Trevor was away for around a half hour. On his return, he gathered our troop and section together in front of the mess area. The sergeant major gave us our orders to make our way to the armored vehicle depot and collect our 90mm Panzers. We needed to do a thorough inspection and be ready for a night patrol. We also had to load up with rations, ammo, and diesel.

Our armored vehicles were all in good condition and painted camouflaged. They each had a small red scorpion painted on the rear with words "Sting One," "Sting Two," and three and four.

The support rifle troopers had a Benz Unimorg troop carrier with words painted on the side: "Scorpion Road Warrior One." The Unimorg Road Warrior Two had the medic, engineers, land mine experts, and ration supplies and was towing a small water trailer.

Just before 6:00 p.m., we reported to HQ to receive our orders for the night patrol. The HQ tent was larger than the rest. Inside there were many folding chairs on a canvas floor cover. At the back of the tent was a screen with a slide projector. There also were many large maps on tripod stands.

I sat in the front row with my ammo gear on, feeling as if I was invincible and going on this fighting maneuver adventure. When all thirty of us were seated, the tent flaps were closed, and it was semidark inside.

Captain Ziggy welcomed us and gave a short speech on what was expected from us on the night patrol. Lieutenant Trevor took control of our mission discussions for the night patrol. While doing his presentation, it was mostly maps and aerial pictures of where the action was. There were red circles where all the bad guys' recorded action was. The red lines on the map were where the prospective ambush locations were. The brown X marks were where the land mines were discovered. The X marks with a circle around them were where the land mines had exploded, causing harm. I counted seven of them.

We were informed it was going to be a half-night's traveling patrol. We had to make camp near Kasane, the tip of the Caprivi, where the Zambezi and Chobe Rivers meet. We also needed to take supplies to our South African Infantry treetop guard post.

After the induction meeting, the nonranking personnel were informed to leave and to prep and wait for our crew commanders' and officers' return. Brian and I and the rest of the bunch made our way to our patrol vehicles.

Being the front armored vehicle was the most dangerous patrol position. In those years the land mines were always set off to explode immediately when driving over it.

Brian and I did a quick walk around our 90mm Panzer and sat inside our driver and gunner seats. I put on my head gear helmet with built-in headphones. I set my radios and positioned my microphone and voice control.

My thoughts were racing, and I was feeling giddy and lightheaded. I knew that tonight's patrol would be an experience of a lifetime. My hands were shaking and I knew this was it.

Brian and I did a quick radio intercom check. I spoke with the other armored vehicles gunners and the support section radio operator. Being the gunner up front in the Scorpion One vehicle, I would be in control of all the communications of our Scorpion unit patrol when our crew commander was busy.

I set my second radio to the HQ frequency listed for the night's patrol. I did a quick check with HQ, saying our vehicle's call sign for the night. "Delta-Alpha, Delta-Alpha, this is Charley-Echo radio check. Over." All was good, and I clearly heard, "Charley-Echo, Charley-Echo, I hear you loud and clear. You are good to roll. Over and out."

Seconds later I heard Greg come through the side door hatch to get in his crew commander position. Soon our lieutenant's voice came out on our vehicle's communication radio frequency. "Zulu-Yankee, Zulu-Yankee, we are ready to roll, Charley-Echo. Let's roll. Over."

Greg took charge of the communications and called out, "Zulu Yankee, Zulu Yankee, we are rolling. Over and out."

My heart was pounding like a Zulu warrior. This would be our first time going on patrol in a danger-one listed zone.

From our Katima base camp, the patrol stretched toward the village of Kasane. This was at the point of the Caprivi Strip, where the Zambezi and Chobe Rivers meet. The distance was around 150 kilometers to Kasane. Around half that distance was a good surface dirt road. The rest of the route was on a hard path between the bushes and trees. The sun was setting fast, and my heart was burning with desire being here and experiencing this new adventure. The night patrol gave a bigger boost of excitement.

While seated in the closed armored vehicle, we had our dim interior light on. We were going through the maps. All the main routes were on this map, which was plastic. I figured out that was to protect the map when it rains. Everyone in our Scorpions unit was issued a map.

While traveling at a mere twenty to thirty clicks per hour, our talk was of the exhilarating moments. Within minutes of leaving the outskirts of Camp Katima, suddenly in front of us were the thick brush and trees. It felt as if we had entered a rain forest, and the bush and trees were larger and denser than what we had ever experienced.

Greg and I opened up our hatches to get into the gunner and crew commander seat position on top of our Panzer. The 7.62mm Browning belt-driven machine gun was in front of me between my legs. I got myself comfortable and cocked it to fire in the at-will position. Greg adjusted the huge spotlights that were above his head.

I looked at him with endless joy. I had a huge smile on my face. Greg said, "You are weird. We are in the most dangerous and extremely harsh land in Africa, and it looks as if you are happy to be here." I said, "Have no fear, bro. We have enough firepower in this Panzer to kill all the Zam-boons that want to pick a fight with us." Greg smiled and said, "I have no fear, Bro-Mike. Let's do it."

I was amazed at the beauty of the land. It was green everywhere, and the after rain, the fresh smell of the trees and shrubs gave me goose bumps all over my body. The red sunset was directly to the left in front of us and the majestic feeling of the African bush was exhilarating.

It was not long before the sun fell off the earth and the early evening was upon us. The cool breeze air was refreshing.

During the patrol every ten minutes we would do a radio check. We were communicating with the other patrol vehicles behind us. We would mention what we saw up front. The sun was now down and it was pitch-black. I felt a little bit hyped up while sitting on top of the Panzer and looking out in the darkness, but everyone seemed relaxed.

On our front armored vehicle, we had a frame with six spotlights shining on the road and in the bushes on the sides of the road. We drove with no headlights, so that the bad guys could not see the two headlights on the vehicle. The bright spotlights shining on the road and bushes in front of us would reflect in a fuzzy way when looking into them. This was to confuse anyone looking at them and wanting to shoot at us. We could see clearly around one hundred meters in front of our Panzer.

We were traveling at a good sixty to eighty clicks per hour now. I slid my night-vision visor down on my communication helmet. The visor was tinted yellow and enhanced the view in front of me, making the light reflection dimmer.

As we traveled we saw many local black people walking beside the road. Greg and I observed their behavior to see if there was any nervousness. When they were friendly and waving at us, we knew that they were locals. Mostly there would be many black mamas carrying large objects on their heads. They would be in groups of around ten walking together.

While traveling at around sixty kilometers per hour, on our third radio we had rock and pop music on our headsets. This was to ease the tension and to keep our minds in check.

When I talked to the troops, the music would cut out, and I would hear only my voice on the radio. When I disengaged, the music would come back on again. We could control the volume of the music, but the radio messages were set loud and clear.

The engine of the Panzer was noisy. With the headset music on, it was a clear sound and jamming time.

Being the front vehicle was awesome for there was no dust hitting our faces. I could feel the cool breeze against my face. We saw a large group of African tribal people walking beside the road. I counted thirty of them. We stopped to ask them where they were going and what they were doing out so late at night. We observed what they were carrying with them. We were polite and informed them our mission was to protect them.

Farther down the route, there was not a soul in sight. It felt as if we were entering a desolate land. Everything in front of our Panzer was quiet, and the night was pitch-black. I was feeling nervous and waiting for the first shot to be fired.

The nicely scraped road ended, and we proceeded on a two-path road leading to the Zambezi River. These paths felt different and strange. We crossed over many small streams and some homemade doggy bridges. During this path routes we received instructions from Trevor from his Panzer on which way to turn, right or left.

It felt as if we were in a safari maze and trying to get from point A to point B.

We passed a small village called Shuckmannsburg on the Caprivi side of the Zambezi River. This post was a few clicks away and opposite Mwandi on the Zambian side of the river.

On the map, our South African Infantry treetop guard post was around three clicks for the Shuckmannsburg village. The outpost call sign was Sierra-Zulu. There were twelve SAI boys there and a medic. They were stationed high up on a treetop post. It was a large enclosed platform with a rotating machine gun in it.

While on route to the South African Infantry guys, Trevor was on the radio with headquarters. It was weird listening in on the communications with them as they gave different codes and ordinance positions to confuse anyone else listening in. It was a simple format that the Terks could not figure out.

It went like this: your position where you were actually located on the map. First A; B-C-D

(A) First communication: you subtract 100 km on your position. HQ receiving would add 100 km. They knew where you were on the map.
(B) Second communication: you add 50 km on your position. HQ would subtract 50 km.
(C) Third communication: you subtract 20 km on your position. HQ would add 20 km.
(D) Fourth communication: you add 30 km on your position. HQ would subtract 30 km.

This was to confuse the Zam-boons and the Ango-lies. They were all dumbstruck and could never find out our true position.

While traveling on the path, we knew that we were not far from the SAI guys. I estimated around two more clicks to go. It was radio silence and waiting for a long radio engage tone. When we were around one click away from them, we heard a long radio engage tone. While in motion we heard three short engage tones and knew that we were around 300 meters from the treetop post.

From the treetop guard post they had a good visual position of our unit in patrol. The bush was dense, and we had no visual sight. They could also hear our unit vehicle closing in on their position. When we heard one engage tone, Brian gave three headlight flashes that we were near. Seconds later, we saw three South African Infantry (SAI) guys come out of the bushes and approach our Panzer. They directed us to park in a formation beside the high treetop guard post. Greg and I gave the introductions while still sitting on top of the Panzer. They were happy to see us; they had been stationed there for five days. This night's patrol was to bring these guys food rations and water.

Within minutes the remainder of our patrol unit was at the guard post, and they made an attack formation around the tree post. We all stayed in position while Trevor dismounted and had brief discussions with the SAI section leader corporal.

Our support section guys dismounted and brought the SAI thier rations and water for the next week or so of guard duty. We stayed and chatted with the SAI guys for around half an hour and continued with our night patrol.

While leaving the treetop post, I had this vision and thought, *When the shit hits the fan, I am sure that they have it a lot worse, being so far from our main camp.* I was feeling great being in an armored vehicle. The only fear was that we would engage in a heavier force mortar attack.

Our Scorpion unit was now traveling in the bush and on a two-path sandy road. Something bothered me; it did not seem right. We were traveling at around fifteen clicks per hour and the path felt kind of eerie. Greg and I consistently looked for any ground disruption on the path. The Zam-boons were targeting these paths more often, setting their land mines on our patrol routes.

I had goose bumps all over my body. Around fifteen kilometers from Kasane, Greg called out on the main radio, "Zulu-Yankee, disruption on the path ahead. Hit ambush formation." Brian stopped our vehicle, sliding the tires in the sand. Our Unimorg Road Warriors One and Two were ordered to drive into the bush and park ten and twenty meters behind our Panzer. The support troopers hit formation in the bush. Our land-mine engineer put on his gear and proceeded to the disrupted path.

While we were waiting, I thanked Greg for seeing the disrupted road first. We were around fifteen meters back from the land-mine position. While the engineer defused the land mine, we were positioned in our Panzer with the spotlights on him, watching what he was doing. Guys like that must have a lot of nerve. If it went off, we'd be protected in our vehicle, but he'd be dead.

It was a large round Russian-type land mine that was positioned in the path in front of us. Our expert engineer took about thirty minutes to dig it out of the ground and defuse it. It looked the same size as a round of cheese. It had a three-inch pressure point in the center of the top. Our engineer said that it was positioned around six or so hours back, and there were three soldiers' footprints around the land mine.

We continued driving on the path for another fifteen minutes. Trevor gave orders to make patrol camp in a position to the right of the path. We spread out in the bush and positioned our vehicles in a surrounding attack formation. Our Scorpion One Panzer was positioned closest to the exit road, in case we needed to get the hell out of there. Our lieutenant was always smart and analyzed the terrain before camp was set up. He would have the four Panzers in a box formation. The Unimorgs were in the center with a large canvas cover between them. This would make a large sheltered area.

The sleeping arrangements for the support troopers, medic, engineer, vehicle mechanic, and Unimorg drivers were between the armored vehicles.

It was around midnight when the patrol camp was made and everyone was scheduled to stand guard. At all times, half of the troop and support section group would sleep while the other half stood guard. On the first night, I was not tired and opted to stand guard first. My beat was from midnight until 3:00 a.m. The next beat was from 3:00 a.m. -until 7:00 a.m.

When the camp was quiet, it was kind of peaceful. Greg, Brian, and I were chatting quietly. It was frightening to know that we were so close to driving over a land mine. We agreed that we had to be on our guard

Trevor did a site inspection that next morning to see that we did not left any evidence of our sleeping there for the night. The support section guys had to clear away our tire tracks with branches until we were on the main road. We traveled to a better road on our way back to Katima Mulilo.

We hustled back to camp, where we were told to stay in our tents with full gear on until Trevor returned. After his debriefing at HQ on our night's mission, our Scorpion unit was off duty until the next morning's patrol. We finally had time to walk around the camp—we could do whatever we liked until the next morning's patrol.

Next to our tents was an open grassy area with a stage and a movie screen. We were told that every night after dark, we would be able to watch movies. We walked around the camp and found the toilets at the other end of camp.

There was a washtub on the side with a concrete slab above the tub. This is where we would wash our clothes. Under the drum contraption was a larger water tub that had clean water in it. After washing our clothes, we would rinse them in the water tub and place them in the rotating drum contraption and spin the water off the clothes. At the same time we would hose the clothes in the drum to rinse them. We would spin the drum by hand and rotate it fast until we were tired and the clothes were reasonably dry.

Being stationed here on the border in the zone one danger area, we got a lot of money. It was called "danger pay."

Later in the afternoon we all went to the canteen. Everything we bought in the camp was duty-free and cheap.

The canteen had crates of beer. We were young and would buy a dozen beers at a time. They cost between fifteen and twenty cents. There were also two pool tables and two table tennis games. There were eight dartboards on the walls and many tables and chairs to sit on. It was a huge canteen. Fifty guys could enjoy all the fun and games inside the canteen. Outside on a grassy area, there were some tables and chairs.

I thought we had ended up in army paradise.

We were sitting outside the canteen with all the guys in our troop, laughing and enjoying our beers. While talking to the lads, we heard three helicopters circle our camp and saw them land near the tents. Greg, Brian, and I left the bunch to go see where the helicopter landing pad was. We first left our remaining beers in our tent and set off with one in our hands.

Behind the last tent, we saw a grass section and the helicopter's large concrete landing pad. At the end of the landing pad was a shallow hangar that could take around four Puma helicopters. Beside the hangar was a small HQ tent.

We walked towards the helicopters on the landing pad. We could see their long rotor blades spinning and winding down. When the rotor blades were stationary, we strolled around the Puma helicopters. A 50mm Browning machine gun was protruding out the side of the large Puma helicopter's open side door. We noticed that the other two smaller helicopters had 7.62mm

Browning machine guns mounted on their open doorways, one to fire left and the other to fire right.

We saw the crew hop out of their bad-bird helicopter. The captain and his gunner walked toward us; the captain looked much older than us. He introduced himself. "I am Kevin, known as Cappie, and this is my gunner, Roy, known as Red, with his carrot-red hair and beard."

We shook their hands and introduced ourselves. He asked us what unit we were in. I said, "I am a gunner in the Scorpion armored Panzer unit in Troop One, in the front vehicle." Cappie said, "Yeah, you Scorpion Troop One boys are always in the thick of it, where all the action is. You guys face the Zam-boons and Ango-lies head on. We have been called many a time by your lieutenants for air back-up to sweep the ambush from above."

He pointed at the 50mm Browning barrel sticking out from the side of the large helicopter. "The same awesome gun as what you guys have in the 90mm armored vehicles. The Ango-lies and Zam-boons fear this gun." Cappie made my day when he told me, "After you guys have been here a while, maybe we can arrange for you to experience a helicopter reconnaissance mission on one of our daily runs."

I was ecstatic, and my heart leaped in my chest, but I kept my cool. "Yeah, Cappie," I said, "Anytime you need a gunner to fill in on your Caprivi Strip runs, I am your guy."

Red asked me where I was from. I answered him, "From the Vaal Triangle, in the Transvaal." He had a big smile and said, "Ya, my bro'er. I am from Cape Town, and Cappie here is from your valley in the confusing Bermuda Triangle, somewhere near the Vaal River." I knew straight out that Red and I would be buddies. Red was a PF (Permanent Force Sergeant). He said, "Cappie is also a PF, and he has been here forever."

The major summoned Red and Cappie to proceed with the debriefing. Red was a hoot and called out to us in a strange manner. "Hey, ma bro'ers. Cappie here goes to his big-cheese boozer. Oh shit, yeah, he is big brass. They have their officers' pub. We sergeants are small brass. I see ya boyz at the beer hole in thirty minutes. I need to do my heli-bird debriefing and I am ready for a dozen beers."

I knew what he meant. Anyone below the lieutenants was not allowed to go to the officers' pub. Greg, Brian, and I made our way back to the beer hole.

We were all hyped up on our exciting experience of talking to the permanent forse heli-bird, bad-boy guys.

Red was not wasting any time and joined us just after his debriefing. That night we played pool and drank our dozen beers each. The following morning I had a bad *babalass* (hangover), but Trevor told us that there was action near Ngoma in the south of the Caprivi at the last village before entering Botswana. Trevor had just come from HQ, having had an urgent early morning briefing. He gave us fifteen minutes to get ready and to be at our Panzer. I was in a bit of a daze, but I got ready quickly, and within ten minutes, Greg, Brian, and I were getting the Panzer geared up with ammo, rations, and what we needed for at least three days of patrol. We always had to leave the Panzer running for at least fifteen minutes to warm up the engine. This gave us enough time to gear up.

We left camp at 5:00 a.m. and traveled full speed to Ngoma. The cool air made me wide awake, and a nervous feeling set in. It would take us around fifty minutes to get there; the road was in very good condition.

It was always a thrill for me to sit on the top of the Panzer while traveling at a fast pace. Brian was a good driver, and his road skills were great. While Greg and I had a good view of the road, and we could see far into the distance. When we noticed any bad sections of road or potholes, we would let Brian know.

The early morning sunrise patrol was giving me the jitters. The cool breeze air was hitting our faces, and I had goose bumps all over. Around halfway to Ngoma we saw many tribal people walking beside the road. They were locals and waving at us as we passed by them. It made me feel happy that we were stationed here in the Caprivi for their protection.

Ngoma was a reasonable-sized village town. When we reached the outskirts of town, some black tribal people were waiting in a Toyota pickup truck beside the main road.

I slowed down and heard Trevor say over the radio, "These guys are the South African Defense Force local informant group." Only then did we know that the army had set up some local informants all around Caprivi. We were directed to drive to the east side of Ngoma. We stopped at a white painted *koeker-shop* (convenient store).

We were stationed just off the main road, where the bush path led into the bush beside the Chobe River.

Trevor entered the koeker-shop with the informant, and their discussions took around fifteen minutes. The shop had an old-style magnetic wind-up telephone and a direct telephone line to our HQ base. The army was smart, setting up these communication points. The Zam-boons and Ango-lies were constantly listening in on our radio communications and trying to locate our positions.

Trevor and the informant came out of the koeker-shop and parted. While standing next to our Panzer, Trevor told Greg to inform the support sections Road Warrior One Unimorgs to drive to the front of our patrol position.

They did so and parked next to our Scorpion One Panzer. Greg discussed the situation with support section leader, Corporal Allen.

Apparently the path ahead of us was in a very poor condition. It was risky and the Panzers could get stuck in the mud. Orders were that the Road Warrior One Unimorg was to proceed down the Chobe River edge path and continue as far as possible. If the terrain was undrivable, they needed to park and disengage—use the "kill switch" on the Unimorg. They had to proceed on foot down the river to Kasane.

A group of around six Zam-boons were spotted coming down the river on a raft. They had shot a few locals dead and ransacked a few village huts. They had less than a two-hour head start floating their raft back down the Chobe River toward the Zambezi River junction.

The Unimorg left our parked Scorpion unit. We saw them disappear into the bush beside the river's edge. At that moment the informant and his buddies drove toward us in his Toyota pickup truck. They parked next to Greg, who was standing next to our Panzer. Discussions were that we could precede one click back on the gravel road and turn right on a better village path. The path continued for around six kilometers east. During the drive the path went up a large hill that was about ten clicks away from Ngoma. Up on the hill, the view of the Chobe River was better, and the position was good to make a patrol camp. We could wait for our support sections guys to return from their search-and-kill mission patrol.

Within minutes we turned around our Scorpion unit vehicles and made our way on the path to the hilltop position. We parked our Panzers in an ambush attack box formation and made camp, setting up a large canvas rain covering between our Panzer Scorpion One and the Unimorg.

In the Unimorg Road Warrior Two vehicle, we had a spare radio pack and a fold-up table with many small folding chairs. In that Unimorg we had a lot of spare gear.

Trevor had set up a command communications ordinance station. He logged our position with HQ and our section leader, Corporal Allen. It was great for Greg, Brian, and me as part of the communications group.

We were now sitting off to the side of Ngoma town, high up on the hill overlooking the river. In the distance we could faintly hear the Unimorg whining through the bush as it went down the path beside the river.

Trevor and Corporal Allen and Charlie, the radio operator, were in constant radio communications. The support section had proceeded well and was now around fifteen clicks away from where they had left the koeker-shop in Ngoma.

From our position, it seemed if they were five or six clicks farther down the Chobe River from our camp position. I had worked out that they were progressing in the bush at around ten clicks per hour. It seemed slow, but they would eventually catch up to the raft-floating Zam-boons Terks going down the river.

It was early morning, and I opted to stand early guard. I had worked out that if our support section caught up to the Zam-boon Terks, it would happen when I was off beat. I could sit and listen in with Trevor on the communications radio wavelength given for this mission patrol.

From Ngoma to Kasane, the distance would be around fifty clicks down the river. We estimated that it would take the Zam-boons around seven hours to get to the Zambezi River junction. It would take our section unit around four to five hours to cover that distance.

They had less than a two-hour head start, and the time distance would shrink. Our boys would catch up to the bad guys around ten clicks before the Chobe and Zambezi River junction.

While I was on my three-hour guard beat, I was listening in on my Panzer radio on the real-time communications. Our boys had done well and were in luck. About three hours on their mission route through the bush, they made it to the better-condition path. They speeded up and had covered about ten clicks in a half an hour. Damn, those Merc-Unimorg bush-warrior vehicles were tough. I could only imagine the thrill the guys were having, going in the bush in those harsh terrain conditions, while traveling at a good pace after the Zam-boon Terks.

Brian, Greg, and I had just come off our guard beat, and we were relaxing under the canvas covering. I was sitting on my fold-up chair with Trevor, Greg, and about eight other guys in our unit. We were chatting when we heard

Charlie come over the radio communication. "We have caught up with them. Through the binoculars we can see them paddling frantically to cross over the Chobe River to the Botswana side."

My guard duty timing was great; they had caught up with the Terks, and the action had started. While communications were in process, the Terks' raft was around one click ahead of our Scorpion Unimorg.

Corporal Allen talked on the radio pack. "It seems as if there are six of them sitting on the homemade raft. The raft seems to be about three to four meters in size, and they have tied six plastic round tubs under it to keep it afloat."

We heard Corporal Allen give the orders "Fire at will at the Terks." We heard the boys open fire and Corporal Allen call out, "We are about fifty meters from the Chobe River's edge and about seven hundred meters from the Terks. They have returned fire."

Most of the section support guys dismounted and had scattered behind some rocks, positioning themselves to return rifle fire.

We heard Corporal Allen say, "Damn, this is funny. The Terks are now in the center of the Chobe River and the strong main current has swept them against some large rocks. When the raft hit the rocks with force, it had catapulted the Terks into the river. The abandoned raft broke into pieces, and the goods that they stole are in the river."

The Scorpion section guys were still shooting rapidly toward where the Terks had fallen in the river. Corporal Allen gave orders for everyone to stop firing and to mount the Unimorg. The Unimorg driver was given orders to speed up through the bush to see if they could get ahead of the Terks floating down the river. The radio communications were constant while the Unimorg drove through the bush. All we could hear over the radio was Charlie calling out the coordinates and the terrain observations in front of them.

In our base camp it felt like an army radio game, where the good guys were after the bad guys and having all obstacles in front of them. We sat glued to the radio communications; none of us could move an inch. Our Unimorg Scorpion section preceded another five or so clicks down the river's edge. The Terks were nowhere to be seen. They must have drowned in the strong current.

The support guys did a reconnaissance walk up and down the river's edge. The Terks were no more. The action came to an end; Trevor gave Corporal Allen orders to return to Ngoma. First they had their lunch and proceeded back to the Ngoma koeker-shop. We also received orders from HQ to stay where we were for the night and return to Camp Katima in the morning. We were all in a good frame of mind and the mood was relaxed. We waited for the Road Warrior One vehicle to return to our patrol camp position on the hilltop. It was just before 5:30 p.m. when they reached us. The Unimorg looked a sight. It was full of mud, and the bush shrubs and tree branches were caught between the suspension and the bumpers and side railings.

Allen and Trevor discussed the maneuver outcome. Allen was certain that all the Zam-boon Terks had drowned. He said, "The way that they were catapulted in the air and seeing them frantically trying to swim in the strong river current and trying to keep their heads above the water, it was obvious that they could not swim." I was a bit envious, listening to the support sections guys describing their awesome Unimorg bush warrior experience beside the Chobe River.

After dinner I was on guard beat from 8:00 p.m. until midnight. After my guard beat, I hit the sack. The next morning, we had a ration-pack breakfast and cleared the sight. It was just after 7:00 a.m. when our unit proceeded back to Camp Katima. The trip back took us around an hour. When we arrived back at camp, we had to spray the mud off our Panzers. I am sure the Unimorg guys had a tough time cleaning their muddy Unimorg.

After lunch, Trevor did a vehicle inspection and informed us, "In the morning, we will be on a patrol to Mpatcha Air Base." We had the rest of the day off, so we did our laundry. After dinner, we enjoyed a dozen beers at the beer-hole canteen. Heli-gunner Red was with us, and we had a good chat and laugh.

It was just after 11:00 p.m. when I crashed in my bed, fairly drunk but down and out for the night. At around three in the morning, I woke up and could hear thunder and heavy rain. This was an angry thunderstorm, and I got shivers from the cool breeze. Only then did I realize that in this part of tropical Africa, when it rains, the heavens open like floodgates, and the rain does not stop for hours on end.

I got out of bed and peeped through the tent flap. Outside our tent, the rain trenches were full and gushing with water. I knew that we were lucky to be on the higher elevated section of the camp, with the rainwater flowing down the trenches.

I climbed back into bed and lay there for a while, but I could not sleep. Greg was awake too, but Brian was sleeping like a rock. I said to Greg, "It is going to be a challenging mission patrol in the morning toward Mpatcha Air Base."

We chatted for a while and Greg fell asleep. I lay in my bed, listening to the rain and the thunder going berserk.

It was just after 5:30 a.m. when Trevor entered our tent. He had his rain gear on and looked totally drenched. He had just come from an early morning HQ briefing. He informed us that our patrol time to Mpatcha had been moved forward until after lunch. We could sleep until 7:00 a.m. breakfast. After breakfast we relaxed in our tent and cleaned our 9mm Star pistols and army gear. The thunderstorm was fierce and didn't subside until after nine o'clock. In some ways it was nice and cool and calm. We were chatting and relaxing on our beds. I read a *Scope* magazine that I had in my locker.

It was just before noon when Trevor entered our tent. We needed to be ready for patrol at one o'clock. We had an early lunch and made our way to our Panzers. It was still drizzling, and we prepared ourselves for a wet patrol run to Mpatcha Air Base.

On this patrol run, there was a Magirus supply truck that was carrying supplies for the air base. We needed to escort the supply truck on that route. HQ orders were that we needed to stay at Mpatcha Air Base for the night and return to Katima in the morning. Like a wet blanket, we left Camp Katima on route to Mpatcha Army Air Base. The road there was always in bad condition. With the heavy downpour of rain that morning, it was going to be a task getting to Mpatcha. The airport was not far from Katima Mulilo. We were told it was around twenty five clicks away.

It was still raining lightly. Greg and I were sitting on the top of the Panzer wearing our poncho rain gear. The wind and rain was wetting my army trousers. I thought, *Damn, a wet and miserable patrol route.* When we arrived here five days earlier, the road to Camp Katima took so long. During that time, I did not realize that our camp was only twenty-five clicks away.

In 1974, the airport was known as Mpatcha Army Air Base. In today's world, it is called Katima Mulilo Airport. In those years, it was a single air strip cut out between the trees, just wide enough for a big Hercules plane to land. Today, it looks four times the size, with a longer landing strip and taxi run-off sections and proper arrival and departure buildings.

While traveling on the muddy road, we descended down a hill and noticed that the bottom section was washed away. There was a stream of muddy water flowing around fifty meters wide over the road. At that moment I knew why we had to escort the supply truck to Mpatcha Air Base. It would be a good opportunity to have an ambush while all the vehicles were in a stationary position beside the road.

Trevor gave the command to do a roadside ambush formation. While we were parked beside the road, Trevor came walking to our Panzer.

The only way forward was for the Unimorg Road Warrior troop carrier to proceed through the slow-running stream across the road. We could assess how deep the muddy water stream was.

Orders were given, and Unimorg parked in the center of the gravel road, next to our vehicle. The guys had trained for these events. The Unimorg had eight gears forward and when engaged, it had eight gears backwards. They had a hundred-meter cable ten-ton winch mounted on the front of the Unimorg bumper axle frame.

The Magirus truck came forward and parked on the hard center surface of the road. The Magirus truck and Unimorg were positioned cab-to-cab, facing each other. They hooked the Unimorg winch onto the Magirus towing eye on its frame. The Unimorg driver and Corporal Allen were in the cab. Two guys were at the rear of the Unimorg, standing on the back flap, holding onto the canvas-covered frame while looking over the canvas covering. The Unimorg reversed and was in position to drive in reverse into the muddy water. Corporal Allen was going to operate the winch from the inside of the cab.

It was a good setup. The Unimorg started to reverse in the muddy water while Corporal Allen was operating and disengaging the winch cable. Greg, Brian, and I could see all the action from our parked Panzer. The Unimorg reversed slowly while the guys at the back flap guided it in a straight left or right position where the road was washed out.

The Unimorg proceeded about twenty meters in the muddy water. The back end suddenly dropped about half a meter. The Unimorg chassis and cab was around a meter from the ground. The water was flowing just below the bottom of the cab door. They proceeded backward, with the two guys at the rear guiding the Unimorg in a straight position. They proceeded further in the muddy water for around another five meters. By now, the muddy water was door height.

Trevor gave orders for the Unimorg to return to the Magirus truck. The muddy road section was too deep and dangerous for the Panzers to cross.

The driver put the Unimorg in extra low forward gear. Allen operated the winch in a pulling motion. The Unimorg engine was at a constant three thousand revs and proceeding forward in the stream and mud. Trevor was operating the winch cable, hauling them out of the mud. It was an experience to see the Unimorg moving toward us with no strain at all. After a few minutes, they were out of the mud and in a stationary position on the hard gravel road in front of the Magirus truck.

Trevor informed HQ that it was not possible for us to proceed further. We needed to return to Katima, but the road scrapers needed to repair the road first when the rain subsided. We made a U-turn, and within half an hour we were back in the Katima base camp.

By mid-afternoon we heard the large Puma helicopter taking some supplies by air. It was just around 5:00 p.m. when we were done cleaning our Panzers and off for the night. We were ready for beers and a good chat. I was getting pretty good at my pool playing and was scoring my winning beers. That night I won twelve straight games and scored twelve gaming-winning beers. Of course I gave Greg and Brian some beers.

I was in my element, and I was so happy to end up here in army paradise and have so much fun. It was two days later when we finally proceeded with our patrol run to Mpatcha Air Base. It was a morning route, and we returned to camp after lunch. The road was resurfaced by then.

The week that followed had many different patrol runs, but there was no Terk action at all. The only word was that Troop Three, the Black Widow guys, had a bit of action on one of their night patrol runs to Ngoma. They shot dead three Zam-boons, with no casualties on our side.

We had done a patrol two days earlier on that same route. It seemed as if the actions were gradually progressing.

Our hair was now longer and some of the boys had beards. We were more relaxed and the tension was gone. Everyone seemed to adapt to the harsh bushland. We were all constantly aware that the danger could happen and change on a dime.

In the beginning of the third week at Camp Katima, from one moment to the next we could feel that the action had stepped up a level. We heard that the Reckies at the Sifuma camp were doing their reconnaissance routes in Angola and Zambia. They recorded a lot of army movement toward the southern part of Angola where the UNITA—National Union for the Total Independence of Angola—tribal people lived in the Benguela and Huambo provinces.

The Zambian army was also growing, and many of their soldiers were in the Caprivi border regions. What were these countries up to, and why would they pick a fight with the people living in Southern Africa, especially with Namibia and the South African forces? We would crush them if they tried anything big with us.

We also heard that Angola was on the brink of war and the Portuguese run government was useless. In the central black-folk African region of this majestic part of Africa, there were too many tribal differences. The killings of the people happened often.

Why was there all this anger in the world? The innocent people living in this majestic part of Africa were trying to protect their livelihoods and their tribal way of life.

Instead, they were dying for no reason at all.

Chapter Five

Katima

My Near-Death Experience in the Caprivi Game Park

On the third Sunday morning at Camp Katima, we received orders to go on a four-day patrol. Troops One and Four were going to make a patrol run together from Katima Mulilo to Rundu. At Rundu we would load ten Magirus trucks with supplies and escort the month's food and drinks supplies back to Camp Katima. Rundu is the largest camp on the border and is in the center position of the Namibian border.

Northern Namibia stretches more than 1,500 kilometers across Africa. The land starts at the Skeleton Coast on the west side of Africa and the Atlantic Ocean. It stretches across Africa to the Caprivi heartlands in the south center part of the African continent.

The large army base at Rundu was beside the strong-flowing Okavango River. Angola was on the opposite side of the river, and the country was in ruins. It was a Portuguese-run colony, and the government was in a dismal state. Many black extremists wanted to overthrow the government.

At the Rundu base camp there were more than one thousand South African Defense Force personnel. Our School of armor One Special Service Battalion (1-SSB) was bassed in Rundu.

Grootfontein in Namibia was our headquarters, where all logistics were handled and supplies were received by train or Hercules planes. From the HQ depot in Grootfontein the supplies were transported by road to Rundu. Monthly, the supplies were collected in a convoy starting from Katima to Rundu and back again.

At Rundu our South African forces had the South African Navy Reconnaissance Corporation (SANRC) boat personnel. They would do their daily watercraft or dinghy runs up and down the Okavango River.

In this part of Africa the river deltas were the best in the world. At some locations the river flowed with strong, fierce currents. At some river bends, it would flow around five hundred meters wide. In this part of Africa the wide section of the Okavango River continued to flow around 350 kilometers long. The wide river section flowed from the village of Nkurenkuru in the west, all the way and passed Andara in the east. This was where the Caprivi Game Park started. The Okavango River proceeds through Namibia into the Botswana heartlands and formed the Okavango Delta and the Okavango swamps.

The endless supply of water served life to millions of wild animals like wildebeest, deer, giraffes, cheetahs, warthogs, and the African "big five"— elephant, buffalo, rhino, lion, and leopard. The Okavango swamps are a wild part of the African land, where many crocodiles feast on all the African animals.

In the Botswana region, you can see hundreds of thousands of deer and buffalo together, flocking the African plains. Nowhere on the planet can you see more animals together in harmony.

The Caprivi Game Park was the total length of the Caprivi Strip. The Strip was a one-kilometer-wide piece of land; two hundred kilometers long, with all the trees cut down and open grassland that stretched in a straight line. This was known as no-man's-land, and it was a shoot-to-kill zone. The Caprivi Game Park is beside it, bordering Angola and Botswana.

Early on the Sunday morning after five o'clock breakfast, we geared up and were ready to roll. By mid-morning we had reached the town of Kongola. There, we would continue with a Hottentot-god tractor land-mine sweeper.

While we were stopped on the main road, Trevor walked up to our Panzer, and we waited for about ten minutes for this contraption to arrive. It was around twelve meters long and looked like a vehicle from another planet. The driver was a local black guy but looked like a bad-ass African warrior. He stopped the contraption beside the road and left the tractor idling as he walked over to Trevor. They greeted each other with handshakes and shoulder bumps and patted each other's backs as they said, "How-zit, ma bro'er?" (How are you, my brother?)

The driver wore leopard-skin pants but had a bare chest that exposed many muscles. He wore black South African army boots and had a long panga knife dangling along his hip from his belt. His body and face had many cut marks. I knew that he had been in many tribal and terrorist fighting conflicts. His name was Benzani, but we all called him Ben. His bad-ass African warrior buddy was called Penswani, known as Pen. He was slightly smaller than Ben and was driving an old Bedford truck with the roof cut off and no windshield. It was loaded up with many old tire rims and the Hottentot-god contraption's spare parts.

There were two other black guys with them who were trekkers. They had old army-style FN rifles with them. The group had four AK-47 assault rifles that were mounted in the doors of the Bedford truck and on the Hottentot-god vehicle's armored steel plate.

These African bad boys were our protection on all the prospective land-mine dirt road routes. Ben and his bad-ass boys did these runs consistently from Kongola to Mashari. Sometimes they would do a run from Kongola to Katima Mulilo.

Ben, Pen, and Trevor talked about the route patrol. We could hear them talking beside our vehicle. Ben told Trevor, "We heard that there is a lot of ambush and sniper action here in the Caprivi Strip. It seems as if the Angolies want to pick a fight with us. We are prepared, and Namibian and South African forces will kill them all."

I could sense that he had a lot of heartache and pain in his life. But he would change from having angry talk to suddenly laughing and be the friendliest guy ever. I summed him up and knew that he was well respected and was a sort of chief in his village.

Nevertheless, I was glad that he was on our side and fighting for the grand people living in this region of majestic Africa. I thought what a privilege it was for us to experience these moments in Africa.

On the side of the main road leaving Kongola, we were positioned on top of the Panzer, waiting for Ben, Pen, and his trekkers to fill up their bad-ass vehicles with diesel fuel that was in a forty-four gallon drum on top of the Bedford supply truck. While we waited, we had an early lunch. We waited for orders to proceed through the Caprivi Game Park.

The Hottentot-god contraption soon took to the road. It kicked up a lot of dust, like a weird dragster. Greg told Brian to keep a visual distance of around three hundred meters behind them. Greg and I and the rest of the troop were sitting on top of the Panzers in a ready-to-fire position. We were informed that on this route, action took place daily.

It was a hot, sunny day with not a cloud in the sky. Ben and Pen and the trekkers were ahead of us. Their mission was to mine-sweep the road in front of our convoy vehicles. This Hottentot-god vehicle and the old Bedford were traveling at around forty kilometers per hour. The landscape was great we saw many bucks and some giraffes. The moments gave us a bit of excitement on this slow traveling patrol route. We felt and behaved like bad-ass bush warriors.

The Santana and Pink Floyd music kept my mood calm, and I was daydreaming a bit. Greg and I observed the larger trees to our right. I told Greg, "The game park looks great." We also saw a few bucks under some trees in the distance. Suddenly, we heard a whizzing sound. The adrenaline in my body went ballistic. We knew that a sniper had fired a shot at us. Greg was fast to react and called over the radio, using the call sign for that day. "Yankee-Bravo, sniper ahead of us, hit formation!" We heard two more whizzing sounds, with one shot hitting the Panzer.

Brian turned our armored vehicle to the right and stopped at the edge of the gravel road. We did not know where the snipers were but assumed they were somewhere in the trees on our right. We were trained that snipers would always strike from a distance to give them time to make a run for it when the action started. I positioned my 7.62mm machine gun toward the far trees ahead of us, aiming just to the right of the old Bedford truck.

I let rip with that Browning machine gun, aiming mid-tree height. I fired in slow motion, until I was in full-action shooting mode. We were trained to shoot consistently for around five seconds and stop. We were to observe any movement for another five seconds. Then, if there was no return fire, let rip again for five seconds, stop, and wait. Greg looked through his binoculars to search for the snipers' movements in the trees.

My heart was in my throat, but with all the machine-gun noise, it was exhilarating to see the tree branches explode as the bullets hit them. During all the commotion, Scorpion Two gunner let rip with his machine gun when I stopped for five seconds. During all this machine gun firing, our support troops dismounted and got into an ambush formation beside the road. They were positioned to stand by and wait for orders.

The shooting stopped, and we observed with our binoculars. The large trees were about 150 meters to our right from the roadside and our stationary position. We saw the four black guys running in the bush toward the trees, as if they were on a battle charge. Greg called over the communications radio, "No firing. Ben, Pen and the trekkers are after them."

They were well trained for they were running in a zigzag through the bush. Trevor commanded us, "Hold your position until Ben and Pen and the trekkers are back."

I had a bad-ass feeling of fearlessness, but I knew I was lucky that the shots had missed me. Greg and I heard the whizzing sound between our helmets. "The bastard almost shot us," he said. We came to realization of what had happened.

My whole body went into overdrive, and I felt as if I was on fire. The adrenaline was pumping through my veins. My breathing was rapid and my heart had a burning sensation. Tears flowed down my cheeks. God had given Greg and me a break. On this day, it was life.

I saw that Greg was crying, and we gave each other a hug and a pat on the back. All went quiet for a few minutes on the radio frequency. We looked though our binoculars, trying to see movements in the trees.

We heard Trevor come over the radio. "Good formation," he said, and he praised us for our sharp alertness on the snipers. He also said, "God is with you guys today, and we are all safe. Thank you Scorpion One; we are proud of you guys leading the pack."

HQ came on the frequency and asked us to stand down until we heard the next shot fired. While we were waiting for orders, Greg and I were discussing from where the shot had been fired from. The trees to our right and the angle from where the snipper had shot at us missed our head gear by centimeters. It was a snap sound in my right ear and in Greg's left ear. The second shot hit the panzer vehicle around three centimeters from Greg's left army boot rest position, and around twenty centimeters from my right army boot normal rest position. The third shot wizzed past me on my left side.

About ten minutes later, we heard six gunshots echoing in the trees. I reloaded my machine gun. Greg laughed at me when I patted the machine gun and said, "Good gun. Good gun." All through my basic training, we were taught what to do when the machine gun jams. Today, it was a good gun.

We stayed in our formation. I was ready to let rip with the Browning machine gun at any time, if need be. About twenty minutes later, we saw the four black guys return through the bushes. Trevor said, "All is safe, and you guys can get off the Panzer to pick up the machine gun shells on the roadside." Trevor made his way to our Panzer and gave Greg and me the locked-finger, "how-zit" handshake and a pat on the shoulder. He had tears in his eyes, saying, "You guys did well. We are all safe." We collected the shells and put them in bins in the Panzer. Two minutes later, the four black guys walked toward us. What we witnessed next made me realize how harsh the conditions were in this part of Africa.

The bad-ass-warriors had the cut-off heads of three Angolan terrorists. They were holding them by the hair in their hands. They had chopped off the heads with the panga knife, and blood was still dripping from their skulls.

Ben said, "One of you is a good shot. You shot the one Ango-lie in the neck. He was the one far away." He lifted the bloody head in front of him, showing where the bullet went through the neck, just below the jaw.

Ben was hitting his chest with his fist like a warrior. "I shoot second Ango-lie in the back and good trekkie shoot third guy up the ass." He laughed and shouted, "Yeah, bro, up da fokin'ass."

All of them lifted the bloody Ango-lie heads in the air while doing a tribal foot-stomping dance.

Trevor told Ben, "We have lost traveling time, and we need to hustle to our night's camp position." This was near Andara, close to the Okavango River Delta. Within five minutes we were all on route. While traveling toward Andara, Greg was smiling at me all through the trip. I guess he knew that he was with a good bunch of army guys and that we all took care of one another. I smiled at him as well, and our conversations were of the Ango-lie snipers and what was happening on this fearless day.

My near-death experience in the Caprivi Game Park made me realize how lucky Greg and I were and that God had been with us today.

It was just after 6:00 p.m. when we reached the Okavango River bridge gate. A path led along both sides of the bridge and continued beside the river's edge. Trevor gave instructions to turn left and proceed to set up the patrol camp next to the river. The campsite was about one kilometer south off the main Rundu route road.

Trevor told us many times, "Camp should always be made in a different location." That night, we were two troops with eight Panzers in an ambush box formation. The view was awesome and the feeling of having more than sixty of us together made the camp feel huge.

While setting up camp, the black guys had disappeared in the bush. When they returned to camp, they were carrying two medium-size deer with them. They had shot them for a *braai* (grilled) dinner.

Those four black guys made a huge fire. They were on the move all the time. The deer skin was cut off and washed in the river and pressed out flat. Salt was rubbed on the inner skin and stretched out on metal crisscross frames. The speed and these guys' work were impressive.

I realized that nothing went to waste in these African tribal countries. Ben told us that his six wives would make pouches or purses out of the deer skin to sell for money. I thought *they are smart African people living here in Namibia.*

The skinned deer was spread out on the cross frames. They coated the Steenbok deer with salt and a powdered mixture. It was a good thing that none of us were vegetarians. I have never in my life witnessed four guys prepared a braai dinner for more than sixty people in such a short time.

Later that night, everyone shook my and Dexter's hands, saying, "Good job. You guys killed the sniper." We did not know who shot the Ango-lie, but everyone said that it was me. The four African black guys also shook our hands. Bad-ass Ben said, "Yeah, you now one of us, killing the Ango-lie."

As it got dark, the large log fire continued to burn. Half the units were on guard duty and the rest were around the huge log fire.

Trevor told us, "On any kill, you guys have relief from your guard duty for the night." So Dexter and I could do whatever we wanted and sleep where we want to. We both made our stretcher beds next to the log fire and beside a huge tree. I felt like a king because of all the attention.

Ben, Pen, and the two trekkers were sitting on some rocks beside the fire; they had a big plastic sheet that they cut up the grilled deer meat. Dexter and I were given the deer's hind legs, which was the best meat on the Steenbok (stone buck) deer. The powder with which Ben consistently coated the meat made the meat tender, with a nice herbal taste to it.

I felt alive, and life was grand.

Ben gave us a metal mug of his homemade hooch. Trevor and Tex, the two lieutenants, joined us with a mug of hooch each. We all said, "Tjords," knocked mugs, and took a big gulp. Oh, my God, it was *mam-poer* (moonshine). It was at least 70 percent alcohol. It had a peach flavor with a hint of orange, and it was strong as hell. It burned down my throat, making me lightheaded. The aftertaste was sweet.

Ben laughed at our pulling faces and shouted, "Yeah, bro, good shit make us strong to fight Ango-lie."

Bad-ass Ben the warrior laughed and smiled at us, showing his large white teeth. He was a character and was always the loud-mouth, in a good way. When he was concentrating, he had a sad look about him. I knew that some evil things must have happened in his life. He looked around mid-forties and had six deep cut marks on his cheeks. His arms had some burn marks where the skin was kind of bulging out very black in color. His chest and arms also had deep cut marks.

But when his buddy Pen did his single-drum fast-rhythm African beat and saw Ben laugh as he did his tribal dance, everyone joined in the laughter and felt the enjoyment.

It was a grand night, and the happy moments next to the river were like no others.

It was late when I finally finished off the half liter of hooch in my mug. My body was warmed up from the hooch, and I don't remember falling asleep.

It was around 4:00 a.m. when Trevor woke the camp. My mouth was dry like a desert. My hangover and the pain in my head were awful. I knew that I needed to do something. I climbed out of my stretcher bed and removed all my clothes and gear. I ran naked toward the river and dove in. Trevor, Tex, Ben, Pen, and his trekkies were laughing at me while shaking their heads.

After a while, Ben came to the side of the river. He waded in to his knees and then stretched his arm out to pull me from the river. Only did I realize the strength in his arms.

Ben said, "Hey, Bro Mike, good thinking, diving into the river to clear the mam-poer head." He removed all his clothes and dove in the river. My God, he had a monster cock on him.

After breakfast we prepared for our journey to Rundu. On route we stopped at Mashari, where Ben, Pen, and the trekkers lived. The Hottentot-god vehicle was stationed there. We proceeded to Rundu. It was around noon when we drove through the gate of a main depot camp. By now we were considered *ou-manne*, with our longer hair. I had grown a mustache. With my bush hat on, I looked tough as nails.

Trevor organized our sleeping arrangements at a site next to the depot. This is where fifty or so open tents were rigged up. A large section part of the depot hanger was made into a mess and canteen hall. We all had lunch and waited for instructions.

In the early afternoon we were rounded up to load supplies on ten large Magirus supply trucks. From the depot's higher elevation, we walked straight onto the back of the trucks.

Our Scorpion unit loaded crates of beer, twenty-four to a carton, on these trucks. There were tens of thousands of crates of beer. We were all in a straight line and passed the beer crates in a zigzag motion. We worked quickly and were sweating from the hard work; some of us took our shirts off.

For one month of supplies, I was amazed at how many beers were going up to the Caprivi Strip area. When we finished loading around 5:00 p.m., the canvas covers were tied down over the exposed crates and ropes were tied to the sides of the Magirus trucks. The drivers were Permanent Forces and they all had longer hair and beards. They moved the trucks away from the depot hangars. I noticed that one truck was a refrigerated truck with all the meat and dairy products in it.

We had dinner and hit the showers. Some of us walked about the large camp and strolled by the river's edge. The camp was well rigged and reminded me of my basic training camp in Bloemfontein. At this Rundu camp, all the guys slept in bungalows.

After dark, when we'd crashed in our tents, Trevor came by in an army Willys Jeep. There were three other lieutenants with him.

They had done the HQ debriefing, and we were told that the convoy would start rolling at 5:00 a.m. A Bedford truck stopped at our tents, and Trevor said, "I have organized more than sixty crates of cold beer for free from the HQ commander. Thanks, guys, for the good speed in loading the trucks."

Trevor and the other lieutenants left in the Willys Jeep. It worked out nicely—we had a crate of beer each. What a treat it was. We gathered around the front of the tents, laughing and having heavenly cold Hansa lager beers.

I told Greg and Brian that we should keep a dozen beers each for the trip back to the Caprivi Strip. We stashed the beers inside the Panzer and covered it, just in case we would get stopped at the gate checkpoint.

It was around 8:00 p.m. when we saw six guys walking toward our tent. One guy asked Greg if we were the 2-SSB Scorpion troop. Greg said "Yeah, Mike and Brian and I are in the front Panzer vehicle." They shook our hands and told us that they were Troop One in the 1-SSB that was stationed in

Rundu. We had been in Bloemfontein at Tempe, doing our basic training at the same time. Apparently 1-SSB was known as the Reptile battalion. And Troop One was the Crocodile troop. They were happy to have met us, and we chatted for around an hour.

Their border runs were boring, they said, and there was not much action around Rundu. They did their patrol runs up and down from Rundu going west, to the Skeleton Coast and back. Their trips could take up to five days.

We talked about our action near Ngoma with our support section chasing after the Zam-boons Terks. The Croc Troop One guys were a bit envious of our having been in Walvis Bay and being stationed at Katima. It was known as the best camp on the Namibian borders. The Croc Troop guys left our tent, and we finished our dozen beers before we crashed for the night.

It was just after six o'clock in the morning when our Panzer took the lead of the long convoy back to the Caprivi Strip. At the main departure guard gate, we had an inspection. They only looked under the vehicle with large mirrors on a pole. We were all good to go. Our dozen remaining beers were good for our return trip. The road trip was different, and we had five large Magirus supply trucks in our convoy. They were between our last Scorpion Panzer, Brad's crew, and our Unimorg Road Warrior One, Allen's support guys. The Tarantula unit was in the same formation as the Scorpion unit, having five Magirus trucks with them on convoy. They were traveling in a separate convoy and left Rundu a half hour later than our Scorpion unit.

The convoy stretched for more than three kilometers. It was sixty kilometers to Mashari to meet Ben and his crew with their mine-sweeper contraptions. They were parked on the outskirts of Mashari on route to Andara and the Caprivi Game Park. The road to Andara was slow-driving. When we reached the Okavango River Bridge, Trevor gave orders that we cross into the Caprivi Game Park and do a roadside stop around two clicks from the crossover bridge. We had ninety minutes to have our lunch, big business, a leak, a smoke, and such.

Before leaving the lunch camp, we always had to clean up the site, but by twelve thirty we were on route to the village of Ishesha. The convoy was doing well until one of the Magirus trucks had a flat tire. The convoy stopped, and we formed a roadside ambush position. The delay was just over an hour. It was a good time to stretch our legs and dismount the Panzer. Some of us also went for a piss and did a bit of walking about, chatting with the other Panzer guys. By four o'clock we were on the road again. We reached Ishesha village within an hour. We drove through the village and made patrol camp on the outskirts of the village.

Apparently, the Tarantula bunch had to keep the half-hour distance behind us. I guess their roadside camp was some distance before Ishesha village. Trevor asked us to give him one of our ration packs each and to put them in the rear of Unimorg Two. When the camp was set up Ben, Pen, the trekkers, and the Lieutenants Trevor and Tex drove to Ishesha village in the Unimorg. Apparently, everyone traded supplies to keep harmony and good relations. They returned with meat, corn flour (pap), onions, tomatoes, peppers, bread, and soft drinks. It seemed to be a good trade, and the locals always wanted our ration packs.

That night we had another big log-fire braai. I enjoyed being in a Game Park and having a log-fire braai in the bush, where the wild animals roamed freely. Ben, Pen, and his trekkers prepared the food for over thirty of us in the camp. During our dinner we had some of our beers. I gave Ben, Pen, and the trekkers two each. Greg and Brian did the same. Their gratitude and the big white-tooth smiles and the hand shake with the shoulder bump and pat on the back was always a friendly gesture.

After our night's braai and beers, we helped clean up the site. Our guard beats were set and issued to us. Our Panzer Scorpion One had the best patrol camp position. We were parked under a large tree, just off the main dirt road. That night our guard beat would be from 2:00 a.m. until 6:00 a.m.

Once on guard duty, Greg and I would place our sleeping bags and pillow on the hatch seats on top of the Panzer. We would get into a comfortable position, and I would cock the 7.62mm Browning machine gun between my legs and know that I was safe and ready for action. We had our helmet headsets on and listened to rock or pop music. The volume was low. Enough that we could chat quietly while on duty. Brian had to sit in his driver's seat and be in a position to make haste if we needed to.

While slouched in the hatch seat, Greg and I looked at the billions of stars in the clear, moonless sky. The sound of the night animals gave me goose bumps all over my body. About an hour into our guard beat, we heard loud animal noises that sounded close—the sound echoed through the silent night and the ground-stamping noise and the bush and small tree cracking sounds were loud and clear. Greg and I visualized what type of large animals would make such a loud sound. I figured it was rhinos, and Greg said it sounded like a stampede of elephants. We heard some growling noises and figured it could be leopards. It was kind of frightening, as it felt as if they were in our camp and would pounce on us, although we knew they were in the distance.

While listening to the animal noises, we heard Trevor come over the Panzer One radio, saying, "Hey, bros, isn't it awesome to be camping here in the Caprivi Game Park? Damn, it makes me happy to be here and experience this." I was quick to answer, "Yeah, Trevor, Greg and I feel the same. We almost want to drive over to the action and see what these animals are up to." Trevor laughed and said, "I am sure we will experience a lot more in the three months stationed here."

We finished our beat at 5:00 a.m. and saw the sunrise. In a strange way, it was calm being in the game park and hearing the animals come alive in the morning. We heard the camp wake up and come alive.

By seven o'clock we were on route to Kongola. From Ishesha it was only a two-hour journey. Not far from Ishesha we saw six giraffes walking over the road and strolling into the bush. We also saw many bucks. On one occasion, in the distance under some trees, we saw three kudus—my favorite deer. Not far from the kudus we saw two black rhinos. We were in wild Africa, and the feeling was out of this world—wild and free.

During the morning's drive, we noticed dark rain clouds in the distance. The cool breeze that blew in my face before the rain came gave me goose bumps all over my body. In Africa, you can smell the moist, cool air before it rains.

We had no Terks' actions on the road from Rundu to Kongola. We felt relaxed and a bit tired from the long journey. At Kongola we parked our vehicles and had a half-hour break. We shook hands with the bad-ass warrior guys, Ben, Pen, and the trekkers. I had this feeling that we would meet again. We stretched our legs and walked around the Hottentot-god mine-sweeper contraption.

Greg and I sat in the tractor seat and looked through the armored glass. It was an experience that felt weird. I was sure that it was a mission to drive this beast at forty clicks per hour and to keep the frame in a straight position on the road. Ben explained how to drive the beast. I looked at his biceps, and they were just as large as actor Arnold Schwarzenegger's. He was a huge, scary, bad-ass black guy that stood around six foot six tall.

We got word that we need to wrap it up and leave in ten minutes. The dark rain clouds were closing in, and we knew that we were going to get wet. Greg and I put our large poncho rain jackets on. About five clicks after leaving Kongola, the lightning was forceful, and the rain poured down on us. It was the first time that we had a heavy downpour on this trip.

While on route to Katima Mulilo, the convoy stopped many times. The roads were muddy, and it seemed to take forever to reach Camp Katima. About five clicks from our camp, the rain stopped, and we had a breather. It was a long trip, driving more than eleven hundred kilometers to Rundu and back to Camp Katima. We did all this driving within four days.

Once we reached camp, we received orders to gather at the stage area. We had a strange feeling that something was not right. Our major informed us that two of our SAI boys had been shot dead and seven were injured in an ambush near Mpatcha Air Base. We had shot dead sixteen Zam-boons and had wounded ten. The Zam-boons were held for questioning. We had found some maps with them, locating their next targets.

We were told that we did well in getting the supplies to Katima Mulilo and the other camps nearby. The SAI were going to help offload the supplies that were on the Magirus trucks.

We were given three days off to recuperate before our next mission. In three days we would get orders to stand a one-night guard beat at one of the nearby Zambezi observation guard posts. After lunch we had to clean our muddy Panzers. After Trevor's vehicle inspection, we were off duty for the day.

In the afternoon, Greg, Brian, and I went to the canteen beer-hole to down some beers. The guys in the camp heard about our sniper episode. We told the other armored-vehicle guys of our Caprivi Strip adventure.

Red also came over that evening. He was impressed by how Greg and I had reacted when we heard the snipers' bullets. It was very late when we finally crashed in our beds.

Chapter Six

Katima

The Most Frightening Heli-Ride of My Life

On the Thursday morning after breakfast, Trevor said, "The Scorpion troop will be standing one night and day guards duty at the Romeo-Bravo observation outlook post."

The guard post was beside the Zambezi River bend, around three kilometers from the main town. We had to get ready to start our twenty-four-hour beat at 5:00 p.m.

We scheduled and grouped the the guys beat with vehicle One and Two together and Three and Four to stand second guard beat. Our time beat was second, from midnight to 6:00 a.m. and from noon to 6:00 p.m. the following day.

What we did not know was that it was going to be an awesome adventure for Greg, Brian, and me.

At just after 8:00 a.m., Red came into our tent and said, "Cappie arranged for y'all to go on a heli-run up and down the Caprivi Strip."

Greg was confused and said, "You mean all of us?"

Red looked at him with a skewed smile and said, "Hey, bro, what's wrong with you, all of ya?"

I was first to say, "Yeah, we can go now. Our Scorpions have to leave for guard duty at five o'clock."

In seconds, we locked up our tent and made our way to the helipad. Cappie was waiting for us and waving. "Come on; let's go."

I had to go through a flight-mission exercise briefing, with me being the one who was going to handle the 7.62mm machine gun. Greg and Brian would be seated in the large Puma helicopter that can seat six people, excluding the door gunner. A medic was also seated with them, in case someone was shot. Our mission briefing was a heli-trip from Katima to Rundu. We would have a refueling break and fly back to Katima.

We made our way to the helicopter. Greg and Brian saw Red strap me in the machine-gun seat at a ninety-degree angle behind Red. He was going to sit as copilot. I heard that he was the backup pilot if any of them were shot. He was a special guy, and I knew why he was stationed so long here on the border.

It was exhilarating, because I was sitting sideways in the left door seat. I was strapped in with shoulder- and waist-harness safety belts so tight that I was part of the chair. The chair was solidly welded on a thick plate that was bolted to the heli-floor. This was not a normal contraption but more like a homemade job. I was so close to the open removed door that my legs and the machine gun were sticking halfway out.

The seat was close to the gun, and the double trigger was about eight inches from my chest. Red slid down a frame above my head. It had a rest for my heli-helmet to lean against.

He told me, "This is the most extreme ride you will ever have. Enjoy and remember you are special." I smiled and gave him gave him the thumbs-up. He said, "The helicopter will fly at a fifteen- to thirty-degree angle. You will experience feeling like you are falling out of the helicopter. As we get to max flying speed, the G-force will make you feel funny."

My heart was in my throat and I was shivering. *What the hell am I doing this for?* I thought. My boots were positioned on two thick metal plates that were sticking out the open door. My boots were strapped to the plate with leather straps and buckles. I was all strapped in for the ride of my life.

The intercom talk was different than that in the Panzer vehicles. Communication was direct, and we all could talk at the same time, just like on a telephone.

Oh, my God, I was so tightly strapped in. All I could move was my arms and hands left to right.

Cappie started the engine to rotate the blades. We all did a quick radio check before liftoff. Cappie told me that we needed to talk all the time. I needed to tell him what I saw on the ground at all times. He said, "If you feel giddy, you need to tell me." He also assured me that Red would be talking to me consistently. He would give me instructions on what to do when we were in flight.

O-h-h-h shit, what have I got myself in for?

The helicopter blades were now almost in full rotation mode. I put the wide helmet visor down. Cappie did a radio check with the other two helicopters. They were in flight first. I felt this springboard lifting feeling. The vibrations and noise was frightening. *Oh, shit, we have a liftoff.* I positioned my head against the frame headrest. It was amazing to see the camp from the air.

Cappie said, "We will be flying at the rear of the formation to Rundu. We will be in the front on the return trip." Cappie did a 360-degree circle around the camp. We went into a fast forward and left-tilting flying mode. We left the camp like a "heli-bat" out of hell. I almost died. The wind was forceful. I heard Red say, "Hey Mike, get a feel of the machine gun. Swivel it max from left to right and up and down about ten times. While you swivel the turret, you need to look at the end of the barrel sight to get a feel for the target you want to shoot."

We were now over a wide stretch of land where all the trees were cut down. The Caprivi Strip was about a kilometer wide and in a straight line. It was no-man's-land, and anyone crossing it at any time would be shot dead.

After fifteen minutes in flight, I was getting used to the feeling of falling out of the helicopter. While flying at a weird angle, I was feeling a bit giddy. Red gave a command to the other helicopters. "This is Tango X-ray. We are going to shoot a burst of rounds and will command when we are done." Red said to me on the intercom, "Go for it, Mike, just like the Panzer—five-second machine-gun bursts, stop, one more five-second burst. Find a large tree on the Caprivi side of the border and see if you can blow it to pieces."

We were flying sideways with the wind hitting the right side of my face. I was strapped in this contraption with an awesome 180-degree view of the ground and trees whizzing below me. When looking left or right, I could see the side of the helicopter. When I looked up I could see the fast rotor blades whizzing above my head. It was frightening, but I felt like a bad-ass eagle in the sky. I swung the gun slightly to my left and lined up a large, high tree. I let rip with the machine gun. What I did not realize was that they have a lot more tracer bullets in the machine gun belt. When I opened fire, I could see a red streak before me. It was easier to line up the target.

It was an unbelievable feeling when I saw that large tree explode as the rounds hit it and the tree fell over. I lined up a smaller tree for the second burst let it have it. I missed a bit, but within a few seconds I hit it and saw the tree explode, lifting up slightly and falling down to the ground.

"Wow that was awesome!" I said. I had a smile so wide that I almost had a jaw lock. Cappie said on the main radio, so the entire helicopter mission guys could hear, "Good shooting, X-ray Bro. The trees have died." I had suddenly been given a nickname, "X-ray Bro," having the call sign Tango X-ray for the day.

It was a long flight to Rundu. About an hour in flight, the large helicopter gunner shot a few 50mm Browning rounds to keep his barrel clean. Where I was sitting and observing his shooting, I could see the rounds leaving the turret in a straight line. He was excellent, shooting around ten rounds and hitting five or so trees. At that moment I knew why the enemy feared the 50mm Browning machine gun. We were now flying opposite the Angola border, and we were close to where the Okavango River crossed over the Caprivi Strip.

Cappie was a hoot and would play with his helicopter. He would fly very close to the treetop level and make a lift high in the sky. He would dive back down to just above the treetops. This was more extreme than any roller coaster ride. I sometimes felt a bit lightheaded from the sudden helicopter movements.

Every time he did this, he would ask me, "Are you with us?" I was enjoying the feeling and would reply, "Tango X-ray. Is that all you can do?"

Oh-h-h-h shit, he did some dog-fighting moves. We were at a reasonable height when he put the helicopter in spiral roll, and we went up and did a 360 loop and straight again. During the loop I closed my eyes for a few seconds. The blood gushed out of my head and made me black out for a few seconds. We came back to a normal flying position. I was back from the dead, feeling extremely lightheaded.

Cappie calmly said, "How was that, X-ray Bro?" I shouted out, "Yeah, awesome!"

I heard HQ on the radio. "Tango X-ray, get into formation and look for the bad guys; over and out." I knew that the major listened in on radio frequency on all the communications.

I was getting used to the sideways-flying feeling, and I calmed down a lot. Every so often Cappie or Red would tell me, "You are doing great. Stay focused." I was consistently giving them messages on what I saw on the ground. Many a time while flying to a higher elevation, I could see over on the Angola side of the border. I saw many reflections of the vehicles driving near the Okavango River.

It was just before 11:00 a.m. when we made a circular flight over the Rundu camp. It looked great from the sky above it and with the Okavango River beside it.

The helicopters landed one by one at a large landing pad near the main camp buildings.

While the rotor blades were winding down, we saw a fuel truck driving toward us.

Red unstrapped me from the gunner seat. We all dismounted and had an hour to kill before our next flight. Red took us to the officers' canteen. We downed three beers each within thirty minutes. We were now relaxed and the fourth beer went down smoothly. I could not stop smiling. Red said, "Awesome feeling, hey, X-ray Bro? Best job in the world, being a heli-gunner."

Cappie and the other two heli-captains joined us in the officers' canteen. We talked with the other "heli-bad boys" and had many laughs. Later, we were taken by two Willys Jeeps with drivers to the helicopter pad. I felt like an officer, having someone drive me to where my next mission would be.

Cappie and the other pilots had their short briefing in a tent next to the helipad. While waiting for Cappie, Red strapped me in the gunner seat as Greg and Brian watched. I saw their envious eyes, but we were all in a happy mood. They knew that being a gunner was the ultimate experience.

When Cappie returned, the rotor blades were winding up until they were in a fast-spinning mode for a heart-pumping explosive liftoff. Cappie had been on the radio with HQ, waiting for orders to proceed to Camp Katima.

I heard Cappie say, "Are we good to roll, X-ray Bro?"

I replied, "Ready when you are, Tango X-Ray Wun" (NATO call sign).

I heard Cappie talk to the base. "HQ, we are good to roll. Over." HQ responded, "You are good for a liftoff, Tango X-Ray Wun."

Oh shit, we did a springboard heli-lift. My heart sank into my butt, and I could feel the G-force upward acceleration—it made me gasp for air.

We were now in the front flying position. I looked over at the Angola side of the border; everything seemed clear. It was midday, the air was crisp, and there was not a cloud in the sky. For the first hour in flight, we were mostly on the Namibian side of the wide Okavango River. Cappie did low-flying skimming-water moves, and then he would take the helicopter high in the sky. I informed everyone what I saw on the Angolan side of the river. It was mostly local trucks on the main road. I also saw a few Angolan army vehicles driving toward a town called Xamavera. Like a falcon falling, we would free-fall dive back to earth and skim the Okavango River. My blood pressure must have maxed out.

I was getting used to the sideways fast-flying motion, and I felt more relaxed. We flew past Muscsso on the Angolan side, where the Caprivi Game Park starts. The Okavango River was now behind us, and we could just see the straight stretch of grassland ahead of us. I noticed a barbed-wire fence around two meters high on the Namibian side of the wide stretch. I knew that it was to keep the animals in the Caprivi side of the game park. I saw many deer and some buffalo, rhinos, and a small herd of elephants.

We were flying high over our South African Reconnaissance Corporation (SARC) camp. The trees all around the camp had been shot down around two hundred meters from the fort walls and barbed-wire fencing. It looked like a sixteenth-century box-style fort with a stockade fence. There was a huge tent in the center with eight other smaller tents around it. There was also a high wooden structure just behind the large tent and there were machine gun enclosures on the four corner posts. While flying over the camp we saw someone waving a black pirate's flag with a gesture, "How-zit, ma Bro's?"

We flew high in the sky for about ten minutes. Cappie informed us that we were a hundred clicks from Katima Mulilo. The remaining reconnaissance route would take about a half hour to get to Camp Katima. Our mood was relaxed.

Then it happened. Red and I saw the movement at the same time. We both spoke on the radio, saying, "Zam-boon troops ahead." Red took control. "They are about a hundred meters in Zambia from the Caprivi Strip. We can see four large troop carriers parked on the roadside, estimated twenty clicks from Imusho."

Cappie was a crazy guy. He made a free-fall dive down to treetop level and made a hard left toward them. We were flying in the Caprivi hot zone and entering the Zambian side of the border. As we flew over their heads, I noticed about twenty of the camouflaged Zam-boon men hit the deck. Cappie called out on the radio, "Hold your fire until they shoot the first shot."

Cappie suddenly did a 180-degree in-flight U-turn. Like a bad-ass eagle in a dive, we crossed back over them. I heard a few gunshots and then nothing.

My thoughts were, "Damn, what is going on here?"

I heard Red's voice over the radio. "The fuckers shot at us." I was shaking like a leaf but my hands were ready on the machine gun trigger to let loose and fire once I got the command to do so.

Cappie swerved back to the Caprivi Strip, and we did a full low-flight U-turn in the open field. He came back lower to the grass, flying about ten meters from the ground. The other two helicopters were high up in the sky, observing the view. We were observing if there were any movements in the trees ahead. I heard Cappie's voice over the radio. "We cannot kill them on the Zambian side, but let's scare them to death." He gave orders, saying, "X-ray Bro, shoot three bursts directly through the trees towards the Zam-boons ahead."

I let rip and slowly moved side to side, shooting as he'd directed. After the third burst, I stopped. During all the machine-gun firing there were many communications going on, and everything seemed to happen in slow motion. I saw many trees exploding and falling to the ground, and I thought my heart had surely stopped.

Cappie lifted the bird up high in the sky and sideways. When the Puma rose up with speed higher in the sky, we could see the Zam-boon men running inland away from the Caprivi Strip.

My hands were shaking from all the action. Cappie shouted over the radio frequency, "Yeah, fuck off, you Zam-boon bastards!"

We were stationary for around twenty seconds as we observed the movement below. We did a hard right and flew back to camp in the front formation. Cappie said, "Good shooting, X-ray Bro Mike. The Zam-boons are running away like skyrockets."

My God, this was too much action for me. I was shaking and felt lightheaded. We were now flying at a high altitude on the Caprivi side of the border. The communications from HQ were positive, thanking us on the good move to scare the Terks from the border.

After another fifteen minutes in flight, I heard Cappie calmly say, "Hey, X-ray Bro, can you see the Ngambwe Falls up ahead?" This was on the Zambian side and not too far from Katima Mulilo and camp. We flew over Katima Mulilo, and I could see many locals waving their hands in the air. I immediately new why we were here, protecting the good Namibian Caprivi people.

We first circled the camp and touched down, safe and sound, on the helipad. We were back in the camp and "home." I had many tears in my eyes from this indescribable feeling.

After we dismounted the helicopters, Major Briggs was waiting for us under the open hangar. He was in constant communication with us and had been listening on the frequency radio on our action with the Zam-boon soldiers fleeing back inland. The major shook our hands; he shook mine last. He said, "Hey, X-ray Bro, if you want to join the Permanent Forces, you are most welcome. Cappie, here, tells me that you shoot a mean target, and you are a natural." I noticed Greg giving me a big smile.

Major Briggs jokingly said, "Red has been here three years, and he is losing his mind. We need to replace him." He gave Red a soft punch on his shoulder.

"Not on your life, Major Bro," Red said. "I am the best you have."

"We all know that Red is here only for the money," Cappie said, "and yeah, he is the best we have." Cappie shook my hand, saying, "You did well today. I think the Zam-boons crapped in their trousers trying to flee from your machine-gun firing. I am sure they are still running away from the Caprivi Strip."

We all had a good laugh. After the excitement of the heli-run, I felt like I was standing on top of the world. I had to go with the bunch to do our flight debriefing. This was in a small HQ tent. It was the first time that I discussed what I had seen. The debriefing was from the time we left camp, the Zam-boon action, and landing back in camp. While we were discussing the trip, many questions were asked. All was recorded on a machine. The major and his three intelligence officers took notes on the helicopter mission. There was a large Caprivi map, with red marking locations on the activity on the Caprivi Strip borders. I saw them make a new red mark location and date and time logged.

After debriefing, Red, Greg, Brian, and I had lunch together. I was beaming like a 1000-watt bulb. In the afternoon, our Scorpion troop Panzer guys and Trevor were in our tent, talking about our awesome day's experience. They were envious of Greg, Brian, and especially my gunner action in the Caprivi Strip.

We were rattling on and on about what we saw. Greg and Brian were in the large Puma and saw the action from above. When I let rip with the machine gun through the trees, they saw the Zam-boons running away from the Caprivi Strip. The way that Greg expressed the action made everyone laugh so much that some of the guys had a gut ache. I was also elaborating while Greg was expressing the actions.

It was a great day for me. The heli-trip was our Scorpion Panzer trump card. We had done it all. At 5:00 p.m., our troop reported to HQ to start guard duty. A Unimorg drove us to the River Bend guard post on the edge of Katima's last village houses. This was where the river turned and proceeded into Zambia. The guard post was on slightly higher ground, about eight meters from the river below. The guard post was about ten minutes' drive from the Katima camp's main gate. We had plenty of time to do the guard hand-over.

Our battalion supports section three Guy's. "The cobra boys" were standing the previous beat. We had a good chat with them before they returned to camp.

They first took us to a large tree not far from the guard post. This tree was around eight feet wide and had a toilet built in it. It had a concrete step and a toilet door on the outer bark section of the tree. Greg opened the latched door. The tree was hollowed out and rectangular like a toilet room. The toilet room was complete with toilet and toilet roll holder. We all smiled when we saw it.

The guard house was huge and had a Browning machine gun mounted high up in a standing position. Through the front opening you could cover a wide shooting range from the left to the right side of the fast-flowing Zambezi River bend. There were six army beds on the side of the guard house with a wide opening at the back. This guard house had a lookout opening that covered the entire river view. The post looked like a Lapa-style hut. It had a camouflaged thatched roof, with netting and some tree branches over it. The sides were thick-beam wooden poles. It had a relaxed feeling about it, and the river bend view was awesome.

Greg, Brian, Dexter, Tom, and I walked down a trail to the river below. It was a steep decline, and the bushes and shrubs were dense. We climbed to a flat section and noticed many hippo footprints on it. We were there for a short while. We went back up the incline with a bit of a struggle and decided to stay at the guard post.

We saw many black mamas walking by us with large wrapped-up items balanced on their heads. Some of the young, good-looking black girls smiled at us and nodded their heads.

We all gazed at the sun setting through rain clouds. The sun's rays reflected through it and on the river bend. The awesome African experience gave me goose bumps all over my body. We all felt free and happy to see this amazing sunset. In that part of Africa when the sun sets, it goes red on the horizon, and the reflections are out of this world. The dark-red reflections through the clouds made our moods so relaxed and free. When I closed my eyes for a few seconds, all my troubles in this crazy world would flow out of my body and into the Zambezi River bend below.

It was a perfect day for us. Within a few minutes, the sun fell off the edge of the earth. My happy sunshine day was gone. As it was getting dark, the full moon was directly above us. The bright moonlight reflected on the flat river bend, flowing from the Ngambwe Falls. There were millions of sparkles vibrating on the water. I noticed fish popping out of the water and creating a small splash. This made my body tremble with excitement, so much so that I had electricity flowing through my body, making me jerk from the explosive feelings in my heart.

No one was talking; we were all amazed at the beauty of the land. We seemed hypnotized by everything surrounding us on this wild African adventure day.

All was calm, and I was so happy to have the opportunity to stand guard beat at the Romeo Bravo observation guard post. During the early night we noticed a group of hippos in the river below us. They were moving closer toward our position. We watched them as they floated on the water and sprayed the water out of their nostrils.

At eight o'clock a Unimorg came up the path toward our guard post. The driver dropped off a large urn of hot coffee for the night guard beat. Times were good, and we all had a large mug of hot coffee each. The wind had picked up some, and it was getting slightly colder. We decided to crash for a few hours' sleep.

At five minutes to midnight, I felt Dexter waking me up, saying, "Beat time, X-ray Bro." I was in a daze, thinking, *X-ray who?* I got my senses right and thought, *Yeah, I am now X-ray Bro.* The other group crashed for the night in their sleeping bags. Our group sipped hot coffee and talked to each other in a soft tone. I hopped on the thick cross beam that was the length of the guard house. I put my folded-up sleeping bag under my bum and rested my back on the beam. I stretched my legs next to the machine gun barrel. The gun was protruding outward from the guard house toward the river. Greg saw how comfortable I was and did the same on the other side. The other guys were leaning against the opening, with one guy behind the machine gun in a ready-to-fire position.

At around four in the morning we heard the hippos splashing in the river. They came out of the river onto the flat section of land that was below us. The hippos sounded if they were fighting for they were making funny noises. We all were afraid. At this time I was standing behind the machine gun, and I pointed it in the direction of the hippos. I looked through the night vision binoculars and could see two large males facing each other. They had their large mouths open, and their teeth were large and round in shape.

Greg and I consistently swapped the position behind the machine gun. We looked through the binoculars for movements in the river.

We also observed the river farther away to see if there were any bad guys out there or any other movement in the water. Back at camp, we were informed that when the hippos make a lot of noise, it is a perfect time for the Zam-boons to cross the river.

Eventually, the hippos calmed down. For the remaining time while standing beat, the moon had disappeared, and the sky was dark, but there were billions of stars. It was dead quiet until dawn. When the sun finally rose, it was a still, calm morning. The animals and reptiles were making their morning noises. A new day was born. The cool breeze made me shiver with excitement at being here. I was feeling a bit tired from the little sleep.

Just before six o'clock we woke the third-beat guys. When they started their beat, we brushed our teeth and hopped into our sleeping bags for a good morning sleep.

Just after 9:00 a.m., a Unimorg brought our breakfast and a fresh urn of coffee. After breakfast we relaxed for a while. Brian had some playing cards with him, and our group played cards until our noon guard beat. Our lunch was delivered, and the afternoons guard beat was relaxing. During the afternoon we saw many local black folk walking by the guard post. Most of the black mamas were balancing many items on their heads. They would all smile and be polite as they walked by us.

At around five twenty we were relieved by the infantry guys. We left the guard post at six ten and went back to camp for our dinner. On the same night we watched an open-air movie. It was the first time at camp that we got steaming drunk. Our troop was off duty for the entire next day. When I woke up, Red was passed out on my sleeping bag on the floor next to my bed. I woke him up and realized that it was way past 8:00 a.m. He was out of it, he was supposed to be on a six o'clock heli-run to Victoria Falls and back.

I knew he was going to be in deep shit for not reporting on time. The army lifestyle up on the borders was relaxed, but the officers did not take this kind of shit lightly. Later that same day, Red told me, "I received my last warning. I will be shipped back home if it happens again."

At this point we had been stationed here in Camp Katima for just over a month and so much action had happened. The days that followed, I would get goose bumps when I thought of my exciting time with Cappie and Red in the heli-run to Rundu and back to Camp Katima.

Chapter Seven

Katima

The Caprivi Adventure Changed My Outlook in Life

We went on many patrols in the Caprivi heartlands in the weeks that followed. Our armored Troop Three, the Black Widow troop unit, was ambushed near the Caprivi Strip and close to a camp known as Sifuma. One support section guy was shot in the lower arm. We also had action on a patrol route toward Mpatcha Air Base. Dexter shot the sniper dead, and the second one was captured and held for questioning

We were now in our second month in the Caprivi Strip. On this day while we were off duty, we got orders to gear-up and make haste to a small outpost camp known as Mturi. This camp was around thirty kilometers from Katima Mulilo. The South African Infantry was stationed there, and their camp was close to the wide-open Caprivi Strip.

While traveling flat out in our Panzers, we got word that the battle was full on. It was speculated that the Zam-boon force was around sixty-plus strong. I knew that they were the same bunch that we scared off on our heli-run when returning from Rundu to Camp Katima. What were these Zam-boon Terks doing? We were more experienced in bush warfare, and for sure whoever was in command of the Terks would send their soldiers to a death conflict. Maybe it was a political move to at least try to shoot some SAI forces, so that the Zambian government could announce an achievement.

That night, I asked Trevor if I could shoot a few rounds off the side of the road on the 50mm and 7.62mm Browning machine guns. I wanted to make sure that my machine guns did not jam. Greg, Brian, and I were in the front vehicle. And when the shit hit the fan, we were going to be first in the line of action.

"Good thinking, X-ray Bro," Trevor said.

We traveled up a sandy path that led up to the Mturi camp for about forty-five minutes. I opened the hatch and shot a few rounds on the 7.62mm gun. Then I slid back in my hot seat and fired a few 50mm rounds just off the road in front of me. This was on the flat, open grassland of the Caprivi Strip.

It was not long before I heard rifle shooting. Greg gave orders to get into formation close to the edge of the open field. The Panzers were in a straight line, moving forward toward the strip. Brian had positioned our Panzer between two large trees on the edge of the strip.

The captain of the Mturi camp was happy to see us. We could see the scared look on the SAI riflemen's faces. Our support section guys did their normal armored ambush field position around the Panzers. During all the chaos, Greg and I were in the Panzer. We received orders from Trevor to "fire at will and pound the Zambian side with high-explosive mortars."

It was now nearly dark, and I could see the hundreds of tracer bullets streaking across the open field of the Caprivi Strip.

My God, what is happening here? I thought. It looked like a full-scale war.

Greg looked at me as a few shots ricocheted off our Panzer. We heard three mortar explosions go off and could see that the Zam-boons were launching them blindly. They landed in stupid locations and in the open field. The closest one that exploded was around fifty meters from our position.

Greg looked through his Panzer sights and gave me coordinate settings on launching my first high-explosive mortar. I heard, " Fire at will." The Panzer rocked as the first H-E mortar was fired. I looked in my sight and saw the trees on the Zam-boon side light up the night sky as the H-E mortar exploded.

Within seconds, the rest of the troop guys let rip and let the Zam-boons have it. The Zam-boons responded by launching tripod mortars toward us. Another one landed around sixty meters to the side of us in the open field. What the hell were these idiots doing?

Full-on battle stations happened for around twenty minutes. I had just fired my sixth H-E mortar and had gone through two belts of the 50mm Browning machine gun.

Over the communications, we got word to stand down and hold position. All was quiet except for a few rifle shots still streaking across that field that were fired from our side of the Caprivi Strip.

Damn, my heart was burning, and the exhilarating feeling was making my body shake. Greg and I popped our hatches open and got in the top firing position. I cocked the 7.62mm Browning machine gun and was ready for action.

We saw some of the Mturi camp off-road biker guys racing across that field. They were firing their R-3 weapons towards the Zam-boon side of the Caprivi Strip. As they disappeared over wide stretch of open field, Trevor came over the radio, saying, "Hold your fire until further orders." He thanked us for fighting off the bad guys.

It was not long after when we heard the three bad-ass helicopters flying low over our heads into the Zambian territory. Their searchlights were shining brightly in the trees. We all held position and felt grand, knowing that on this day's conflict, we had kicked ass.

Trevor mentioned to our unit on the troop-to-troop vehicle communications, "The action may return."

My heart was in my throat, and my body was trembling. About twenty minutes later, the night-mission helicopters' noise was gone, as they returned to Camp Katima. All was good.

We received orders to move back and continue all night long on a patrol, up and down on the Katima Kongola main road. I felt as if I was in a war movie and in the main event. At around 5:15 a.m., we heard the three helicopters fly over our vehicles toward the Caprivi Strip. They were doing a visual sweep-up operation on what had happened the night before at the Mturi camp and beyond.

It was just after six o'clock when we got orders to return to Camp Katima. During the drive back to camp we learned the outcome of the previous night's action. We sadly had lost six SAI guys in the Mturi camp, and there were seventy-odd Zam-boons dead. The word was that there were body parts scattered about that could not be identified. I guess the H-E mortars were the bad boys and made a bloody mess when they exploded. We had also hit seven old trucks that were Zambian soldiers' carrier vehicles.

In our Scorpion troop and support section unit, no one was shot or killed.

At Camp Katima, Trevor and Major Briggs rounded up our Scorpion unit in the mess hall. The major shook our hands and congratulated us on the fighting that had taken place the night before. Trevor was always emotional, and while giving us a prayer, he choked on his words and tears rolled down his cheeks. I too had heartaching thoughts, and tears rolled down my cheeks. The happy feeling in my heart, knowing that we had such a grand, caring guy as our lieutenant, was mind-blowing.

We were given time off for the day and had to wait for further orders from our HQ.

During the day, we spoke with Red. He had been in the morning reconnaissance mission. They did the observation heli-run over the camp. He told us that we had pounded the sight, and it was a bloody mess. The burned-out trees and smoke could be seen for many miles away. The Off-road biker unit had given them the dead-body count and the ground destruction that had taken place.

In the week that followed the Mturi camp fighting, the Caprivi seemed to be in a no-action calm state.

On Saturday, our Scorpion Troop One had to stand guard beat for two consecutive days and nights at the Alpha Bravo treetop post. This guard post was around ten clicks away from Camp Katima and beside the Zambezi River, opposite Sesheke. Our Scorpion troop was taken to the guard post in a Unimorg. It was just past 5:00 p.m. when we arrived at the treetop post.

We had taken ten extra 7.62mm Browning machine gun belt cases with us. Troop Five, the "Corral Snake" guys, were relieved from duty. During the conversation with them, we learned that many Zambian soldiers had just arrived in Sesheke. We told Troop Five about our heavy action the week before, and it seemed if they were envious that our Scorpion One guys got all the action.

The Alpha Bravo guard post was mounted high up in a massive tree, about twenty meters off the ground. The guard house platform had wooden steps with a rope rail, leading up to the platform guard post. The steps formed a spiral incline to the top of the tree where the guard house was.

Inside the guard house were six sponge mattresses. There were also two 7.62mm machine guns mounted on a rotating bucket-seat frame that could swivel 160 degrees. There was a telescope and three day/night vision binoculars. From the scenic outpost the view over the river was grand. The Corral Snake guys returned to camp. We hauled all the ammunition up to the tree post with a rope pulley and bucket.

Food rations and a large urn of coffee also were hoisted up to the treetop post. At the bottom area, there was a barbed-wire section that could cover the wooden steps below. This was to keep the bad guys from trying to climb to the guard post at night.

These South African forces guys thought of everything. On the side of the post was a small opening to be used as a toilet. The toilet section was enclosed with wood. About two-thirds of the observation post protruded out over the water, including the toilet. We had to squat inside the enclosed toilet to have a shit. When we lifted up the toilet seat, it was only an open hole where the shit or piss fell straight down into the river below. And big ol' log shit would float away down the river current. You also could feel the wind blowing up your asshole while dumping your log shit. When pissing through that toilet hole, the wind would spray your piss onto the water below. There was a spray bottle of disinfectant to use in the toilet hole after you have done your business, to keep the smell neutral.

In the tree house we had a metal washing tub with ice in it. We got the ice and tub from one of the cooks in camp. We all had smuggled beers in our backpacks and sleeping bags. On these beer-smuggling episodes, our corporals were quiet as mice. We never told on each other. I was with a bad-ass group of guys, and we always looked out for one another.

At sunset, it was beer time. The mood was happy and the talk was great.

We rotated the guard beat from our last beat at the Romeo Bravo post. Scorpion vehicle One and Two were now on beat until midnight and vehicle Three and Four were from midnight to 6:00 a.m.

After dinner, the Scorpion Three and Four guys snuck in their sleeping bags to sleep. Greg, Brian, Dexter, Tom, and I were on beat. We watched through the night binoculars what was happening on the Zam-boon side of the river. We could see many of the Zambian soldiers sitting by campfires, eating and drinking.

Then it happened: my heart raced with the fear in me. While Dexter and I were sitting in the machine-gun seats, we heard gunshots. Greg and the other guys looked through the binoculars at the Zambian side of the river. Zam-boon soldiers were shooting some rounds in the air. They were also doing some funny fire-warrior dance. I was ready to fire the machine gun, but Greg said loudly, "Stand down—they are all drunk and being stupid."

This went on consistently, with those idiots doing sporadic gunshots in the air. Through the long-range night binoculars we could see them well enough to see their ranks, or stripes.

Greg and I watched soldiers doing stupid drunken dancing. We saw young black tribal girls do a suggestive hip-shaking dance. Their naked boobs were flopping in the firelight as they danced with fast, vibrating shoulder movements. They had short grass skirts that hung on their hips. Their feet shuffled and bounced. The soldiers were all sitting on rocks drinking whatever was making them aggressive.

Our eyes were glued at the tribal lady warrior dance. After about ten minutes of dancing, a tall black guy with camouflage trousers and a hand gun got up. We knew he was the big cheese of the crazy soldier group. He was bare-chested and started to feel these girls as they were dancing suggestively around him. He danced a bit with his hands in the air while shooting a few shots in the air with his handgun, and then he grabbed one of the black native girls and forcefully pulled her skirt down. She stood naked in front of him, looking frightened by his aggressive behavior.

He removed his trousers. What happened next made me feel all funny inside. Five soldiers got up and lifted the naked girl in their arms. We could see that she was screaming and her body was frantically trying to get loose from the awful Zam-boon soldiers. They held her legs and arms stretched wide open.

With our binoculars, it seemed as if they were ten meters in front of us, so Greg and I could clearly see. The "big cheese" guy repeatedly raped the girl. At the same time, he was hitting her face and spitting in her face. I could see the pained expressions on her pretty face. She had endless tears running down her cheeks. Her mouth was bleeding from Big Cheese Guy whacking her as he frantically raped her with speed.

I had this weird feeling that this was her first time. She looked frightened and in shock. Monster-cock guy did it to her solidly for a long time. It looked as if her body was just flopping and that she had passed out from the pain. He stood over her, shaking body and shouting at her. He was worse than an animal.

Oh, my God, I thought. *It's not over yet.* Six soldiers got up and stood behind this animal. They removed their army trousers. This act went on continuously for more than two hours. None of them cleaned themselves until they were done with her. I could see blood coming out from between her legs. Her head was bopping about in a trance or passed-out state. They had no care if she died from these evil acts.

Greg and I stopped watching, and I said, "Oh, God, I want to say the words. We are here to protect the local people living peacefully on the riverbanks of this wonderful land."

"Why are these extreme acts of violence happening?" Greg asked.

We could not believe what we had just seen. From that instant, we had a bit more hate in us.

When the animal Zam-boons were done relieving themselves, they threw the girl's naked body on the ground and pulled their trousers up. Mike's thoughts were, *don't these animal people clean themselves?* They kicked dirt on her body, lying motionless on the ground. She was in a bloody, messy state.

We saw them shouting at the village people and showing them with their arms that they should leave the young girl on the ground. She lay there beside the fire, and no one could help her. I had a feeling that the tribal people were threatened and was hiding from the soldiers.

I wondered if she was dead. We could not see any movements from her at all. We all cried like babies. After about five minutes, we saw her arm move. The tears flowed down my cheeks like a waterfall. My prayers were answered; she finally moved. The brokenhearted naked girl slowly rolled herself on her belly. She tried to stand up slowly, but her legs could not hold her up. She collapsed on the ground. My thoughts went ballistic. *"Dammit, get up, girl! Get away from there. The animals may come back for you!"*

Finally, she slowly crawled on her hands and knees, flopping two times on her belly to the ground, while moving slowly toward the river. In pain, she lay in the water for several minutes. She slowly washed the blood and dirt from between her legs and her naked aching body. She was crying endlessly while shaking her head from side to side.

When I gazed at her face, it was the saddest hollow look that I had ever seen. I just wanted to kill all those bastards that did this to her. Greg was always in control and said to all of us on the beat, "What we have witnessed tonight stays with us. There will be no shooting across the river unless we are under attack." We all agreed, and for the rest of the short beat, we were mostly quiet with our sad thoughts.

The midnight beat started there shift. We told them what had happened and told them no shooting unless we were under attack.

While lying in my sleeping bag, the noise across the river was still going on in full force. I could not sleep. My thoughts and heart were sad, knowing what they were doing to the young black girls in these tribal villages.

Why do people in power do such acts of violence? Why harm the happy normal folk living here in majestic Africa or in this wonderful world we live in? I wondered why I was seeing such acts of sexual violence in front of my very eyes.

It was long past midnight before I finally fell asleep, but I awoke suddenly around five thirty with a wary feeling. I lay there for a while and then got up. The river looked so calm and peaceful that I could not believe the extreme events from the night before. After breakfast, we strolled around the Alpha Bravo guard post. About fifty meters away was a small Caprivi tribal village. The guys met the chief, who said around sixty village people lived there. The chief was a peaceful guy. His English was fairly good. He told us that our sergeant major took good care of them.

I asked him, "How does the sergeant major take care of your village?" He went quiet for a while and then spoke in a black language to an older white-haired black guy, who then left us. The chief said, "You wait and see." A minute later, two young good-looking black women joined us in his *kraal*. They both had young naked babies with them, sucking milk from their exposed breasts. The two baby boys looked of mixed blood, and they seemed to about three months old. The two women wore colored-bead dresses, and they looked nice and clean and respectable. Their large boobs were visible though the top beads around their necks.

Chief said, "My two daughters are Sergeant Major's temporary wives. He makes me two boy children to become clever warriors." He smiled and said "My girls get plenty of good food for our village and some money too. Sergeant Major love to have sex. Every week he come and keeps my two girls happy. You will see tonight; he come and say to you that he inspect the village. He does not go back to camp until morning. He have best kraal here and love to fuck my daughters together. We know one day he will leave this place. I hope he make me many clever warrior children."

We left the chief's kraal. I smiled at Greg, saying, "Maybe this is the humane way to keep the tribal people happy."

That night around six o'clock, the sergeant major parked his Jeep next to the big tree. He waved at us as we stood on our beat and shouted from below, "Here to do my regular village inspection." Greg waved back; the sergeant major disappeared down the path to his two wives for his Sunday-night sexual pleasure.

We all laughed and knew that the sergeant major had been here too long, getting involved with the local village women. That night, the same action across the Zambezi River was going full on. We did not look much at the campfires but more around them and observed any actions or movements in the river.

The following day I could not wait to go back to camp. My mood was different. I was glad to be at the Romeo Bravo treetop guard post and see the nice river below; the surroundings were great. What we had witnessed on the Zam-boon side of this majestic river was awful. My heart was sad, and the bad memories of that horrible night's events haunted me all through my Caprivi Strip adventure.

The weeks that followed were calm with not much happening in the Caprivi heartlands. The patrol runs were every other day or night. On our time off, we watched movies and drank a lot of beer. The camp had only about ten movie reels. We saw *The Sound of Music* and *Mary Poppins* more than five times each. I remember that Julie Andrews was the star, and when she sang, the happy mood in the camp was like we were all floating on a cloud. We were now on a countdown, as our duty here on the border was coming to an end. We had around twenty days left on our three-month border duty.

Just after 7:00 p.m. we were returned to Camp Katima, tired and hungry. We had just driven through the camp gate when HQ informed us there was action near a small island known as Hippo Island. Hippo Island was about fifteen kilometers from our camp. It was on the Caprivi side of the Zambezi River and farther down past the Alpha Bravo treetop guard post.

The SAI guys were doing a foot-patrol mission. They were ambushed just as it was getting dark. Our Scorpion troop unit with support sections set off to Hippo Island. We had to drive much of the way through the bush, as there was no road to Hippo Island.

Brian drove the Panzer over the rough terrain and smaller trees. When we smashed into them, I could see them break and flop over and go under the armored vehicle. The ground was uneven, making the Panzer rock from side to side. Greg gave Brian directions on the land map in front of him. We also had to drive through a shallow stream.

It was now dark, and we could hear a few gunshots echoing through the trees. The bad guys must have heard the humming of our vehicles. Suddenly, all went quiet.

By this time, our Panzers were around five hundred meters from the river's edge. On the radio communications the South African Infantry guys were holding ground about fifty meters in front of our vehicles. During these observations, we were all wary. We could not see or hear any action beyond our view.

Trevor and I were on top of the Panzer. I was ready to fire the 7.62mm machine gun. We gazed through our night-vision binoculars. Our support section guys slowly made a foot-patrol sweeping movement through the bushes toward where the SAI guys were holding ground. We were the back-up and waited for instructions.

Trevor was consistently in communications with HQ and the SAI and Scorpion section radio-op.

It seemed as if the Zam-boons had retreated and crossed back over the river. It was not long before we heard the bad news. An SAI lieutenant was shot dead, and two SAI section guys were wounded severely. At that time, there were no Zam-boon casualties.

Our medic attended to the wounded. We were in the observation stance for around two hours, waiting for orders. During this time, our Scorpion section guys did a sweep up to Hippo Island and back. They found the crossover location where around ten Zam-boon soldiers had come over the river on their *maccora* (this is a carved-out tree boat, like a canoe or kayak.) There were blood marks, and it seemed as if there were some Zam-boon casualties.

We were instructed to wrap it up and return to Katima base camp. The Scorpion Two Benz-Unimorgs loaded all the SAI guys. On this run, I had not shot one round—that seemed strange.

On Sunday we traveled on patrol to Mpatcha Air Base. We were about halfway there when we got orders from HQ to proceed to Kongola. There was action at the Reckie Sifuma camp. We needed to go there as backup. This was where Angola, Zambia, and the Namibia Caprivi Game Park met at the Kuando River. This river flowed into and through the Caprivi Strip.

On the early morning patrol to Mpatcha, we left camp around five o'clock. An hour into our patrol route, we received the HQ orders: "Make haste to the Sifuma camp." It was around 11:00 a.m. when we got to Kongola. We traveled on a smaller dirt road to the Caprivi Strip and Camp Sifuma.

Before crossing over the Kuando River, we had to go down a scary descent and drive over a dodgy metal frame bridge and back up the other cliff. The metal bridge had twelve-by-ten-foot wooden planks inserted into a metal base. It was wide enough for the Panzers to cross with no hand railing on the bridge.

The bridge length was around fifteen meters long and looked unstable. Greg, Brian, and I were the first to cross in our Panzer. We sat on top of the vehicle in our ready-for-action position. We could hear the wood creaking and the bridge moving as we slowly proceeded over it. When we looked over the edge at the deep gorge below, we saw loads of crocodiles splashing frantically. My heart rate accelerated. In a panic, Greg told Brian to hustle over the bridge. Luckily, he could not see the snapping crocs in the river below. I am sure he would have crapped in his trousers from fear.

We never told Brian what was below until we crossed over the bridge and parked the Panzer. It was one of the most nerve-racking experiences in my life. The armored vehicle only had about eighteen inches per side to stay on the plank bridge. I had envisioned of the Panzer falling in the gorge and Greg, Brian, and me doing the croc-snapper tap dance, just like the Bugs-Bunny cartoon. Once over the bridge, it was easier for the rest of the vehicles to cross. Greg and I stood on either side on the bridge and showed the drivers a more center position to drive over. Before driving to the Sifuma camp, we first looked at all the crocs in the river below. There were more than fifty large snappers.

It was another ten minutes of driving on a hard sand road. We saw the Sifuma camp in the distance. It was fort-style wooden camp that was formed like a box. It was on the Angola side of the Caprivi Strip. I remember flying over it in the helicopter when we did our run to Rundu and back. The trees had been shot down around the Sifuma base camp. It looked more like a sixteenth-century fort, with all the trees chopped down and imbedded in the ground, with sharp pole points sticking upwards. The corner platforms had sharp pointed poles around them, with steps leading up to the guard posts. Inside the corner guard posts were 7.62mm Browning machine guns. They had the same style swivel chairs as the Alpha Bravo treetop post. There were two layers of razor-sharp coil-style barbed-wire fencing on the ground outside the wooden fencing around the camp.

In the center of the camp was a large tent with many smaller sleeper tents beside and behind it. There were around thirty hard-case Reckie boys stationed in the camp that could sleep fifty Reckies. There was also an underground ammunition depot that was under the large mess tent. I saw a 50mm Browning machine gun mounted high on a solid wooden pole structure beside the large center tent.

The Sifuma camp was the Reckies' HQ, where they kept all their supplies when performing their reconnaissance patrols into Angola and Zambia. I gathered that thirty of them were on a mission. We were position to park our Panzers in-between the corner outposts. Our Panzer was in the hot position again, at the far end of the camp, facing the Angola border.

We stayed in our vehicle positions while Trevor had a quick meeting with the Reckie captain. It was coming on lunchtime, and we were all gathered in the large tent and had lunch. The Reckie captain, Trix (his call-sign name), stood up and told us why we were there.

"Two days in a row the Ango-lies have attacked the camp to capture all the ammo stashed in the bunker. The last action was this morning at four o'clock. On the morning raid, twenty-four Ango-lies were shot dead. One of our Reckies has died and two are seriously wounded." He showed us on a large map. "They are getting smart and pounding the camp with tripod-launch mortars."

While driving into the camp, I did notice many explosion holes and a few in the camp. Most were around the outer perimeter of the camp fencing.

Captain Trix said, "We have set booby traps in the trees and around the camp perimeters. There is one trip wire across the road leading to the camp. We have word that the Ango-lies are going to hit the camp hard tonight. We all have to be prepared for the worst. Nothing happens during the day. We should all rest and sleep because tonight is going to be like a New Year's fireworks display."

All the Reckie guys looked bad-ass and were mostly big, muscular guys. Some had ammo belts crisscrossed over the sleeveless battle dress. Most of them had tattoos everywhere and had long hair and beards. I knew that they were wild bunch.

They all wore faded camouflage clothes and had panga knives on the side of their army belts. The Reckies also were heavily armed with 9mm Star pistols, just like we had. Just about all the Reckies had long stiletto knives on the left sides of their belts. Their R3 folding buttstock rifles were hanging by a strap off their backs. They all spoke a kind of broken English, reminding me of my school time in Durban, as they used a lot of slang words. I knew that they were in the thick of all the ground action, being stationed here on the border. Many of them had leopard-skin caps on their heads that only the Ango-lie officers wore.

Greg, Brian, and I crashed in one tent, and I fell asleep until dinner. Afterward, we walked around the camp until dark. Then we had to mount our Panzers. We were ready and in a firing position to shoot the 7.62mm machine gun when the action started.

We all received orders to fire a few rounds in the bushes ahead of us. We had to aim a bit higher so as not to set off the trip wires. The noise was frightening with everyone shooting at the same time.

We were consistently in radio communication with each other. We talked to the Reckie HQ on what we observed in the bushes. Greg and I were now wide awake and had our rock music on to calm down our nerves. That night we saw hundreds of trees shot down outside of the camp and many splintered stump trees. We had to sit and wait, knowing that sometime during the night, the action was going to happen.

Trevor and I always had a premonition that something was going to happen soon. On this night, Trevor had just said to Greg, "I feel it is time; be on your guard." Greg and I looked through our night-vision binoculars and all seemed peaceful and quiet. I looked at my watch; the time was 2:57 a.m.

I was feeling a bit wary. It was just after 3:00 a.m. when a trip-wire explosion went off and lit up the night sky. It was about three hundred meters away from the camp and toward the Scorpion Two Panzer locations. Trevor was right on. His gunner, Dexter, let rip with his machine gun, shooting three bursts of fire into the trees ahead of them. Two mortar explosions landed about fifty meters away from the camp. I knew that those idiots could not set their distance correctly and were launching the mortars blindly.

The two corner Reckie machine-guns posts were shooting consistently. Trevor gave me orders to shoot three bursts of machine-gun fire in front of me, then wait, and then three more bursts. This was to ensure that no mortars were launched from the Angolan side. As I was shooting, Greg was watching for any movement in the trees. I looked at the two Sifuma camp corner posts. The machine guns kept firing. It seemed like ten munities had gone by with continuous firing going on. Then a command was giving to stand down and wait. At that moment, it felt as if we had been dropped in a full-battle war zone.

The camp suddenly went quiet. I looked toward the machine-gun post to my left. The machine-gun barrel was red from the continuous shooting and smoke was rising from the barrel end.

We were told to "hold position, and do not fire any rounds." The Reckies were going to do a reconnaissance sweep through the trees and around the camp.

Greg, Brian, and I continued to communicate on our vehicle radio. After the shooting noise and then the sudden quiet, I was feeling all hyped up. It was the most exhilarating machine-gun noise we had ever heard. We were on standby orders until sunrise.

During the early morning, we could see that many more trees around the perimeter had been shot down. It felt as if we were in a corner with the bad guys trying to kill us. What were these stupid Ango-lies thinking? There were ten dead and mutilated bodies near our camp. Three tripod mortar launches were found in the woods. One had a mortar in it that was not fired. We heard that the Ango-lies were shot dead before launching it.

We stayed three more nights at the Sifuma camp, with no action reported. During the day we would sleep, and at night we were on guard beat all night long. It seemed that the bad guys were out-gunned.

During our stay at the Sifuma camp, the three helicopters did a reconnaissance aerial sweep above the camp and beyond. This happened at odd times, three times a day. We could hear Cappie giving reports on his observations to HQ at Camp Katima. On Thursday morning, we were given orders to return to Katima. After our return, our troop was given two days off with a two-day pass to Katima Mulilo.

On the first day, our troop went into the town center to buy ornaments and stuff to bring back home. We were driven to town in two Bedford trucks.

It was our first time to linger in Katima Mulilo. We walked around feeling free, like the locals did. We got many handshakes from the local townspeople. We felt special knowing that we were in the Caprivi for their protection.

On Sunday night, Red got drunk. While driving the helicopter crew's Jeep, he went off the road inside the camp, hit a tree, and ended up in a ditch. On Monday he was put in the lock-up for five days, charged with destruction of army equipment.

The days were getting closer to our leaving Katima. I felt both happy and sad. I knew that all the guys who were there for a year were going home, and maybe I'd never see them again.

Red was released from his lock-up on Saturday morning. Cappie had arranged for me to do one more heli-run to Victoria Falls and back. This was going to be a two-hour reconnaissance flight.

At around 5:00 p.m., the three helicopters left camp, flying east. We were in the front helicopter, leading the pack. It was the best time of day to see the falls in full flow. The sun was setting and gradually going red, and it was a fantastic scenic flight. I felt on top of the world and had goose bumps all over my body. Cappie flew low, skimming the flat water and flying fast just above the Zambezi River, toward Victoria Falls.

We did this low, sweeping, side-to-side flight until we were at the falls, and then he made a high-elevation lift. I could see the wide crack in the earth. The falls were more than two kilometers wide and the spray from them made a large rainbow over the falls. The sun was becoming red in the sky, with many streaks of sunlight shining brightly against the scattered clouds.

I had tears in my eyes because of the beauty of this wonderful African continent. I thought, *why is all this fighting going on in this majestic part of Africa?*

Cappie did a 360-degree flight over the falls. He said, "Hey, X-ray Bro, not many folks have seen a sunset like this."

Red said, "You have made our heli-runs special. Good to have you with us, X-ray Bro. We will not forget you."

On our return flight, Cappie said, "Hey, X-ray-bro, you have seen it all. It has been a treat having you on our heli-runs."

I was choking with endless tears, as the wind blew them into my long hair. I could not talk at all. My life had so many special moments. I was sobbing like a child from the feeling in my heart. After a few minutes, I was calmer. I said, "Cappie and Red, thank you for making my life worthwhile. I will never forget this magical moment. Thank you, thank you, and thank you for having me."

That Victoria Falls trip was so peaceful and so special. I cherish that moment as the best feeling in my entire life. The memories of that special day are in my heart forever. On that sunset day, I was on top of the world, looking from above. My body still gets shivers and I feel lightheaded whenever I think of that special day.

During the last week at Katima Mulilo, we did two more patrols runs. We were in luck, as there was no action recorded at all. Our amazing Scorpion unit was spared, with not one guy being wounded or killed. God was their looking after us. Many times I heard the streaking bullets whiz by me, but I was wearing my invincible suit of armor—our training to survive in this amazing part of Africa spared us. My Caprivi adventure changed my outlook on life. I was not a young boy anymore. I had become a man.

It was on the Tuesday morning when I saw General Botha for the second time. He gave us a border-duty defense badge and a thank-you-and-good-bye handshake. The badge was in a small case that looked like a pen holder. It was the imprint map of the Caprivi Strip. It was so special for we had been ninety-three continuous days in the Caprivi heartlands, protecting the local tribal people.

Later that morning, we saw the Bedford trucks come into the Katima base from Mpatcha Air Base. Crew-cut boys were getting off the vehicles. I noticed the young boys of Troop One, the Scorpions, looking wary yet excited.

Of course we had long hair and Windhoek lager beers in our hands, shouting, "Yeah, hooray! We are outta here!" We mounted the Bedfords, and I sat by the open flap at the back.

Cappie and Red came over and gave me the special handshake, saying, "One day, you will visit Katima again. Take care."

Like a strong Victoria Falls breeze, we were gone—it all happened so fast. I have never returned to visit Katima Mulilo, but I have traveled five times from South Africa to Victoria Falls by touring bike. In 1985, on one of my Zimbabwe trips with friends, we did a four-day ferry "booze cruise." This was from Lake Kariba down the Zambezi River to Victoria Falls. We stayed at the Elephant Hills Resort and did a two-day trip in the Wankie Game Park.

On that trip we did one of the most daring white-water-rafting paddles. It was in November, when the river and the falls are in full flow. On those white-waters events on the Zambezi River, you go over five large decent gorges, where the raft is in a vertical drop between the rocks and gushing water. It was a thrill, knowing that the raft could capsize and we would be catapulted into the fast-flowing water below. It was the best water excitement in the world.

That trip to Lake Kariba and Victoria Falls was my best African holiday experience in my life—but bear with me. My thoughts went haywire for a while; let me recap what happened next in my army life.

When we reached Mpatcha Air Base, the Hercules planes were revving the propeller engines to fly us out of the Caprivi Strip. It was a sunny day, and my thoughts went back to when we arrived here in the Caprivi. Damn, we'd landed in a thunderstorm and were leaving on a day with a clear blue sky. The Caprivi Strip and heartlands can have opposite extremes in weather.

It was late in the afternoon when we returned to the Rooikop camp. It felt strange to be back in the desert. When we were back at camp, I phoned Steve and asked him if I could stay with him until I started work. He was okay with it.

We had three days to chill out at Rooikop base camp before the train would bring the next bunch of army 2-SSB boys to the desert. Major Briggs gave us all a one-night pass to go into town. Greg, Brian, and I got in touch with the girls, and we were hungry wolves, ready for sex. Our group in the Bedford truck stayed one night at the Swakopmund party house.

My excitement could not be stopped and the feeling of having sex was out of this world. In the morning, we left the girls really early. We needed to be back at camp by 7:00 a.m. Jessie was crying as the truck left the party house.

On the last night at the Rooikop camp, Greg, Brian, and I got steaming drunk. We had Sundowner beers and passed out on the Rooikop rock. On Friday morning, we saw the new lot of 2-SSB boys come to the Rooikop camp. We were all taken to the train station. The long train journey—it took us five days—was back to Bloemfontein in South Africa. It was sleeping time, chilling-out time, and playing-cards time.

On Wednesday we had returned to the large 2-SSB base camp. We all stayed one night there and got our discharge papers the following morning. My last day in the camp was over. I gave Trevor, Dexter, Tom, and the troop unit guys the good-bye handshake. We all exchanged addresses and the guys were gone in the morning. That night, I was on the same train as Greg, going to Johannesburg and Pretoria.

Before leaving camp, we gave Brian the good-bye handshake. He was going on a train the following morning to Port Elizabeth. Greg and I thanked him for his excellent Panzer driving skills. That was the last time in my life that I saw Brian.

It was an overnight train ride to the Transvaal. In the morning, I got off at the Vereeniging train station. I gave Greg a hug and the good-bye how-zit handshake. Greg was on his way to Pretoria. He was the last of the good guys of our Scorpion Troop One bunch.

Life is strange because I did see Corporal Greg again.

Chapter Eight

Civilian Street

I Was Wild and Carefree—Life Was a Breeze

It was about 9:15 a.m. when the train gave a jerk and left the Vereeniging station. I stood on the platform and waved good-bye to my close army buddy Greg. I grabbed my duffel bag and took a taxi to my brother's house. Steve and his hot wife, Jenny, were living at a coal mining colony. Their red-brick house was old, but it looked respectable. They had a big garden, and there was a single garage next to the house.

I knocked at the front door, but it took a while before Jenny opened the door. She looked as if she had just climbed out of bed. We had never met, but her eyes opened wide and she gave me a hug. "Mike, you have arrived!" she said as she grabbed my hand and led me into the house.

She was wearing a see-through nightie. I thought, what the hell is going on here? I left my duffel bag in the living room as she led me to the kitchen. I sat down at the wooden table.

She walked around in her nightie, making me a cup of coffee. She gave me cookies and a glass of orange juice.

I had just come out the army and could not stop staring at her naked body through her nightie. While walking this way and that way, she noticed that I was gazing at her body. She smiled, saying, "It's okay. Steve is at work all day, and we can spend the day together."

After we had our coffee, we went to the living room and sat on an L-shaped sofa. We talked for a while about my army experiences and my experiences on the border in Katima Mulilo. She seemed to be so interested. She was teasing me, and I felt uncomfortable gazing at her almost-naked body.

I came to my senses. I got up and said with a sigh, "Jenny, where am I sleeping?" She said, "Down the passage, second to the right." I knew that I had to try to keep out of her way; she was Steve's wife and the situation was a total disaster. Why would she be so daring with me?

I had a shower and changed into my regular clothes. When I saw Jenny again, she had dressed in proper clothes, hot pants and a thin blouse. She asked if I wanted to go shopping. "We can drive around the town and have a late lunch," she suggested. She showed me a few nice places in town.

That night when Steve was home, I thought that he looked so much older than I'd remembered. He had a mustache and long blond hair over his shoulders. We chatted for a while, and we made our way to his garage. Steve started to work on his Sunbeam Alpine sports car. I was jabbering away about my army experiences, but Steve was not really listening much.

I stayed nine frustrating days at my brother's house. When Jenny and I were alone while Steve was at work, she tried many times to invite me to have sex with her. In the mornings, Jenny would be in her see-through nightie. I was young and highly sexed up, and It was such a torment for me.

Finally, on Monday morning I reported to Iscor Works to start my apprenticeship training. For the first month, I stayed at the apprentice hostel. It was nice having my own room and freedom to do what I wanted to do. My room was on the third floor of the six-story hostel building.

The apprentice hostel had a large mess hall; the food was pretty good. I was getting US$ 150.00 per month for the first year apprentice pay. In those years, everything was dirt cheap, and I worked out that I could save more than half my salary.

On my first day in Vanderbijlpark, I visited Elise and heard the shocking news. A year earlier, while I was staying with my aunt Carry-bitch and her family, late at night my cousin Marius was having sex my sister. Elise was so dumb not to have Marius wear a condom. She later fell pregnant with my Cousin Marius's child.

While I was away for the year of army duty, no one told me the news. When my aunt Carry-bitch found out that Elise was pregnant, she blamed her and threw her out on the street. Steve took her in until she had the child. She lived with Steve and Jenny at the colony until the little girl, Natasha, was born. She had the baby girl in late August while I was in Namibia at the Rooikop camp. Why did no one write to me about this?

Apparently, when the little girl was three months old, she developed a fever. My sister did not have the money to pay for medical care, so she did not take her to the hospital. It was a very sad morning when Elise woke up and found the little girl had sadly passed away.

I tried to figure out where I was on the border at the time Elise lost her little girl. I worked out that it was around the time we had the heavy fighting at the Mturi camp. Our Scorpions were shooting across the Caprivi Strip, pounding the Zam-boons with our H-E mortars.

I focused on reality and gave Elise a hug. I was holding her tightly in my arms and kissing her forehead. Elise burst into tears. "I am so sorry," I said. She calmed down and showed me many pictures of her little girl, Natasha. Elise was now living with a girl from the salon where she worked. The flat was just above the shopping center.

I was young, and my thoughts were explosive. I was going to beat the crap out of my cousin Marius when I finally saw him. During the pregnancy and after the birth, Marius never once contacted my sister.

While I was at the apprentice hostel, I applied for an Iscor flat. I was lucky to get one, although in a scummy area. This was where all the Iscor Works operators stayed and was known as "Kok-a-lols." I was happy for it was my own pad. The two-bedroom flat was a bit small but a good size for a single guy. It was in a government-style dark-brick building. I was on the corner, on the ground floor. My parking space was in front of the flat. I felt lucky to have the corner flat.

With my US$600.00 savings of army danger pay, I bought a new double bed, cupboard, dresser, and curtains from an Indian bazaar. I bought some cheap crockery, cutlery, a kettle, a toaster, and pots and pans. At a pawn shop I bought a fridge and a crummy two-seat sofa, a bean bag chair, a coffee table, and a cheap record player.

I was going to start my "Civvy Street" life independently. I was not going to ask favors from anyone, especially from my weird family.

In the first two months in Civvy Street, I caught the Iscor bus to work and back. I was living with the basics and saving money.

By the third month, I bought a 1969 British 250cc BSA motorbike from a guy at work. The bike was in a poor condition, but it was wheels, so I was mobile. It cost me another US$ 15.00 to put the old bike through the test and on my name. Over the following three months, I paid the seller US$ 120.00 for the BSA bike.

Life was lonelier than my army days. I had two friends from work, Brian and Richard. We would go out every Friday and have a few beers at the Killarney Hotel's "whites only" men's pub. These pubs were always just off the street and at the corner of the hotel.

I was driving the bike without a license. In those years, the cops were slack. My hair was getting longer, and I looked older than my eighteen years. When riding the BSA bike, it was like riding a monster vibrator. When the bike was idling, the damn thing would rattle and shake and vibrate. It felt as if I was riding a jackhammer. Cor dammit, the vibrations would consistently give me a hard-on. The bike had a small oil leak. I thought, *Yeah, typical British shit*. It was a cheap bike, but it had character.

On a strange Friday after work, a bunch of us decided to go to a barn party. The party was on the outskirts of town at a small barn house. The barn party was about twenty kilometers from Vanderbijlpark. It was just after five o'clock when we got there.

I was wilder and feeling more carefree. I had named my bike the Rattlesnake. I painted a small snake on the rear mud flap above the back taillight. On the side of the gas tank, I had painted "N F, N R" as an abbreviations for the girls—"No Fuck, No-Ride." When guys asked me what the initials meant, there was always laughter. Most girls, however, would shake their heads.

Ten of us guys from the apprentice training center hung out together. In the barn house there was a long shanty bar and a large wooden dance floor. All around the sides were many cheap plastic tables and chairs. We arrived early and sat down in a good spot near the entrance. By six o'clock, the barn started to fill up. We saw an old Bedford bus arrive, and many tight-jeaned chicks climbing off the bus. I guessed the barn owner was picking up all the farm girls on the roadside and loading them up to have a blast at the barn party.

The beers were cheap. We were all on our fourth round when the bus arrived. The music DJ was pretty good, and the type of pop music he was playing had a good rhythm. I was sitting at the corner of our table, with my legs crossed and my boots resting on the table.

It was around eight o'clock when I noticed five girls walk together through the barn door. They all had tight-ass bodies. As they made their way to the bar for some drinks, they were laughing and seemed carefree. They stood at the bar, moving with the rhythm of the music and facing the dance floor.

Brian and I were watching them. I noticed one short, slim, sexy chick looking in our direction and then chatting to her friend. She had ankle boots over her stovepipe jeans. She wore a red polo-neck top with a denim jacket. Brian and I talked about how sexy these five girls looked. As we were sizing them up and gazing at their tight-jean bodies, the short skinny chick was looking at me in the eyes. She had a pretty face and a wild look about her. She had wavy light-brown hair that was shoulder length.

I gave her a bit of a head lift and a full-on smile. Oh gosh, she smiled back and talked with one of the girls standing next to her. The two of them giggled and smiled in our direction.

I thought, *Wow, it has been many months since I've been to a party.* Seeing all these sex-hungry girls made me quiver with excitement. My monster cock was dry as a bone, hungry for a steaming hot wet patch. From the time I landed back in Civvy Street, I'd had no relationships. I only did the pubs where the pool-playing guys hung out.

I was ready for good sexual action. The way "good-looking" was smiling at me; I could sense that this sexy girl was curious about my smiling gesture. While gazing in her eyes, I downed my beer. Like a released spring coil, I stood up and walked over to her. She was good looing and her facial expressions were wild and daring. She had slim legs and very tight jeans on. While glaring down between her legs, my boner stretched against my zippered jeans. Her boobs were medium-sized that fit her bean-sprout body well. The way she was dressed would make any guy only think of giving her one. I had a feeling she had had sex before and was on the lookout for a satisfying guy like me, to give her a "full service."

I was smooth and knew how to break the ice. I stopped in front of her and just gazed at her slim, sexy body, making a slight gesture. She frowned in response, seeming to wonder what I was staring at. Not saying a word, I just smiled at her and gazed at her body up and down. I was shaking my head slightly.

By now all the girls were looking at me strangly, as if they were thinking, *what is he doing?* I said to the bean-sprout girl, "Wow, you look great. Do you want to dance?"

She had a big smile on her face but was a bit flustered, softly saying, "Yeah but not with you." I knew she was giving me the cold shoulder and playing hard to get.

"I am Mike," I said. "And you are …?" She was a little hesitant and nervous, shaking her head from side to side. I noticed all the girls around her were smiling and giggling.

She put her hands on her hips. She stood facing me with an angry expression. I was sizing up looking at her from her shoes to her head. She shook her head and said in a husky voice, "You won't leave." I said, "Not until you dance with me." She gazed at me and said, "I am Violet, and these are my friends, Joyce, Hailey, Trish, and Annabelle."

I shook hands with the girls first and held Violet's hand last. I slowly pulled her toward the dance floor, saying, "Let's dance." It was my lucky moment for the music changed to a slow dance. I held Violet's left hand, ready to do a slow two-step. I placed my right hand behind her and slid it slowly down to her lower back. As we slow-danced, I pulled her body slowly toward my body until her firm boobs were brushing my chest. She was shivering but showed no resistance.

Her right hand held me tightly just below my rib cage. We did a few floating moves around the floor. My head was beside hers, brushing her cheek as we glided on the slippery floor. Violet's long wavy hair tickled the side of my face. Her perfume was making me feel giddy. I could feel her nervous body vibrating as our bodies interlocked.

Her perfume smelled nice, and her slim body gainst mine was giving me the jitters. She was not resisting at all. I could feel my cock expanding tight against my jeans. The music was a bit loud, so we did not talk much. We were dancing in rhythm as if we had done this dancing for many years. She was so light in my arms, and I was daring, pulling her floating body tighter against mine. I could hear her heavy breathing as her face touched my neck. Violet was squeezing me, and I knew she was excited.

As we floated around the dance floor, her crotch was tight against my right leg between her thighs. My bike keys were in my pocket, rubbing against her crotch, making her right hand shiver while holding my back. I could feel her body shaking slightly against mine. My right hand slid lower, and I gradually wedged my middle finger between the top of her bum cheeks. My hand pushed her crotch tighter between my legs. Her boobs were rubbing against my chest as we glided across the floor. Violet could feel my rock-hard monster-cock bulging against her inner thighs. I felt her hand slide to the center of my back; she dug her nails into my spine.

I wondered what her thoughts were. Her lips touched the side of my neck. Violet was breathing heavily and seemed to be ecstatic. I was sure her thoughts were sexual. I could feel her pushing her crotch against my bulging jeans, showing no resistance at all. Our bodies were vibrating.

In a moment we both moved our heads back at the same time, gazing in each other's eyes. She had large gray-green eyes and protruding lips, and her mouth was open. My left hand released hers. In an instant, I slid my hand around until my fingers were stroking the back of her head. At that moment, our lips touched, and we had an open-mouthed French kiss. The tongue-sucking sensation made electric vibrations flash through our bodies. This was making us shiver, and we could taste the beer in each other's mouths.

The dancing stopped, and we were now in a body-lock full-on kissing position. My right hand pressed her tight ass hard against me. I could feel her body twitch and shiver. We didn't care who saw us. At that moment, we heard some cheering from the bunch of apprentice guys who were with me. We also heard the girls clapping and laughing.

I heard one girl call loudly, "Violet, what are you doing? You hardly know the guy." We released our long French kiss. I could feel Violet's body trembling against mine. She was in shock, looking at me with a slightly frightened look. I was holding her in my arms with our bodies pressed tightly against each other. Her face was inches from mine.

I knew I had to be cool, and I broke the ice, saying, "Wow, you make my whole body tremble." Violet gazed in my eyes, but she was frowning and still in shock. I smiled and grabbed her hand. We walked to where the guys were sitting. Her hand was shivering. I pulled a nearby chair for her. I sat on my chair and pulled it against hers. I looked at Violet's girlfriends gawking at us and said, "Hey, Joyce, Hailey, Trish, and Annabelle, come and join us." I nudged Brian and said, "Hey, Brian, what's wrong with you? Make the girls feel welcome."

When I looked back at Violet, she was smiling widely and nodding her head. I gave her a cool smile as she slid her shivering hand in mine. This was fast action, and I could feel that she felt good with me. The other girls joined our group. Trish sat next to Violet, and I heard her whisper in Violet's ear,

"Mike is a catch, hang on to him." I knew what she meant and felt Violet's hand squeeze mine a bit.

We chatted like we were an item. I could feel that she liked being with me. I bought a round of brain-damaging shooter drinks for the girls and for Brian, Richard, and me. Brian sat next to Hailey, and Richard sat next to Trish. We had more beers, and Brian and Richard bought the next round of shooters. Violet and I had many dances, and my buddies danced with the girls. I could sense that Violet was getting a bit tipsy. I got her a Coke. We were talking loads while having many kisses in between our talk.

While having another slow dance, my monster cock was hard against Violet's body. Her bums were squeezing and thrusting slightly with her pussy rubbing against my bulging cock. I could sense that she was ready to have sex. It was now around one o'clock in the morning, and my mood and thoughts were only about sex. I could feel that Violet was getting horny as we kissed and sucked each other's tongues. Her body twitched against mine. After our hot slow dance, Violet sat on my lap, putting her arms around me and kissing me.

I felt brave and asked Violet, "Where do you live?"

She answered, "Not far from here. I live with my aunt and uncle on a plot."

"Would you like me to take you home?"

She was daring and said, "Okay. Let me tell Trish that I am leaving." Violet returned and said, "Trish wants a lift home too."

I was surprised that Richard was not with her. Violet and Trish must have thought that I was driving a car. I said, "I am here on my bike, and we will have to go three up."

Trish looked wary but said, "It's okay, but please drive slowly."

I only had the one helmet. I asked Trish where she lived—it was five kilometers from the barn party, in the opposite direction from where Violet lived.

I kick-started the old Rattlesnake BSA bike and got into a riding position. Violet was wedged tight against my back. Trish was behind her, holding on to the crash bars. I heard Trish say, "My God, this bike vibrates a lot." I smiled and answered, "Yeah, it's my Rattlesnake bike." Violet looked at the "NF, NR" painted on the side of the tank and asked what it was. I said, "No Fuck, No Ride, but tonight is different for I have two girls on my bike." While driving away, she nudged me on my back.

We were all high as kites, the Rattlesnake bike roared to the road. I was driving around thirty to forty kilometers per hour to Trish's home. Violet had her hands around my waist and was wedged tightly against my body. We dropped off Trish and then went to Violet's uncle's pad. I could feel Violet's body and boobs wedged against my back. Her face was sideways and her hair was flopping beside it. We were cruising along, with the cool night breeze hitting our faces. A few times I felt her squeeze my member. The vibrations on the seat were making Violet's legs shake and squeeze against mine. I knew that this Rattlesnake bike was vibrating her pussy, sending endless electric thrills through her.

We stopped outside the gate. Violet climbed off the seat and stood next to the bike. In the moonlight I saw her face shiver. She was a little tipsy and asked me, "Do you want to come inside?"

I stood beside my idling bike, shivering from the exciting ride and cool night air. I said; "Your uncle and aunt might not like me coming in so late at night."

She asked me to turn off the noisy bike engine. I did so and put the bike on the side stand. I leaned against the bike with my butt sideways against the seat.

Violet stood between my legs and held me around the neck. I put my hands on her butt and pulled her closer to me. We kissed. She released my lips and said. "My uncle and aunty are working night shift at Iscor Works. They will be home this morning at around seven thirty." She smiled at me and said, "Come on. Let's push your bike to the back of the house."

We pushed the bike around the back and parked it outside the kitchen on the concrete slab. We entered through the back door. We took off our shoes and made our way through the dark to the living room. We sat next to each other on the sofa.

Violet whispered in my ear, "I sleep in one room with my younger cousin Sheila. She is thirteen years old and asleep. I have two boy cousins Brad and Bruno, nine and eleven. They sleep in the third bedroom."

Violet got up and placed her finger on her lips so I would be quiet. She disappeared down the hall. After some time passed, I heard her close two doors. I knew that we were going to have sex and that Violet was making sure no one heard us.

I was feeling excited and nervous. After a few seconds, Violet came into the living room. She had a blanket and two pillows with her. I helped Violet spread the blanket on the carpet. She put a pillow at the top and center of the blanket. She placed a small hand towel over the center pillow. Violet stood up and looked at me nervously. The outside veranda light was shining through the curtains, making the room bright.

Violet removed her denim top, polo-neck, and bra. I gazed at her large nipples sticking straight out. I removed my clothes and placed them on the sofa. Her jeans and panties came off while I was removing my jeans and jocks. We were both naked and nervous.

Very quietly she lay on the pillows and blanket and opened her legs. She moved the center pillow under her lower back. I was ready for action and knelt in front of her open legs. She had an awesome slim body, lying naked in front of me.

It was many months back that I last had sex. We had sex, and the cool weather made the mood more exciting. Afterward I walked naked to the bathroom to clean up my sweaty body. Violet got up, kissed me, and walked naked down the hall to the bathroom. When she returned, I was lying on the sofa with only my jocks on. Violet put on her panties on and lay on top of me, putting the blanket over our bodies. We chatted and kissed for a while. Violet said she was working as a supermarket cashier but wanted to become a hairdresser. She told me she was seventeen, going to be eighteen in December.

We started to French kiss, and we were in the mood. Damn, it was rising and getting hard again. We had sex one more time that took longer. When we climaxed, something did not seem right. Violet's cousin Sheila was gawking at us all the while I was having sex with Violet.

Sheila jumped up, holding her hand inside her panties. She left the living room. Violet ran naked down the hall after her. I wondered if she had been masturbating while looking at us having sex. I thoughts, *Violet must be in trouble with her cousin.* I put my clothes on and lay on the sofa. Violet came back to the living room, wearing her nightie and clean panties. She sat next to me on the sofa and started to cry. I put my arm around her shoulders. I knew that Violet was confused.

She told me, "Sheila was sitting on the sofa watching us while we were having sex. She was masturbating, and it must have been an eye-opening experience for Sheila. She is blackmailing me for money or she will tell her parents what we did."

I thought, *the little bitch*. I came up with a plan and asked Violet if she wanted to move in with me. I told her, "We are now an item, having had sex two times on this early morning."

Violet's face lit up like a light bulb, and she said, "Yeah, I was going to move out anyway." She had a big smile on her face, saying, "Wait here. I am going to pack my suitcase, and we can leave."

I thought, *Wow, in my life things happen to the extreme. I met Violet last night, and this morning she is moving in my pad, and she is going to live with me.*

As I waited for her, it was getting light outside. When she came into the kitchen, she was dressed in her party gear with a white shirt. She had two rucksacks and a medium-sized suitcase.

Violet wrote a note for her aunt and uncle and pasted it on the fridge. She wrote in the letter, "I will be staying with a friend and will visit you all next weekend to explain."

We walked out the kitchen door towards my bike. I kick-started the BSA bike and left it idling to warm up. It was a stubborn bike for it would die on you when you tried to ride it while it was still cold. I would normally leave it idling for around ten minutes.

While waiting for the bike to warm up, I strapped one rucksack on my chest. Violet had the other rucksack on her back. She wedged herself tightly behind me. She positioned the suitcase on her right leg, and her left hand held me on my crotch.

I looked toward the kitchen door and saw Sheila standing there in her nightie with her hand in her panties, looking bewildered. I frowned at her and thought, *why is she holding her gash? What is with her? Is her pussy itchy?* I called out to her, "Don't be a little bitch. Don't be a tattletale on Violet and me fucking in the living room."

She glared at me and pulled a funny face. Violet said, "Let's go, I need to leave this place." I knew that Violet was not happy living with her aunt and uncle and family. I hit the accelerator, and we were like a noisy rattlesnake in motion, hitting the road. Violet had tied her hair in a ponytail. The cool breeze was chilling our bodies, making us jerk.

I drove to the main tar road leading to Vanderbijlpark at around 120 kilometers per hour. At the traffic light on the outskirts of Vanderbijlpark. I took a different route that would bypass the main entrances into the town. I knew the route well and figured that there were no early morning cops on that route. I was driving without a license and had a girl behind me without a helmet. As I drove, I kept a lookout for any cop cars. I thought *What if I am caught? How would I talk my way out of this situation?*

It was just after six thirty when I parked my bike in front of my flat. When we entered the flat, Violet said, "Nice pad." We put her gear in my room. We were both hungry, and I made us sandwiches and coffee in the kitchen. I put the music on, and we sat in the living room and did our thing. We were both tired from the all night's excitement and decided to bathe together. We fell asleep in bed until noon.

My life was changing again. Violet was the first girl to live with me in my flat.

When we woke up, we had a good chat about Violet's wanting to become a hairdresser. I told Violet that my sister was a qualified hairdresser and that I would ask if there were any openings for a beginner.

Later that afternoon, we had lunch at KFC just down the road. We went into a pawn shop, and I bought a small helmet for Violet to wear. We drove to where my sister was working in the shopping complex.

It was a great weekend for us. My sister said that they were looking for a beginner that could start in the mid-year apprenticeship training. Violet, Elise, and the salon owner discussed her apprenticeship opportunity. She was hired. All that she needed was to produce her O-level certificate and a recommendation that my sister signed.

Violet was over the moon and was smiling from ear to ear. She needed to give one month's notice at her supermarket cashier job.

On Monday at work, the guys thought I was smooth. They thought it was cool for me to meet Violet on Friday night and have her shack up with me for the weekend.

Having Violet living with me seemed to be great—until she started to complain a lot. It started when I would go alone out with the guys from work on Fridays for the boys' pool and drinking session. When I got back home a bit drunk, she would go ballistic at me. She would say, "You leave me all alone here in the flat and have fun with your guy friends. You don't care for me."

I was young and thinking, *what's with her? I never did complain when she goes out alone with her girlfriends.* Her mood changed after the following Friday. It was as if someone had changed Violet's thinking. She was bitchier and extremely aggressive all the time. I was confused by her actions. At almost nineteen years old, I just wanted to enjoy life and have fun. I was not ready to settle down and struggle with little money, being a first-year apprentice. Violet seemed different.

I tried to explain to Violet that everything takes time, and why the rush of being so possessive of me? I was faithful to her, not flirting with girls. At all the parties and discos we went to, I would get many suggestive stares from all the pretty girls. I was Violet's guy, and I never thought of having more than one girl at a time.

My nineteenth birthday came about, and the arguments gradually increased. Violet started her apprenticeship, and she seemed to fit in well. We were still having a lot of sexual intercourse. That was about the only pleasure we had together.

Around the end of June, everything fell apart. We were at a discothèque having fun. Brian, Richard, Violet, and I were together as a group. Violet was wearing a sexy black miniskirt with a matching tank top. She looked awesome. I was thinking, *I am so happy to have a good-looking girl like Violet.* I was dancing with her, but she was being a bit bitchy with me. I sat down at our table and downed my beer. She sat next to me with her sulky face and her arms crossed. I was trying to talk with her, but she just ignored me. I thought *what now?* I got up without telling her where I was going and walked to the toilets. When I returned, Brian and Violet were not at the table. I asked Richard where they were, and he pointed nervously toward the dance floor. He looked worried. Violet was dancing suggestively with Brian. I was fuming but kept my cool. The song ended, and the next one started. I sat there in anger and downed my beer

Brian and Violet had four dances in a row before they came back to the table. I kept my cool and asked Violet, "Do you want to dance the next one?" She looked at me, evilly, and said no. I gazed at Brian, and he seemed to be in a different mood. I knew that something was not right. I tried to make peace. I got up and went to the bar to buy a round of drinks for all of us. When I returned to our table, I saw Brian sitting with his chair close to Violet. I could see his hand squeezing her leg under the table.

I came up behind them and poured a beer over Brian's head. I knew that we were going to box. I quickly put the other beers on the table, and Brian stood up, wiping the beer spillage out of his eyes. As he looked at me, I decked him with my elbow on the side of his face. He went airborne, landing on his back on the next table. He was lights-out.

I was fuming mad. I could not grasp what was going on. Violet seemed to be the perfect girl. I turned back and felt Violet slap me across my face. I grabbed her wrist forcefully, making her know that it was enough. I lot of people gathered around me. I waved with my left hand, indicating to all that I was cool. I said that the guy I whacked was being fresh with my girl.

I pulled Violet by the arm and forcefully walked out of the disco with her. Richard was a good-thinking guy. He grabbed the remaining three beers I had bought and followed us out the door.

As I got outside, I had a go at Violet. I shouted, "How can you let Brian hold your leg while I was buying drinks? You are a cheap whore?" Violet started to cry. I was fuming and said, "What is it with you and Brian?" As she cried, she confessed, "Last month when I was out with my girlfriends, Brian was with us. I was drunk and went home with Brian, and we had sex."

I blew my top with anger and was now in a crying fit. "How many times have you had sex with Brian?" I asked.

She was stupid, telling me, "Four times."

I went ballistic and said, "We have been having sex at least ten times a week." I was in a dismal state and asked her, "Why are you fucking both of us?"

She was more stupid, telling me, "I enjoy having sex with both of you."

My mind went blank. I screamed at her, "You are a little whoring bitch. Over the last month or so, you have been bitchy to me. In the meantime you were fucking with Brian." I was tripping out. During all this time, Richard stood to one side, listening to our conversation. I looked at him and asked loudly, "How long have you known this?"

He was wary of my rage but confessed, "I only heard about it tonight, when you were in the toilet. I did not know; I swear." He gave me one of the beers as a peace gesture. I downed the beer in one gulp. I was angry and threw the empty beer bottle, smashing it against the wall of the disco. Violet stood in front of me, crying and trying to grab and hold on to me. I thought, *Why me? She seemed to be such a nice girl.*

In a rage, I said to Violet, "Tomorrow morning I want to see you and Brian at my pad at nine o'clock to collect your things. Tell your fucking lover boy I want to talk to him." Then I told Richard, "Let's go to the Killarney Hotel pub. I feel like getting drunk." Richard gave me Violet's beer, and we both downed our beers. I said to Violet, "Your lover boy can have you. You are a little whore. Go fuck with him tonight. We are through."

Richard told me, "See ya there at the Killarney." I left Violet standing at the disco doorway, holding her mouth with both her hands. I got on my BSA bike and kick-started it. I drove off slowly on my bike, spinning the back wheel on the loose gravel before proceeding to the tar road. When I was a distance from the disco, I slowed down to wipe all the tears flowing from my eyes. I was in a sorry, sad condition. The tears streamed out of my eyes, down my cheeks. The wind blew my sorry, sad tears into my long hair that was flapping under my helmet. It was the first time I had been ditched by a girl. That night when I left the Killarney Hotel pub, I was piss-drunk. For the first time, I rode my bike home in a death ride. I remember leaving the hotel but not getting home.

I woke up in my bed in a fright and realized I had passed out with my clothes on, lying on the top of my bed. I looked at my watch. It was just after 7:00 a.m. I was in a dismal state. In shock, I thought, *where the hell is my bike?* I raced to the front door—the BSA bike was nicely parked in my parking space. I frowned and thought, *I am pretty good at riding the bike in a piss-drunk state.*

It was just before nine o'clock when Violet, Brian, and his older brother Vince parked his car in the parking lot next to my bike. It was the strangest sight to see Brian and Violet standing together, holding hands. Brian had a bad cut on his cheek, and his left eye was swollen and a bit blue in a complete circle. Vince came up to me and said, "No fighting."

I told him, "All is cool. I just want to ask your cheating brother, why with my girl, Violet—why?"

Vince turned to Brian and asked him, "Why?" Brian looked warily at both of us and said, "Because we clicked, and I love her." Violet was clinging to his side like a little whore.

I don't know why, but at that moment, I felt relieved to hear those words. I knew that I was so lucky not to marry a girl like this. I stood in front of Brian and held out my hand. I gave him a handshake, saying, "Good luck." Then I whispered near his ear, "The little bitch was having sex with both of us at the same time. You both have a good fucking life together." I shouted, "Violet will never change and will fuck with others while you build true love." I walked toward Vince and said, "Your brother is an asshole."

He smiled at me and said, "I know." I gestured that Brian should stay outside while Violet and Vince got her stuff out of my flat.

Before they left, I gazed at Violet while she was staring at me. She gave a wary small smile. I smiled back and that was it; I was all by my lonesome again.

Before leaving for my call up duties in the army for the year, I signed a five year contract for two six months bonuses. At the end of June, Iscor paid me a six-month bonus for the first year's army service agreement back-pay. After taxes, I was paid US$ 620.00 for the first year. I would get the same the following year at the end June.

The following day I sold my Rattlesnake bike to an older biker dude who collected old British bikes. He paid me US$ 160.00, giving me a US$ 50, 00 profits. I was over the moon. With all my savings from my first six months of working and with my bonus, I had saved just over US$ 800.00. I bought my first car, a 1973 Ford Cortina. It was blood-red in color and had wide wheels and chrome rims. It also had a free-flow booster exhaust and a wood-rim steering wheel. The seats were black imitation leather and a bit worn out. The car drove okay; I knew I had a good buy. I paid US$ 630.00 for it. The Ford cost me US$ 40.00 for tests and car regestration. At the same time, I got my civlian driver's license. I was now car-mobile.

It was weird time in my life. My girl messed around and ditched me. I sold my Rattlesnake bike. I bought my first car, and I received a weird phone call at work, all within one month. The army had informed me that I needed to report for an army at Waterkloof headquarters. I was going to Wonderboom Air Base to fly up to the border. The sergeant major told me, "There is a lot of fighting up on the SWA (South West Africa) and Angola border. The MPLA (Movement Peoples Liberation of Angola) in Angola is going to war with UNITA (Union of Total Independence of Angola) and FNLA (National Front for the Liberation of Angola). Civil war is going to break out. You need to report for duty at Waterkloof on the twenty-second of August before lunchtime. You need to be in full bush army gear."

I would receive my weapons on that day and go for practice shooting the same day. He told me that my recommendation was good when I did my service in Katima Mulilo. He informed me, "You will receive your duty papers in the post soon for a three months-plus call of duty."

The following day I got my call-up papers. I informed Iscor of my army call-up. I was told that my apprenticeship would be on hold until I returned. After my army duty at the end of the year, I had to do progress training the following year to catch up.

It was a strange week for me. On Saturday night while clubbing, I met an awesome-looking Afrikaner girl, Kristina. She was with a large group of girls. She had a firm body and long, straight blonde hair to her ass. She also had big-size boobs and a firm, tight round ass.

I asked her out, and we met on Sunday at a shopping mall.

She was hard to get, and I struggled like hell to have my first kiss. After six consecutive days of dating her every night, we finally had our first French kiss. We were alone in the drive-in theater. It took me around ten minutes to warm her up, with a lot of resistance from her, before we French kissed.

She had a split personality. While we were tongue kissing, she was groping me as if she was in heat and wanted more tongue down her throat. That night in the drive-in theater, we had sex. She was the weirdest girl I have ever been with. Before sex, we played the rock, paper, and scissors game, with the loser removing his or her clothes. After we had sex, it was a disaster. She had wet my car seat completely, and I did not have a towel with me, I felt as if something was not right.

As I climbed off her naked wet body, I could not see the speaker next to my window. I did not realize, but the car's hand break was not all the way tight, and the car had gradually slid down the drive-in hump to the driveway. It was close to the car behind me.

I got up and climbed into my front seat. The car behind me could see my naked bum as I climbed back on my seat. I heard a soft horn and saw a quick flash of lights from the car behind me. The guy shouted from his open window, "Cor-dammit, you are a champion, making so much noise and having sex for so long." Kristina was in shock, and she lay still. I shouted back, "Yeah, she was awesome."

While sitting naked, I started the car and drove out of the drive-in theater. Kristina was in shock and said, "We are driving naked in your car."

I laughed and said, "Yeah, you have squirted both of us totally wet with your cum juices."

She was a hoot for she said, "Yeah, but that was the first time I had cum."

While driving back to my flat, she covered her pussy with her hands. She lay flat on the car seat beside me. Her large naked boobs were bouncing about as the uneven road surface made them flop. Every now and then, I would gaze at her flopping boobs and her awesome, extremely white naked body next to me. It was an awesome feeling, driving home naked.

I parked the car in front of my flat. I climbed out and walked naked around the car and opened her door. She said, "What are you doing, standing naked outside?"

I looked around the parking lot and said, "There is no one here. Come on; we need to have a bath and get dressed and put dry clothes on." I pulled her off the seat. She was resisting a bit but came anyhow. While she was standing naked next to my car, I opened the rear door and got our dry clothes out. I closed and locked the doors and grabbed her hand and said, "Come on, before someone sees us." I opened the door to my flat and we stepped inside. I locked the door behind her.

We had a bath together. I softly washed her back, her awesome boobs, and the rest of her body, and then I washed myself. As we climbed out of the bath, she was smiling. We got dressed and chatted until I took her home, just before eleven. While driving away from her folks' house, I thought, *I best not to contact her again.*

At the Iscor apprentice training center, Brian and I talked on the surface only. I heard that he was not living with his brother anymore. He had applied for an Iscor flat, and Violet was living with him. He no longer came to our Friday night pool gatherings. I guessed he was under lock and key. Richard and I were now best buddies and going out every Friday night, clubbing and hitting some discos.

I was enjoying my time alone and was gearing myself up for my army call-up. I was keeping myself fit and doing a lot of push-ups and sit-ups and daily doing a ten-kilometer run.

It was now the beginning of August, and I had three weeks left before I would report to the army base at Waterkloof.

On the last Sunday night before my army duty, Elise and I had a dinner together. Later that night I packed my army gear clothes in my duffel bag. I ironed my browns and bush jacket. It was winter, and so it was cold at night. I cleaned the flat and got rid of all the goodies in my fridge and defrosted it. I made sure that I was good to leave the pad for three months-plus. My sister said that she would clean the place once a week, while I was away. She would also pay my debts

On Monday morning four o'clock, I folded all my bedding and put it in the cupboard. I locked my flat and drove off to pick up Elise. We drove to

Vereeniging train station, where I bought a ticket to Johannesburg. That was that; I was ready to go.

I gave Elise a peck on the cheek, and she begged me to be safe. I always had premonitions and knew there was no bad karma going up to the borders to fight for what was right. By six o'clock that morning, the train gave a jerk, and I was in motion toward Pretoria, the capital of South Africa. I saw Elise waving good-bye and blowing me kisses. I felt all grown up, and my seven months-plus in Civvy Street had been awesome.

Chapter Nine

Ruacana and Angola

Life Was Grand; We Were Border Patrol Bush Warriors

It was just after 10:00 a.m. when I arrived at the Waterkloof train station. I took a bus to Waterkloof headquarters. To my surprise, there were over one hundred souls at HQ. I presented my registered call-up documents for Sergeant Major DeKlerk to sign.

After lunch we were all taken by coach to Wonderboom Air Base, where we received all our remaining gear, a 9mm Star pistol and empty magazines. My army gear was a bit faded, and I looked rough with my long hair under my bush hat. We were taken to an army shooting range and a target practice range. There were homemade targets shaped like men that would pop up and down again. There was also an obstacle course, where we had to climb over field obstacles and shooting targets at the same time.

It was great. I was in fit condition while running through the timed shooting trails. We continued with lectures, border reconnaissance training, and night exercise, nonstop, until 11:00 p.m. half the guys with me were in a bad state, throwing up from exhaustion.

I thought, *I am in a pretty good shape, compared to most of the guys with me.* That night we slept in tents near the shooting range. None of us had been informed where the base was or what the name was. It was like we were on a secret mission and doing army training and practice shooting.

On the following morning we were all sectioned off in different groups. Three of us were selected to become full corporal armored Panzer crew commanders. We had to do an induction course that was seven days of solid lectures and training. They had a Panzer for the practical training. Gosh, it took a crew commander six weeks to learn what we were doing in seven days.

It was an extreme crash course. We were getting up at 4:00 a.m. and going back to bed at 11:00 p.m."

I always had observed how Greg was performing when we were up on the border at the Katima Mulilo camp patrols. On the eighth morning, just after breakfast, the captain of the induction training course gave us our results. I was shocked at what I had achieved. I was glowing like a 1000-watt bulb.

I was first out of the guys doing the crew commander course, with an 88 percent pass. I was second, with 96 percent pass, on my shooting target course. I had the sixth highest fitness pass rate out of the more than one hundred souls coming from Pretoria and surrounding cities.

We were presented with our new ranks. I was now a full corporal and received two sleeve stripes and six that I had to sew on my shirts and bush jackets.

After breakfast we had an HQ meeting. We were all loaded in two Hercules twin-prop planes flying to Grootfontein Air Base in Southwest Africa, Namibia.

I felt as if I had never left the army for Civvy Street. None of the guys who were with me in this army duty in Pretoria had been with me when I did my basic training.

It was now Friday at the end of August. After lunch, we boarded the planes, and the two Hercules fat bad-birds took to the skies.

It was late in the afternoon when the Hercules planes landed at Grootfontein Air Base in Namibia. We were rounded up and preceded to a huge hangar. As we entered through large open sliding doors, we saw more than two thousand souls standing in tight formation. I had the jitters and knew that this was a different ball game than what I had previously experienced.

At the front end of the hangar was a high stage, where many big-brass-guys were sitting on chairs. There were several microphones mounted on wooden podiums where the "big cheese" would give their speeches. There were a few big-brass generals at this large gathering.

We all got in a formation and lined up. I was lucky to be in the front row of our hundred or so guys coming from Wonderboom Air Base.

It seemed as if we were the last to arrive. General Botha stood up and told us that there was extreme fighting going on in Angola and that this was real-time action. We needed to stop the atrocities that the MPLA movement was causing against the people living in the south of Angola.

This was not a defense operation but more like picking a fight with the Angolan MPLA bad guys.

At first, the SAI names were called out, and I saw many guys filtering though the lines as their names were called. They formed into their units and left the hangar. Next were the engineers, the Para-Bats. As they left the hangar, we moved closer to the stage.

I was hyped up and tired at the same time. It was a weird feeling seeing General Botha again. He said, "The Auxiliary and the Tank Divisions have been deployed, and the armored 1-SSB and 2-SSB will be on standby until orders have been clarified on when to deploy the battalions in Angola." It was just a matter of days or weeks before the movement would proceed.

They first read out all the units' names in the 1-SSB and the guys formed a marching platoon. They left the hangar to an area staged for them at the Grootfontein sleeping tent depot.

At around 8:00 p.m., something good happened. The 2nd Special Service Battalion (2-SSB) names were called out, Troop One Scorpions Panzer. My name was read out first: Michael, Dexter, Josh, proceed forward" I was again in the Scorpion unit and going to be the front leading armored vehicle, Sting One. Dexter was my gunner, and we had a different driver named Josh. Greg was now a sergeant and was in Sting Two. Trevor was still our lieutenant, which was great. In our Scorpion armored unit, there were five new souls. Brian, our Katima driver, was nowhere to be seen. I had thoughts that maybe Brian had eloped with his Namibian sweetheart, Greta, in Walvis Bay. They seemed so much in love.

All the other armored troop and section names were called out. Most of our unit guys who were in Katima Mulilo eight months back were on this call-up duty. I was over the moon. When we all stepped out of the parade line, we gave each other hugs and the how-zit handshakes. It was a thrill for me when Trevor came up to me and gave me a hug and a handshake, saying, "How-zit, X-ray Bro? I see you have stepped up in life and you are now a crew commander and a gunner."

I knew what he meant. I was the only one who had done both training in our Scorpion unit. My buddy Greg had also stepped up higher, first being a corporal and now a sergeant. He was now second in command of our Scorpion unit. Life was awesome.

We were rounded up fast and taken by Bedfords to a large base camp on the outskirts of Grootfontein. I was thrilled to be with my buddies who had been with me at Camp Katima.

Trevor always took good care of his Scorpion unit and had organized many crates of Hansa beer for us. The first night at the Grootfontein base camp, we laughed and told great stories. I showed the guys a picture of Violet and me on my Rattlesnake BSA bike. Violet was wearing hot pants and a halter top. She was sitting reversed on my lap, facing me, with her legs wrapped around my waist. I was driving with no helmet, and my hair was long and over my ears. I wore boots and shorts but no top, and I held a beer in my accelerator hand. She was French-style kissing me, and her tongue was sticking out while I was sucking on it. It was a prize picture, and the guys were amazed at the life I had in Civvy Street.

Everyone said, "Damn, she is a hot babe. We are all moving to the Vaal Triangle."

Trevor showed us a picture of his awesome-looking wife. He said that she was nearly five months pregnant. He was hoping to be home in December, when she gave birth.

Over the weekend we received our armored vehicles, and the Panzers were the same ones as in Katima. They had new German Ferret engine in it. We were told that they had more horsepower and lasted longer. I also noticed it had new tires.

Before we arrived on the border, our vehicle had been shot by an aircraft armor piercing bullet hole hrough it. The closed-up hole was on the side of the rotating turret and went through the gunner seat position and out the rear side of the gunner seat. It was patched up with gray plastic steel. The outside patch was painted camouflage. While sitting in the gunner seat, the hole was clearly visible. There was a 60mm filler mark covering the hole. Dexter and I scratched our heads. We knew the gunner had died in the seat with a hole through it.

We were kitted up big time with extra rations, ammo, and gear for a long trip—for six weeks. We were going to travel deep into Angola.

Our troop and sections had extra men. There were now two medics, two mechanics, one land-mine engineer, and two addition drivers. One was driving a diesel fuel tanker and the other a Magirus truck that carried all the supplies. Our Unimorg Road Warrior Two was towing a larger water trailer.

On Sunday night, Lieutenant Trevor got orders that we needed to make haste to Ruacana. The location on the map was on the border of Namibia and Angola. Trevor had a debriefing with our troop's corporals and Sergeant Greg. We received our maps and our call signs for the entire mission.

These call signs would stay for the entire time we were here on the borders. Our vehicle radio call sign was Sierra Wun (Scorpion One) and my name call sign forever was Mike X-Ray Bro, being the crew commander of the first vehicle.

It sounded so cool when I heard over the radio communications, "Sierra Wun Mike X-ray bro—do you hear me? Over." I would say, "Sierra Wun Mike X-ray Bro—I read you loud and clear. Over."

I would always get goose-bumps when I heard my Scorpion vehicle call sign. Greg was Sierra Two Golf. Trevor was Sierra Tree Tango, and vehicle four, Corporal Brad, was Sierra Fower Bravo." Our armored support section corporal Allen, Unimorg Road Warrior One, was Sierra Romeo Alpha Wun. The radio op's name was Charlie, call sign Sierra Romeo Charlie Wun.

One Monday morning at five o'clock sharp, we were all loaded up and ready to roll. It was a grand feeling for me to lead the pack out of the Grootfontein base camp.

Our unit was now a longer convoy and we felt different than our previous time in the Caprivi. It was also feeling weird handling most of the crew commander call sign communications. Being in the front vehicle was an exhilarating feeling.

These Ferret German engines had less noise. Our driver Josh was impressed, and our top speed was around 110 kph on a straight road.

The tar road was in a fairly good condition, and we were doing well on our travel time toward Ondangwa. It was just after 6:00 a.m. when we drove through Tsumeb on route to Ondangwa and then onto a gravel road to Ruacana.

The traveling distance for the day was going to be around 520 kilometers, which would take about eight or nine hours with our scheduled stops. The weather was nice and cool, and it was a treat sitting on top of the armored vehicle, having a few beers that I had stashed in the vehicle. I was listening to some heavy rock music. Dexter and I were in a good frame of mind, and we clicked. I knew he was the best gunner in our unit. I was happy and lucky to have him.

During the trip we stopped two times on the roadside for the boys to do their business, having a tree piss or a bush shit. At our second roadside break location we saw high fencing. We could see on the map that we were passing the top part of the Etosha National Game Park.

Just before noon we stopped outside Ondangwa and had lunch beside the tar road. At around one o'clock we sheared off left and were on a smaller national road having two-way traffic. This road was in poor condition, and in some places we had to slow down to ten kilometers per hour.

Our driver, Josh, was a good guy, but he complained frequently, "My back hurts and the constant straight road is boring." I told him, "Josh, zip it and stay alert at all times. There's no need to complain. This is the beginning of the trip and the driving will get a lot worse." He got the message and never complained again.

We arrived at the Ruacana junction roads at five o'clock. We proceeded left off the road and drove another five kilometers into the bush on a hard path. We ended up on a ridge that was high up on a mountain, with a gradual decline leading to the valley below. We knew that there were two centurion tanks high up on a ridge. They were camouflaged and in a stationary position under some larger trees and shrubs. Our position was between the two tanks.

When our Panzer stopped, I looked through my binoculars at the valley below. In the far distant haze, I could see the large Ruacana Dam catchment wall. The Cunene River and Ruacana waterfall was below the mountain. I was experiencing so many sweet adventures.

A chill ran down my back, and knew I was back in majestic Africa.

We made camp and did the same configuration to move out the location in formation, in case the shit hit the fan.

While the unit was setting up camp, Trevor, Greg, Brad, and I sat on the large rock overhanging the edge of the mountain to observe the terrain below. We were all in a good mood. I felt more grown up, knowing that I was now ranked and had to give the troopers orders.

Trevor, Greg, Brad, and I walked to a tank that was closer to us. Golly gosh, it was awesome to see this bad-boy tank. It looked much larger than our armored vehicles. The five tank guys greeted us. They were all Permanent Forse guys and looked like a bunch of bad boys.

We all had mustaches and fairly long hair. I guess we also looked the part. Trevor asked many questions on what was going on in this part of Africa. We were told that the infantry below at the lake catchment wall was consistently under pressure, with much sporadic shooting happening at night. The MPLA wanted to blow up the lake wall.

On some days the tanks were given coordinates to fire the mortars at the Terk positions below the mountain and valley. The following day we were relieved by Troop Three, the Black Widow unit. We were ordered to make our way down the mountain pass toward the Ruacana Dam wall. It was a narrow, twisting road that hugged the mountainside. Only then did I realize how high up Ruacana was on the mountain. We had to crawl down in extra low gear.

Dexter and I were on our guard, sitting on the top of the vehicle. Around halfway down the mountain, we came around a bend, and I heard a few shots whiz by us. Shit, I knew it was a sniper shooting blindly at us.

When I looked left up the mountain, the sun reflection was in my eyes. I quickly shut the visor down and said on HQ communication, "Ambush on the left or the front. Hit formation." I then heard a thud. I wondered why Dexter was not shooting the 7.62mm machine gun. While giving orders on the main HQ radio, I glanced over at Dexter. Shit—he was shot in his arm. I instantly gave orders "Sierra Wun gunner down. Sierra Two gunner, get in position, snipers to the left -- Fire at will."

I heard Greg's gunner shooting three bursts of machine gun fire. While he was firing, I slid Dexter down in his hatch seat. I heard two more shots ricochet off the Panzer. I leaned over and got in position to fire the machine gun. With my helmet visor down, the view was good. I watched for any movement on the mountain and down the valley.

These guys were good; I could not see anyone. I thought, *yeah, the snipers always shoot from a distance. Yep, the fucker shot at me again from the valley below.* I positioned the machine gun farther down the road and fired a short burst. "Around three hundred meters away in a tree below the mountain, I saw the sun reflect on something in the tree. While everyone was firing, I heard a few more shots around me.

In an instant, I said to Josh, "Close your driver's hatch. The sniper is straight ahead of us." I swung the 7.62mm machine gun straight ahead and let rip toward the sun refection in the tree. I saw that Ango-lie sniper fall out the tree onto the rocks below. I gave orders to stop firing. I looked through my binoculars, keeping my right hand on the machine gun trigger, ready to fire. I gave orders: "Hold your fire." I was watched for any movements in the valley below. All was quiet.

All I could hear was Dexter's groaning and crying from the gunshot wound. I leaned over and removed his army jacket and put pressure on his wound. The bullet had gone through the lower part of his bicep muscle. I told him, "You are good, Dexter. It's just a flesh wound." I was still observing the trees down the mountain. Shit, there was only one of the bad guys.

During all the communication, the support troopers were in a formation around my Panzer. I gave orders for the medic to make haste to attend to Dexter. He was in shock and shivering excessively. When I told him it was a flesh wound, he said, "Yeah, I got shot and survived, and oh shit, it hurts." He was so lucky for the bullet didn't hit a bone. I told him, "I got the bastard in the tree below. All is good."

At that moment, Trevor was standing next to us. He bent down and held Dexter's hand, saying, "God is with you today. You will be okay." Trevor gave me a hug and said, "God is with you too, X-ray Bro. I saw many bullets whizzing past you, and some ricocheted off the Panzer."

I told Trevor, "I could not see where the bastard was shooting from with the sun in my eyes. Luckily, I saw a reflection in the trees."

We counted six bullet marks that had ricocheted off the armored vehicle. One was inches from where my right boot rested in the crew commander seat.

The sniper also almost hit our driver, missing the open hatch by about two inches. Josh thanked me so much for instructing him to close his bullet-proof hatch.

It was a good day for our unit. Trevor was always alert and I knew that he was one of the best we had. The medic instructed the support troops to take Dexter to the Unimorg mobile unit.

Trevor decided to take command of the front vehicle. I was now in the gunner position while we proceeded down the mountain. When I mentioned to Trevor that it felt great being back in my old gunner position, he smiled. I said, "Yeah, this is the spot for me. Give me a machine gun between my legs, and all the Ango-lies better run away."

I was a bit shaken up by shooting the guy who had tried to kill me. Seeing him fall out of the tree was frightening. My machine gun rounds had whacked the tree, vaporizing the tree branches in a mist. It was like a flash picture was taken, and the visions were branded in my brain for life.

Around mid-morning, we arrived at the SAI-2 unit. We made camp where the hot-spot ambush location was. This was near the village of Calque.

I did not realize until later that we were now in Angolan territory. We were stationed to stay there until further orders. It was a bit boring at the dam wall; we were not moving. Dexter was getting better, though, and on the third day, we got a replacement gunner for me. It was in the afternoon when we saw an army Willys Jeep arrive at our base camp.

Colin was a PF gunner and a corporal like me. He looked a few years older than I and had been three times up on the borders doing his duty.

I felt good to have someone experienced as my gunner. He seemed a nice guy.

Trevor informed me that I was in charge of the Scorpion One vehicle. Colin was only relieving Dexter until he was fit for our mission. Dexter was in a good enough condition to travel with the medics in the Unimorg during our mission in Angola. He was on light duty for two weeks until the medics released him for action.

It was hours after Colin had arrived when our unit got word from Grootfontein HQ. There were extreme acts of violence in a UNITA village next to Chiange. We were all informed to gear up and leave the Ruacana Dam location immediately.

At 4:00 p.m. we traveled on a secondary badly scraped road toward the village of Chitado.

We were all feeling the pressure of traveling in Angola. In my thoughts, I knew that all over Angola it was civil war zone. All of us had an uncomfortable feeling about being here, and we were more on our guard. It was as if we had traveled into a more desolate land, and the uneasiness was felt by all.

We passed the Chitado village at around 6:00 p.m. and preceded about ten clicks farther. It started raining heavily, and Trevor decided to make camp. While driving, Greg and I notice a reasonable spot just off the road where we could set up camp for the night.

While the unit was preparing the campsite, Trevor had a brief gathering with all the ranked guys. We stood away from the unit near a large tree.

Trevor had a dismal look on his face when he informed of the mission ahead. "A village near Chiange is where the action happened a few hours back. Many of the local tribal people were killed, and the MPLA forces decapitated most of them. The area is now recorded and documented as an act-of-war massacre."

We had our ration-pack dinner, and guard beat had started. I was on four-hour guard beat, from 2:00 a.m. to 6:00 a.m. It was a miserable night, as a misty rain was falling. At around 3:00 a.m., Trevor came to our Panzer and informed us, "Be ready for we are riding out at 4:00 a.m." He woke up all the guys who were sleeping to tell them to get ready.

I knew the sooner we made haste toward Chiange, the better chance we had of catching up to those cruel animal people. The distance to Chiange was around 220 clicks to where the action was recorded. While on route, we heard HQ call out our Scorpion Unit calls signs. "Sierra Uniform, make haste to Chiange, and do a sweep-up operation." We were traveling at a fast pace, the sky got lighter. When our patrol passed Otchinjau, we heard two helicopters in the distance flying toward the location of the fighting.

We were lucky that the misty rain had stopped. The gravel road was good enough to average around 50 kilometers per hour. Just before 7:00 a.m., we were on the main tar road from Cahama, traveling to Chibemba. We proceeded to where the Calculivar River and the secondary road met. We were now in the hot zone and on our guard in a ready-to-fire position inside the vehicle. I could see a lot of smoke in the distance.

My hair seemed to stand on end, and I had a wary feeling. *What will we find at this remote village?* I wondered. We drove on a sandy path and hit formation next to the river below the large village of Chiange. I slowly proceeded in the front formation until I could see what was on the hilltop.

My heart was in my throat, and everything seemed to be dead quiet, except for the humming noise of the armored vehicles.

I heard Trevor say on the radio communication, "Sierra Wun Mike X-ray Bro, do you have a visual at the site on the top of the hill?" Greg and the rest were around fifty to a hundred meters behind me. The support section guys were in formation just behind our armored vehicle.

Seconds later, we saw what had happened. *Oh shit! No-o-o!* What we witnessed next was awful. I almost threw up when I saw it. The village on the hill was a disaster, and the cannibal guys were gone. It was very quiet, and all the mud huts on the hill were either burned out or destroyed. I gazed in disbelief at the village. I focused first to see if there was any movement in the bushes, but there was nothing. I instructed Colin that we needed to pop up on top of the Panzer fast. I said that he should get in the machine gun firing position.

We did that. I had the binoculars with me, and I scouted a 360-degree view to ensure that the area was safe. I flagged the support section leader Allen to spread his men out and to do a sweep through the village. I saw a few guys throwing up at the sight in front of us. I was upset and shouted at Corporal Allen, "Get your men in order and do a sweep up. They may still be hiding in the trees ahead."

I gave a command for the other armored vehicles to get in a battle formation in case we were bombarded with tripod mortars. As I gave my command, the tears were running down my face at what I saw.

It was a small village of maybe fifty or so local people living on a hilltop above the river. Like a flash imprint in my brain for life, I can still envision the massacre and the destroyed village. It was unthinkable what these inhumane African people did to the peaceful tribal village people. All the tribal men were slashed with panga knives, and some were tied to wooden poles in the ground. All of them were mutilated, and their dicks were cut off. This seemed to have happened while they were still alive, with the blood oozing out between their legs.

The young children lay scattered around the krall huts, and some were burned inside the mud huts. The small children were shot in the head or back, probably as they were running away. The teenage girls were the worst sight. Most of the children were shot in the head and we could see that there was, acts of sexual abuse was performed on these young girls.

The girls all lay on a pile next to a bloody, dirty sponge-style mattress. The flies were everywhere and the stench was horrendous. No words can describe the evil acts.

The village women were the worst sight. A lot of them were tied with rope to the trees. All were shot in their heads. Their breasts were cut off and thick branches had been forced up their vaginas. The chief and his wife were tied on two crisscross pole structures that were buried in the ground in the center of the village. His head, arms, and legs were chopped off and lay scatted on the ground beside his body. His wife had many cuts on her face. Her breasts were cut off, and a large tree branch was shoved up her vagina. It was up so deep with endless blood around the thick branch sticking out between her legs.

All the cattle were slaughtered. Many parts were cut off in an inhumane way and some of the meat was cooked for a feast. Burned half-eaten meat was around a bon-fire. We all kept our position, and the radio communication was quiet. Trevor commanded us to stay focused and maintain position in our vehicles. He asked Allen if the support section had found any survivors. There was no one.

We did an analysis of how many regime soldiers performed these acts. The engineers and the support section guys estimated around thirty of them. They were all on foot. We figured out that they must have come down the river on some form of raft. I was on top of the armored vehicle all the time. I looked around the site for any movement. I had cried so much that my body had no more tears to shed. I felt hollow, and I could not grasp what type people would perform these sadistic acts of violence.

Trevor had informed HQ of the extreme acts of violence. We were told to do a two-day reconnaissance mission around the area but to leave the slaughter areas "as is," in case there was any disease that might spread from those who were slain.

At the slaying site the support section was instructed to do a further reconnaissance mission around the larger village of Chiange.

We all moved back toward the Chibemba road. We made camp just off the Calculuvar River in a patrol-fight formation. This was on the opposite side of Chiange and the river, just off the roadside. At our patrol camp, our talk was on the acts of violence that had taken place. Trevor was consistently on the radio ops communications with HQ. We were advised to hold position and be vigilant, as the bad guys might still be in the area.

That night we were on a four-hour guard beat. It was one of the worst nights in my army life. My heart was hurting. During the night I only slept about two hours. My thoughts were exploding and I was nervous that we might engage in fighting with the MPLA soldiers.

On the second day, late in the afternoon, our Scorpion support section guys returned to camp. We were informed that the regime soldiers had taken the train to the slaughter village. They dismounted about five kilometers from the village. There were footprints and a few burned-out fire places next to the river.

They built a wooden raft to float down to the Chiange village. It seemed as if they had returned on the same route to board the train going back to

Chibia. Corporal Allen informed us, "We found the second trail of footprints around ten kilometers north of Chiange. This was leading from the river to the train tracks."

On the second day at the campsite, we had many gatherings with the local village people. On the third day we made our way up to the town of Chibia. In this larger town we had a meeting with the local UNITA army. The UNITA leader, Dr. Sevimbe, had traveled down from Lubango to meet with us.

After our town council meeting, HQ in Grootfontein informed us that we needed to retreat to Ruacana and wait for orders. The Cubans were in Angola to support the MPLA forces. It was now the middle of September. We heard that the UNITA officials were forced out of Luanda, the capital of Angola. The central part of Angola was now a hot-zone fighting area.

On route back to Ruacana, we talked about the Angolan government being overthrown and that no one could control the events that followed. What would be sorted out, regarding Angola's future?

The constant driving and the monotony made all of us restless. It started to rain, and it was miserable trip. While traveling from Otchinjau to Chitado, Scorpion Four, Brad's Panzer, went off the road and got stuck in the mud. The patrol stopped, and it was a task for the Unimorg to winch the Panzer back onto the road.

We lost around two hours traveling time. When we arrived at Ruacana, we held position on the mountain overlooking Angola. We made camp in between the two Centurion tanks. It was a treat to have a campfire dinner with the PF tank guys.

In the morning, we were up early. The unit vehicles looked a sight, and we had to remove all the mud from the vehicles.

We were stationed for more than two weeks on the Namibian border and did daily patrol runs up and down the border. These were from Ruacana to Ongenga to Ondangwa and back. We also did two three-day runs to Rundu and back to Ruacana.

It was also a treat to do a border patrol run from Ruacana through Angola and to a town called Foz-do-Cunene on the top end of the Skeleton Coast National Park.

We were more relaxed and had a wild feeling. On the routes, the village's koeker-shop exchange trading was becoming our normal patrol routine. During this time up at the border, we drank beer consistently. Every time we passed through Ondangwa or Oshikati, we would stop at the koeker-shops. We would trade our excess ration packs for supplies. It was always a good trade, getting a kilo of mielie-meal and a dozen local Hansa or Elephant beers, plus some meat, herbs, and spices. We would also trade for a box of tomatoes and a bag of onions and some green peppers for two ration packs. Sometimes we combined the ration packs, and it was a big feast time.

During those runs when we made a bush camp at night off the main roads, we would shoot a few stone bucks and have a braai at night. We would have a typical South African feast—braai meat with mielie-pap (corn flour porridge) with tomato, onion, and green pepper gravy poured over the pap.

Those roadside feasts were grand. We were bush warriors, and we had a don't-care attitude. We looked rough as hell. When I was on the ground walking about, I had the Panzer submachine gun hanging off my back. On my wide army belt I had two extra 9mm submags hooked next to my Star pistol mags and water bottle.

When we had a feast at night, we'd play rock music. We did have a good formation camp set up, just in case the bad guys wanted to pick a fight with us. Trevor was always in communication with HQ on where the action was. He always told us that we were here in the thick of things, and we would go where the fighting action was.

It was a wild and carefree time in our lives. The mood was great, and there was always laughter. At night, after we made our roadside patrol camps, it was the best time of the day.

I remember doing my guard beat at night on the Panzer, slouched on my sleeping bag and pillow on the hatch. I would gaze at the night sky and see billions of stars shining brightly.

After the sun fell off the end of the earth, I could hear all the wild animals doing their bush-hunting attacks for food. Many a time we heard lions. We knew they were miles away but felt so close that the hair on our necks rose like a Mohican path.

Those roadside camps made us feel like bush warriors taking over the wild African land. All the guys in our Scorpion unit became bush-warrior blood brothers. While going for a night piss or dump we would always go two by two. One guy had a piss or dump and the other kept watch. We would always be safe and inform the guys on beat where we were. The bush open toilets were always kind of sectioned off, with a rope tied between and around trees, not too far from patrol camp.

In all the time I was up on the borders and doing patrol runs, we never once had an incidence of someone's going astray and shot at night.

We had been on the borders for just over a month when everything changed. We had just returned from a long-haul patrol run to Rundu and back to Ruacana. It was late in the afternoon when we heard the word on what was happening inside Angola.

It was now early October, and the South African Defense Force (SADF) was to launch an operation know as Savannah (Task Force Zulu). We were going to Luanda from the Angolan province of Cunene. Our armored 1-SSB was traveling through the center part of Angola known as Huambo. Our 2-SSB was traveling a coastal route known as Benguela.

At the Ruacana junction, we waited for another two days for the battalions. On the last morning, we did a short patrol run to the Ruacana Dam catchment and back to Ruacana junction.

Chapter Ten

The Angola War

Our Trip through Angola towards Luanda

It was raining when the rest of the battalion joined us at the Ruacana junction. It was now the entire Two Special Service Battalion on convoy, leaving together and traveling into Angola. With us were many Magirus trucks that carried most of the food and ammunition supplies. There were also four Unimorgs that were rigged up with rocket auto-launch mechanisms. They could shoot forty rockets in a sequence launch. The rockets could demolish an area the size of a football pitch. Their maximum range was over fifteen kilometer away.

The Artillery, with their 150mm explosive bombs, arrived around half an hour later. They would leave the convoy separately in two days' time, after our battalion had departed

We felt we were ready and would launch a full-scale war with the bad guys. In the days that followed, we received orders to do inspections on our vehicles and to load up weapons and rations for four weeks, minimum, bush patrol. I noticed many large camouflaged diesel fuel tanker trucks in the convoy.

On the departure day just before dawn, the Reckies first did a scout maneuver down the mountain to see if there were any Ango-lie snipers on our route road.

Dexter was released and was back with me in the armored vehicle. It was around 6:00 a.m. when our Scorpion Troop One led the convoy down Ruacana Mountain into Angola. I was in the front vehicle, and our route was toward Cahama. The battalion was moving together into Angola. While traveling down the mountain pass, Dexter and I were sitting on top of the Panzer, having a few beers and listening to Santana rock music. We were leading the pack. I noticed he was a bit uneasy.

Radio communications were minimal. Every now and then I had to give Trevor an update on the road conditions and what I observed in front of me. This was from my Panzer to his. Then he would do a direct communications to HQ, to Major Van Zyl, who was in charge of the convoy. Traveling was slow and the light rain was gloomy. I guess the longer the unit is mobile, the slower the convoy moves. It was pretty boring with nothing but road in front of us.

On the first day, the convoy stopped around 5:00 p.m. outside Lubango. We set up camp in different locations and formations. This was just in case we had a night attack.

That night our big brass had a meeting with the UNITA soldiers. Their captain in charge of UNITA decided to join our convoy to Luanda. At this time we received communications that the MPLA were retreating all their forces out of the south to regroup around Luanda and surrounding urban locations.

The MPLA must have heard that the South African forces were traveling north to Luanda, the capital of Angola.

We stayed one day and night in Lubango and then departed for Benguela and Lobito. The UNITA soldiers in their pickup trucks traveled in front of my armored vehicle. The trip took us two days to get to Lobito by the coast. We made camp next to the ocean.

The experience of seeing the ocean was just what we needed. We'd been traveling for many days in the harsh Angolan bush. It was now the middle of October, and the full-on rainy season was here. Major Van Zyl gave orders that we would fan out and take different routes to Luanda. We were all tired, and I could see that Josh was a bit exhausted from driving the Panzer on these long, slow trips. We were told that the following day, we would rest to freshen up. We were also informed, "From now on, we need to be on the lookout for land mines on the gravel roads and ambushes near the towns or river crossings."

It was late in the afternoon of our resting day when Trevor rounded our Scorpion crew commanders and section leader. We gathered in the temporary HQ tent.

He gave us our route orders for the following day. Apparently, the heavy fighting was at the Nhia and Longa Rivers. The rivers were around 290 kilometers south from Luanda. The UNITA forces were in stalemate with the

MPLA at the River Longa. They were also experiencing sporadic attacks from the rear.

Our SADF had to do a sweep-up operation from Lobito to Wama and all the land mass area from the coast to the tar road leading to Luanda. The five troops and support section units all had a different route to travel for the sweep-up operation through the villages. This was to ensure there were no MPLA stationed behind us. We would all regroup in three days' time at different locations beside the Nhia and Longa Rivers. This is where the UNITA was holding ground.

Our Scorpion unit route was from Lobito to Bocoio, and we had to proceed to Chila, Atome, and Catanda. This was our first day's route. It was now full battle stations. We had to travel fully loaded and needed to be prepared to fire if any gunshots were heard.

That last night outside Lobito, we had a good time together. We felt that some of us might never return home after this trip.

All five troops were together at a roadside camp outside Lobito. Most of the troop guys that were with me were the same as those who had been in our advanced training at the School of Armor. Greg and I had a chat with all the other troop guys.

In my thougths I new that some of the lads might die in this Angolan war. This part of Africa had so many problems, but we South Africans were going to die for a cause we didn't understand.

It was around 9:00 p.m. when our Scorpion Panzer One guys were informed for our guard duty. Beat would start at 2:00 a.m. and last until 6:00 a.m. It was a good time to stand beat for we knew that Trevor would round us up before sunrise and have a quick breakfast and move on our patrol route.

During our beat, Dexter, Josh, and I talked a lot. At about four thirty, I saw Trevor walk up to our Panzer position. I thought, *yep, we are leaving early, and our guard beat is shorter.* Trevor said, "Hey, bros, we are out of here at 5:00 a.m. Have your breakfast and gear up to leave camp." I knew from that moment onward we were going to be exposed to ambushes or gunfire battle stations in the hot zone. Every morning before going on patrol, I always gave my guys in our Panzer an encouraging pep talk.

On this weary morning while waiting for our Scorpion unit to prepare for the road trip to Bocoio, I gave Dexter and Josh a pep talk, saying, "Remember, we are trained for this mission to Luanda. The Ango-lies are idiots and stupid.

We can be smarter and better than them. We are all going home after this South African Savanna task force Zulu war mission. Be alert and have good vision on today's travels ahead of us. Today is going to be a good day. Have faith and keep your thoughts clear and positive."

In the Panzer, we would pat each other's shoulders as a good-faith gesture. They both thanked me on our vehicle radio, saying, "Thanks, X-ray Bro, we will not disappoint you." It was minutes when I got orders to roll. Trevor said, "Sierra Wun Mike X-ray Bro, are we ready to roll? Over." I gave the command, "Sierra Tree Tango, we are rolling. Over and out." The UNITA pickup group was now traveling between our Unimorg vehicles.

The secondary tar road from Labito to Bocoio was in a reasonable condition. We traveled for about an hour and a half to get there. We turned left on a gravel road to Chila. We stopped about one click from the tar road.

We had a roadside piss. Trevor, Greg, Brad, and I had a discussion beside my Panzer on what lay ahead of us. The dark rain clouds were not far away from the ocean, west from our position. Dexter and I put on our poncho rain gear before getting in position on top of the Panzer.

While on route to Chila, the heavens opened and the rain came down, buckets full. We did not realize that the road surface was clay, and the driving conditions became like an ice skating rink.

Great, this is all we need on this first trip, I thought. Josh was pretty good at judging how the road surface was, and we crawled along the road. The rain continued all the way to Chila. It was difficult to stay on the slippery, muddy road. At two places, the Panzer went sideways, but we never left the road.

As we traveled slowly through Chila, we saw all the local village people cheering and dancing as we passed. Trevor said, "This is a sign." He was smart, saying over the radio com, "Sierra Wun Mike X-ray Bro, if you approach the next village, do an observation to see if the village people are friendly. If not, you know that the village may be an ambush or is destitute. Over and out."

It was just after 1:00 p.m. when the rain became a slight drizzle, but the road was still muddy. At a flat section alongside the road, we stopped for lunch. An hour later, set off we set off for next village of Atomy. On this stretch of muddy road, the conditions were worse. It took around two hours to drive about thirty clicks. Our Scorpion One Panzer looked like it had a mud bath. Dexter and I were also a bit wet, and the mood was somber.

Driving through Atomy we had the same reception, with all the happy UNITA folks dancing, clapping hands, and cheering at us as we drove past them.

On route to Catanda, we saw around thirty UNITA African folk walking beside the road. I ordered Josh to stop the Panzer. I gave the rest of the unit orders to stop around fifty meters apart. This was in case the folk tried to attack us—not that it would be wise to do.

They were carrying many items with them. I asked if there was a leader or chief with them or someone who could speak English. I also said they should keep their distance from our armored vehicle and that just one of them should walk toward me.

An older chief walked up to our Panzer. All the while, Dexter had the machine gun pointing at the group on the other side of the muddy gravel road. I asked the chief, "Why are you walking toward Atomy?" He spoke pretty good English and answered, "There is MPLA fighting north of Catanda, and they heard that the MPLA was moving south toward them. I am moving my village people south, away from the fighting."

I answered him, "How far ahead of Atomy is the fighting?" He looked a bit puzzled but answered me, "About two weeks' walking distance." I estimated that to be about 240 clicks away.

The chief gave me the answer that I was looking for. He said, "We heard that some MPLA have been coming further south, and some village people have been killed about one week's walk from here."

I looked on the map. "Yeah, there is the River Queve that is around 150 clicks from our position." I relayed the chief's information to Trevor and then thanked the chief for his help. I asked him, "How far south are you taking your village people?"

He said, "To Huambo, where my brother lives."

In a second, I felt the desperation of these kind black UNITA folk, trying to survive what was happening to them in Angola. I looked at the map and could see that they would have to walk more than three hundred kilometers from Catanda to the town of Huambo. I informed him that our army unit force was from South Africa and that we were there to protect them. "We will stop the MPLA people killing the UNITA folk living in the south of Angola." I said.

He smiled so happily and bowed his head many times. It was pitiful, and my last words to this brave chief were, "Good luck, Chief." We proceeded to travel toward Catanda. My thoughts were, *some folks will take extreme measures to survive.*

Trevor was amazed at the courage of the UNITA folk, trying to stay alive in their country while having tribal unrest and the slaying of the peaceful village people. The road toward Catanda was in a better condition. It was just before 5:00 p.m. when we traveled through Catanda. The same greeting of the happy folk made us realize why we were fighting in Angola.

We set up camp about a hundred meters from the road in the bush. The first night sleeping in the bush gave us the jitters. I had a feeling that tonight would be okay. I was first guard beat from 6:00 p.m. to 10:00 p.m. Trevor informed me that there would be action tomorrow. He said, "We are close to where the ambush sites were recorded over the last month or so."

That night, we heard HQ inform us that UNITA was holding ground and pushing the MPLA northwards toward Luanda. After my guard beat, I could not sleep well. It was way past midnight when my eyes finally closed.

With all the communication on ambush locations, we knew that most ambushes happened close to where the road crosses near the rivers. Our first river on the route was the Queve River. Trevor said, "I want to leave early, before sunrise, so that we can be there by early afternoon."

The road toward a larger village called Uku was in a good condition, and we averaged around forty clicks per hour. By mid-morning we had gone through Uku, and the same UNITA folk were happy to see us traveling through their town.

With all the rain the day before, it was a difficult road to travel. I noticed that the road had many pot holes, as well as some vehicle tracks coming out of a bush path. I stopped the convoy unit and asked for the land-mine engineer to make his way toward our front Panzer.

"I don't know why, but the sudden vehicle tracks bother me," I said.

Trevor joined our engineer, and the three of us assessed the fresh vehicle tracks on the road. We gathered that they were around three hours old and that there were three pickup vehicles. From the path, Trevor and I decided that the Panzer troop guys should sit inside and get prepared for battle stations.

When we were about five clicks from Conda, I suddenly got a chill and told Dexter and Josh, "I feel that something is not quite right in this village ahead of us. Be prepared for the worst." I got on the radio with Trevor and told him the same thing. I instructed Josh to close his hatch and to look out for land mines on the dirt road. I instructed Dexter to cock the 50mm Browning and to wait for orders. We were moving at about fifteen clicks per hour.

I was consistently looking through the enhanced vision sights at the road and in the bushes ahead or us.

The UNITA pickup trucks behind our Unimorgs were informed that there might be action ahead.

By golly gosh, I was right. While approaching Conda, it seemed different. There were no townsfolk doing their happy dance as we approached the village. I gave Josh orders to proceed slowly and to keep focused on an escape route. Time seemed to be in slow motion. I could see the tense look on Dexter's face. I informed Trevor that I was going to give a short 50mm round burst, shooting toward a white building between the trees to my left.

I instructed, "Dexter, shoot three rounds of the 50mm Browning gun toward the side of the building". Soon after, I saw the side of the building explode and fall over. I was right on; we had surprised the Terks. The firing of rounds toward our vehicle came full on.

Josh quickly proceeded into the bush as I gave orders to the unit behind me. "Hit a staggered formation; ambush ahead." I then gave orders to proceed forward and do a sweep-up formation through the village. The support troopers and UNITA soldiers dismounted their vehicles and made a formation behind the Panzers. I saw some movement to my left. I gave instructions: "Thirty degree on the left is a pickup truck." Dexter was positioned in the turret and let rip with the 50mm Browning gun. Damn, the truck exploded—and all hell broke loose.

We proceeded slowly through the bush, and when we reached the small village, we saw many camouflaged MPLA running away from the village. I gave Dexter orders to fire again. We both moved fast and positioned ourselves on top. Dexter let rip again, and I saw three MPLA soldiers shot and fall to the dirt. I looked through the binoculars and gave Dexter instructions where to shoot. At this time our Panzers were four abreast and proceeded forward at a fast pace. The support section and the UNITA soldiers were sweeping up just behind the Panzers.

Within minutes, we were through the village and regrouped. All the remaining bad guys were running through the dense trees and bush at the end of the village. We stayed in formation at a fifty-meter distance from one another and stopped at the end of the village.

Trevor gave orders for the support section and the UNITA soldiers to do a reconnaissance between all the buildings, in the bush, and around the village. We were trained to analyze the surrounding situation first to ensure that we did not have a counterattack from behind.

My heart was pounding as I looked through the binoculars in the bushes and trees in front of our vehicles. Trevor called out on the radio, "Good thinking, Scorpion One. You guys did well. The maneuver was a success. We are good, with no casualties."

The support section leader came on the radio and said there were six Terk-soldiers dead as well as two Cubans, who looked like instructors. In the Toyota pickup truck there were five Terks killed when it blew up. "It seems there were around twenty-five to thirty Terks in this ambush group," Trevor said.

I patted Dexter on his shoulder and said, "Good shooting. The first kill is always a fearful sensation, but the objective is to protect and to outsmart our enemy. No one in this ambush has been wounded or killed." Dexter smiled from ear to ear. I knew he was a smart gunner, and I was happy to have him in our Scorpion One vehicle.

At that moment we heard Trevor give orders for the support section and UNITA soldiers to make haste and proceed on foot through the brush and trees and to find the Terks before they reached the River Queve.

The support section and UNITA guys were in constant radio communication with our unit. It was not long before they found the footprint trail and proceeded after them.

Trevor discussed with HQ the ambush sweep-up operation. Our Scorpion unit regrouped and proceeded on the Condo road to the River Queve Bridge. We were in constant contact with the support section radio op. Just over an hour later, they reached the River Queve. The MPLA Ango-lie Terk soldiers were gone.

Greg informed HQ that the Terks had left the river on some form of raft or boat. HQ gave orders to wrap it up and proceed to Gabela. Our support section and the UNITA soldiers made their way to our position at the bridge. They loaded up, and we proceeded northward. The Terk action at the Conda village gave us all a hyped-up feeling, knowing that we were well armed for any action in the danger zone. The road toward Gabela was in a reasonable condition.

Just after 4:00 p.m. we reached a T-junction from Sumbe to Gabela. Our unit turned right and traveled another five minutes towards Gabela. Trevor gave orders to turn left in the bush and to proceed about hundred meters from the gravel road. We made night camp not far from the junction near Gabela.

That night we all felt the pressure of the hair-raising experience. It was a moonless night for our Panzer guard beat. The rain clouds were gone, and the black night with billions of stars was clear and calm. I slouched on my sleeping bag on the top of the Panzer and looked up at the pitch-black night. It was always an exhilarating feeling to hear the nights sounds of the animals and the crickets in the bush. It made us feel like wild African bush warriors—there was no other place in this wonderful world that gave such a feeling of being in the wild and free.

The most frightening sound is the male lions roaring at night. The roar echoes and vibrates through the night for more than six miles. When you experience the lions' night sounds, the hair on your back and neck rises up in a cold chill. Your body goes into overdrive with endless goose bumps, from your toes to your head. It is a frightening, ecstatic, nervous feeling like no other.

That night we had only three hours sleep before we had orders to leave. I thought, *Is it today that we will encounter the hot-zone war action?* Dexter, Josh, and I were all cleaned up and had our ration-pack breakfast. We were ready to roll at 5:30 a.m. Just before seven o'clock, HQ told us to do a patrol run from Gabela to Porto Ambiom "T-junction" and back. This route was over two hundred kilometers, round trip.

We were to check the train that traveled daily from Gabela to the coast to Porto Ambiom and back to Gabela. While traveling on the road though the mountains, we crossed a train track two times. At the second crossover point, we parked the convoy on the side of the road. We were in a stationary ambush formation.

Our Scorpion One Panzer was always in the thick of it. The support section guys cut down a reasonably sized tree and dragged it on the train line about ten meters in front of our Scorpion One Panzer, facing the trains approach. We felt like American cowboys on a train raid. We sat on top of the Panzer, ready to let rip with the 7.62mm machine gun, if need be. Trevor sat on top with Dexter and me, waiting for the train's arrival. It was a good time to chat and relax. It was just after nine thirty when we heard the train approach us from a distance. The support troopers were behind our Scorpion One Panzer in a ready-to-fire position.

The train slowed down, and we heard four hoots of it horn. The train came to a halt around twelve meters from our Panzer and just about touching the log across the tracks. It was an old train that pulled four open-interior carriages behind it. Trevor and the support section guys walked up to the train engine. I saw the black African driver pop his head out and wave at us with a friendly but frightened look on his face. I heard Trevor ask the driver, "How many passengers are in the carriages?" The driver said there were twenty-five. At this time we saw many black African folk peeping out of the carriage doors.

Trevor asked, "What goods are you transporting to Porta Ambiom?" The driver looked bewildered and said, "Not much, my boss. We normally take goods daily from Porta Ambiom to Gabela."

"Come on down and show me what you have in the carriages," Trevor said. The driver did so. As he did, he spoke in his black language at the African folk gawking at them. The people moved back inside the open carriage doors. From our Scorpion One vehicle, I saw two support section guys climb up and enter the carnages.

After the inspection, all was good, and the driver and the boys returned to the train engine. The boys removed the log across the tracks, and the train set off slowly, passing our Scorpion vehicle. As they passed us, the African black folk waved at us.

I knew that we had scared them at this roadside crossing. Trevor walked to our Panzer and said, "Hey, Bro Mike, all seemed A-okay on the train."

We set off toward Porto Ambiom. It was a mountainous route and the traveling pace was slower. Dexter and I enjoyed the ride. The road twisted and turned in the dense mountains. The mood was happy and good. We were also on our guard in case we are ambushed on this route.

It seemed peaceful, with not a soul or a vehicle in sight. We stopped for lunch at the T-junction leading to Porto Ambiom. We could see the ocean in the distance.

Trevor decided not to go to Porto Ambiom. While driving back to Gabela, we stopped three trucks and six vehicles. All was good. At around 4:00 p.m., we stopped the old steam train at the second crossing that was closer to Gabela. It was the same train driver. The train had seven carriages hooked up behind it. There were just a few local people and supplies traveling on it. The four extra carriages behind the African folk had cattle, pigs, and bags of corn flour in them.

Later that afternoon we made camp just north of Gabela. The UNITA soldiers informed us that the local people on the train said there was a lot of fighting going on around a hundred clicks north of Cabela. Trevor informed Greg, Brad, and me, "Tomorrow will be a different ball game. Be prepared for HQ mentioned that the MPLA and the UNITA/SADF forces are at war and in a stalemate position at the River Longa. That is about ninety-five clicks ahead of us." He was always positive and ensured us that we would all be going home after our border duty.

We were told to be ready for 5:00 a.m. departure and to be ready for action.

After our breakfast the next morning, I gathered Dexter and Josh together and together, the three of us put our arms over each other's shoulders in a hug.

I gave a little speech. "I trust both of you to be alert and be safe," I said. "We will look after one another and our Scorpion unit buddies. This is it, guys; it is what we have been trained for. We don't know what to expect, but I know and feel that we will all be good, and we will make it home. Take care, guys. Trevor, Greg, Brad, Allen, and I are your commanders. If you guys need to talk to anyone, please speak freely. In our Scorpion Panzer One, I am always here for you guys." We released our shoulder grips, and we did the "how-zit" handshake and the shoulder-bump, good-friend-gesture hand pat.

Chapter Eleven

The Angolan War

In My Life, There Is a Guardian Angel Looking after Me

We departed before dawn the following morning towards Quilenda. It had rained during the night, and the road was in poor condition. It took us just over two hours to reach Quilenda. While driving through the village it looked a bit desolate. The local folk were in a somber mood, and I noticed the weary looks on their faces. Nevertheless, we waved at them and they waved back. It was now the last week in October.

The road to the Nhia River was slightly better, but the traveling was slow. We arrived at the Nhia River Bridge at midday. All was quiet, and we did a formation just off the road, parking our vehicles about one hundred meters from the bridge.

The UNITA soldiers with us proceeded with their pickup trucks toward the bridge. We waited for more than an hour before we received orders from HQ. "Proceed to the Longa River Bridge and go down a path to where the Longa River forks away from the wider Nhia River."

We could not hear any gunfire. Trevor mentioned on the radio that the fighting would most probably be at night. We were the first unit of our South African 2-SSB to arrive at the river's edge. We knew that the other Troops Two to Five would be stationed in different locations up and down the Longa River. I looked on the map at where our locations were. I knew that we were in the center, and it was most probably where most of the fighting action was.

The town across the River Longa Bridge was where the MPLA were based in Mumbonda. It was only around five or so clicks from where our combat position was.

Just before the Longa River on the gravel road there was a large tent. This was where the UNITA HQ was based. We stopped next to the tent. Trevor came forward and shook hands with Captain Mbawani. He was in charge of this UNITA outfit.

They were in the tent for around ten minutes, discussing where our stationary battle station would be. When Trevor came out of the HQ tent, he walked up to our Scorpion One vehicle and said, "Take a left down this path and find a good position between the trees, not far from the tent. Position the Panzer just above the path in case we need to haul out of here. You also need to have a good view of the river."

As usual, Trevor had our Scorpion One Panzer nearest to the exit road and main gravel road leading to Mumbonda. We proceeded down the path for about one hundred meters from the UNITA HQ tent. We found a great spot. Dexter and I hopped off the Panzer, and we cleared the rocks and stones and brush. Josh slowly positioned our Panzer on this slightly higher ground next to two very large trees. We had a good view of the river below. There were not many trees to obstruct our view. Behind the Panzer was a slight descent, where we could set up our small three-man tent and campfire position.

Dexter and I climbed back on the Panzer and cut off the few branches that obstructed the full view of the river. We both said at the same time, "Awesome spot," and we had a good laugh about our speaking in unison. I told Josh to set the Panzer gearbox in differential gear-lock and then engage the hand break, and turn off the engine.

After we parked in a good getaway position, we put our camouflage netting over the Panzer and camouflaged it with some twigs and branches. We did a good job of hiding it from the bad guys across the river and from a bird's eye view from above.

The UNITA foot soldiers were based about three hundred meters in front of our formation and closer to the river. Their small group position was stretched out as far as the eye could see. It felt different having the black UNITA guys with us in our battle formation. We had never trained for this kind of combat

After setting up our small canvas tent behind the Panzer, Trevor informed us over the vehicle radio, "I want everyone in Scorpion unit to make your way to the UNITA HQ tent." We all had to walk there and wait for our next command.

It was not long before Trevor gave us orders on what needed to be achieved before nightfall. Our command camp was going to be a practical format and in a way that we could clear our site within an hour, if need be.

Orders were to set up our Scorpion unit (HQ combined with the mess tent). This would be set up around fifty meters behind the UNITA HQ tent and close to the main gravel road. The support section's Unimorgs, the two Magirus trucks, and the diesel fuel tanker had to be positioned around the HQ/mess tent. This was also a bit away from the roadside and in-between the trees and shrubs.

Next, the engineers, medic, vehicle mechanics and Magirus and fuel-tank drivers had to set up sleeping quarters, plus a trench to lie in when the fighting started over the river toward our position. They also needed to have a good view of the Longa River.

The support section riflemen had to make sleeping quarters between the Panzers, plus dig a trench to lie in when the fighting started. The section leader, Allen, and the radio operator, Charlie, had to be between Trevor's and Greg's Panzers. Lance Corporal Tom, with his tripod belt-driven R-1 machine gun, had to be at the end of the Scorpion One defense line.

Trevor was a good leader and his battle skills tactics were unusual. I am sure the officers above him were impressed with his tactical formations. Behind our Scorpion unit battle line, there was an escape route between the trees that led to the HQ tent and the main road. This route between the trees was marked with yellow luminous ribbons around the trees for a night escape, if we needed to get the hell out of there. Trevor thought of everything. At the river's edge, there was a wooden floating platform hidden between the bushes.

There was also a ribbon route between the UNITA trench dug-in forces toward the river to have a shit or piss at night. When you have your dump, big ol' log shit would float away from the platform down the river, never to be seen and no smell at all.

By 4:00 p.m. our defense position was completed. Trevor, Greg, Brad, Allen, and I took a walk to the main road. We spoke with the UNITA captain Mbawani in his sleeping tent that was opposite the path and closer to the road leading to Mumbonga.

He was in constant radio talk with many journalists in Luanda who were observing the real-time action there. While listening to the chaotic talk, it seemed like there was a massacre in the streets of Luanda.

Trevor gave us a list for our guard duty schedules for a week. He also gave a list to the captain to review our schedules. The guard beat was now twenty-four/seven, and it was six-hour beats at a time. At any given time, half the Scorpion unit was on beat, and half were off. We also had schedules to eat in the mess tent at different times or to eat on guard beat.

We met many of the UNITA soldiers, and they were all friendly. Most of the talk was about the continuous fighting over the river. They were happy to have us there. Greg and his crew were on the same schedule as our Panzer One, and our guard beat was from midnight until 6:00 a.m. It was just after 5:00 p.m. when Trevor, Greg, and I walked to Captain Mbawani's HQ tent. Their radio communications were going on consistently. Around half of the communications were in their black language and the other half in African English.

While sitting on stools in the UNITA HQ tent and listening to the radio, we could figure out what was going on in real time in Luanda, the capital of Angola. Captain Mbawani also translated for us when the communications changed to their black language. It was frightening to hear the radio talk. Everything seemed to be in a hyped-up communications.

Captain Mbawani said there was a lot of fighting going on in the north of Luanda. The mercenaries and the FPLA and Zairian troops were in full battle. The Portuguese had abandoned the Angolan government, and UNITA had been ousted from Luanda. It was now in MPLA control. There was fighting in the streets all over Luanda; it was in disarray and out of control. During all this radio chaos, Captain Mbawani told us that the action happened every night next to the Longa River. He estimated that there were over one thousand MPLA on the opposite side of the Longa River. Every night the UNITA soldiers shot some MPLA soldiers crossing the river to our position.

Then he said, "Tonight you will see the action, and everything will be different. We now have you, the South African army, with us. They don't know you have arrived, and they will have a big surprise when you shoot the big guns."

It was nearly 6:00 p.m. and the start of our Scorpion unit's guard beat. Trevor left Captain Mbawani's tent to start his beat. Greg, Allen, and I stayed for a while longer. Just before dark, we returned to our vehicle. I decided to have my dump shit down by the river's edge before it got dark. I was thinking, *someone may think that I am a Terk and shoot me.*

Dexter said, "Let's all three walk together to the river's edge. That way we won't feel afraid in the dark." It was a smart move, and Josh, Dexter, and I made our way to the river's edge toilet. On the way down we saw a few UNITA soldiers, and they gave us the African one-two-three handshake. The UNITA soldiers said "Thank you boss, tonight we show the Terks who we are and that this is our land." I realized again why we were protecting these grand African black people living in this part of majestic Africa.

All they wanted was to live peacefully. Why were there differences of who controlled the land? Most of the folks didn't give a damn about the Angolan government, but they would fight to protect their villages and what they had.

Dexter, Josh, and I had our big dump shit and piss on the homemade platform toilet. We made our way back to our Panzer just as it was getting dark. We made a small fire behind our tent for our ration-pack supper and coffee. It was not long before we heard some shots streaking over the Longa River toward the UNITA soldiers below us, where they were dug in their position near the river's edge. After that, all was quiet for a long time. It felt scary, knowing that the MPLA were shooting blindly over the river. I thought that a stray bullet might kill me. *What a bummer, dying that way.*

Our spot between the trees was good, and our tent was well protected behind our Panzer. Our little fire behind the tent was not visible from the Longa River. We did well at protecting ourselves behind our Panzer. On this first night at the stronghold defense position, we tried to sleep but could not. The strange environment and excitement kept us awake.

Dexter, Josh, and I played card games in our tent, having a rigged-up extension wire with a 12 volt light, with a switch connected to our radio input wires. This was long enough to stretch from the Panzer to our tent. It was a dim light that would not reflect through our thick canvas tent. But it was good enough to see clearly inside the tent.

At 11:50 p.m., we got in our positions for guard beat on the Panzer. We did the radio changeover with Trevor, Brad, and Allan, who had been on the first beat. I had my sleeping bag under my bum on the hatch and got myself in a good slouched position. With the night vision binoculars, I did a slow observation of the opposite side of the Longa River. The moon was fairly bright, and I made markings on my map at the different sections on the opposite's side of the river.

Dexter was also in a ready-to-fire position with the 7.62mm Browning gun cocked. We knew that soon we would hear gunshots fired over the river. Twenty minutes later, we heard a sporadic burst of gunfire hitting the trees below our position. I logged the position where I saw the gunshots. A few of the UNITA soldiers returned fire. I noticed that they too were shooting over the river blindly.

On the radio, Greg said, "Hey, X-ray Bro, did you log the position where the shots were fired?" I answered, "Yep, it is around twelve degrees to my right and in a cove next to the river."

Greg said. "It's time we show these bastards who is the boss. We are going to wait five minutes, and then Scorpion Two will shoot one five-second burst, and Scorpion One, shoot your first burst, and we will follow until both gunners have shot three bursts each. We will wait for a response."

Scorpion Two let rip with the 7.62mm machine gun toward the opposite cove location. It was now a different ball game, and the continuous machine gun firing was exhilarating. About five single shots fired blindly in return and then nothing from the MPLA side.

After three bursts each, the night went still, with only a few shots fired from the UNITA soldiers below us. I guess the whole camp was awake with all the machine gun firing going on from Scorpion One and Two Panzers. We heard the UNITA soldiers below us cheering and shouting after the commotion we had caused.

Greg came over the radio "I think we have picked a fight with the enemy." It was not long before we heard Trevor on the radio, saying, "Good tactics guys. We will see what their response is." During the long six hours of our beat, there were only a few shots fired from the MPLA side of the river. The UNITA would respond with return fire.

It was now the beginning of November. Late in the afternoon, we heard that the artillery had reached the Nhia River. They were going to be stationed there, and their position was around four kicks behind our dug-in location next to the Longa River.

In the few days that followed, a lot more sporadic gunshots were fired at night over the Longa River wacking the tree branches close to our Panzer position.

From one day to the next, the action increased and became full on. I had a feeling that a lot of MPLA had arrived across the Longa River at their stronghold in the town of Mumbonda.

The MPLA were now launching tripod mortars and small artillery mortars.

At night the streaks of the auxiliary bombs from our South African Defense Forses were screaming over our heads into the distance and then would explode five to ten kilometers away. The sounds that echoed through the night gave us an exhilarating feeling—this was war time. The night sky would light up like the end of the world was near.

During the day, it was sporadic gunfire here and there. At night, it was big bad guns doing their thing. It was like a chess game, and either side was in a stalemate. The Unimorg's forty rockets were launched in sequential order and would streak in staggered rocket launches that were awesome to view. At least twice a night we received coordinates and orders to fire a few high-explosive mortars toward the outskirts of Mumbonda.

Every night we could hear the radios from one campsite to the other. It was now early November, and Cuba had agreed to send twenty thousand troops to Angola to support the MPLA regime. On November 9, 1975, the first wave of Cuban combat troops arrived. They came by vessel and were based in Luanda. I thought, *Oh shit, we are going to have full-time warfare. We will fight until the last man stands.*

On November 10, Cubans and MPLA pushed the FPLA and the Zairian troops north, out of Angola. On November 11, we heard that Portugal formally had transferred sovereignty to all the Angolan people, leaving the country in the hands of three groups—MPLA, FNLA, and UNITA—to fight and proclaim Angola as the People's Republic of Angola.

On November 16, the Russians arrived to support the MPLA. They were going to train and instruct the MPLA on how to fight. We wondered who the hell we were fighting in support of the UNITA forces. The Communists had arrived, and we expected there would be more intense fighting.

On the Nhia and Longa Rivers, the fighting had stepped up a level. We engaged in more extreme day and night bombardment. We held our ground, and daily many UNITA and SADF guys were killed. Our Scorpion unit felt the pressure, and some guys went "bomb-happy" (went crazy). When the bomb landed and the explosions went off, some would panic. Some of our support section guys were getting trigger-happy, shooting at anything they heard.

Trevor maintained order and always ensured us that we would get out of this mess. We held position and our artillery consistently pounded the MPLA coordinate positions.

At this time in my life, I was carefree and my hair was over my ears. None of us shaved, so we all had short beards. We looked rough as hell. Our daily clothing was bush hat, army T-shirt with the sleeves torn off, bush browns trousers, and black army boots. I carried my 9mm Star pistol in my army belt on my right hip; my army stiletto knife was on my left hip. The 9mm submachine gun was around my shoulders, hanging on my back. Around my belt, I had ammo pouches that carried eight pistol magazines and four submachine gun twenty-five-round mags and my water bottle. I was well prepared to fight off anyone trying to kill me while I walked in the bush.

Going for a shit was difficult. We had to make our way to the river past the UNITA soldiers and shit into the river, then wash hands with our water bottle, and proceed back to our stronghold position. I never did shit at night. I was nervous that someone might think I was a bad guy and shoot me.

Our Scorpion One Panzer had endless extra 7.62mm cases with two hundred rounds per case. It was the most boring time in my life, waiting for shots to be fired and return the fire.

One day, however, late in the afternoon, I was almost shot dead. I had just come back from my shit by the river. I was walking with Dexter, and we were climbing up the incline toward our Panzer location. Shots suddenly whizzed past us, with some whacking a tree in front of us. Dexter and I ran up the hill and dove behind a large tree. As we crawled, we looked back over the river to try to locate where the shots were being fired.

We knew that we needed to cross the path and get to our Panzer. We lay there for a few minutes with our hearts pounding, and we both knew how lucky we were. We dashed over the path and heard two more shots whiz by us. We made it to the rear of the Panzer and climbed inside. Josh was sitting in his driver's position and had the binoculars with him. He shouted out, "Where the hell, have you guys been? The Terks have been shooting at our Panzer location."

Dexter was agitated and said, "Damn, we can't even go for a shit anymore." During all this chaos, I heard Trevor's and Brad's vehicles shooting across the river.

I got in my crew commander position as Josh scouted where the MPLA were shooting. "Good work, Josh," I told him. "Where are these guys locate?"

Josh said, "See those two large trees together in the center part of the river? They are about ten to twenty meters to the right of the trees."

I gave Dexter the sight position, and we let rip with a high-explosive mortar. We hit the spot, and the explosion was massive. I gathered we must have hit a machine gun post or something larger. It was obviously something metal.

Trevor said over the radio com, "Good shooting, Scorpion One. You guys are supposed to be off guard duty. I could see you guys running from the incline, and it was close—you guys were almost shot. God is with you today."

My heart was pounding, and I was in a bit of shock, thinking, *damn, that was close. We need to find a different and safer route to the river toilet.*

It was a scary yet boring time of our lives. Dexter and I came up with a plan to keep ourselves busy. I started to train Dexter on how to be a crew commander. During the day he studied the theory books, and I would show him all the crew commander practical skils that he needed to know. It was my way of staying sane.

We would change gunner positions on alternate days. I would be in the gunner position with the 7.62mm Browning gun between my legs. Dexter would practice his crew commander coordinate bearings. Many times I shot the 7.62mm and the 50mm Browning machine guns. I enjoyed shooting the high-explosive mortars at night. It was the best feeling in the world, sitting behind the 7.62mm Browning machine gun, on top of the Panzer.

The sound of the gunshots became normal. I guess we were all a bit bush-happy from hearing gunshots twenty-four/seven. It didn't bother us at all. Many times the gunfire whacked the trees around us.

By the end of November, we had been in Namibia and in Angola for three months on border duty. By chance I was sitting in the gunner position on top of our Panzer as Josh, Dexter, and I listened to Santana music on the Panzer radio. It was a moonless night, but the stars were sparkling, and the mood was happy.

It was on this weary Friday-night guard beat when the shit hit the fan. Suddenly, there was the sound of gunfire across the Longa River. Sergeant Greg was on beat on Scorpion Two, and I heard him call out in a panic, "We are under attack from the Ango-lies across the river! Fire at will!"

The Ango-lies opposite the river let rip with machine gun fire. At the same time they launched mortars toward our dug-in position. I heard many shots whiz by and whack the trees around me. A few mortars exploded around twenty to thirty meters in front of my Panzer. I let rip with the 7.62 mm Browning toward the continuous bullets streaking over the River. The fighting action was more intense, and the MPLA forces gave us a full-on battle. It was not long thereafter when the SADF launched artillery fire across the river toward the MPLA positions.

At that moment I stopped firing and looked through the binoculars at the explosions on the MPLA positions. The UNITA soldiers in front of us were dug in next to the river. They were rapidly shooting. Through the binoculars, I looked left and right, up and down, at where all the explosions were lighting up the night sky. I saw a mortar hit a MPLA tripod machine gun position. All the sandbags and about six soldiers flew in the air in a fire-ball explosion. They were dead.

I felt as if I was in a movie and the action was all around me. The SADF artillery was pounding the opposite side of the River Longa. The sound of those big guns screaming across our heads made me think, *you guys have picked a fight with the wrong crowd.*

The night firepower went on for many hours and came mostly from the SADF side. During all the chaos, we heard over the radio com that the Cuban forces were opposite our position and were fighting alongside the MPLA.

It was a frightening night. At some stages, the firing would slow down to only a few shots. During that time, Dexter and I changed gunner positions so that I was in my crew commander seat.

Trevor constantly kept us in the right frame of mind and would ask if anyone had been shot. This action happened until morning. At sunrise, all seemed to have calmed down, with only the odd shot being heard.

It was just after 7:00 a.m. when the medic and the support section guys did a sweep-up operation through our camp to see how many were dead. It was a sad morning; there were seventeen UNITA soldiers dead and six SADF boys. Our Scorpion One unit was all okay; no one had been shot. The armored unit, Troop Two, the Tarantula guys, was on the opposite side of the road from our position, and six of their SADF guys had been shot dead; four were wounded.

During the morning, Trevor came up to the individual Panzer and support section guys and made sure that we were all good. Our Scorpion One guys were off guard beat, but we were still in our positions to fire at will. Trevor gathered us with him behind the vehicle; he wanted to talk to us together. "You guys did well, and none of us is dead," he said. Tears ran down his cheeks, and we all could not stop crying. We huddled together, and the tears just flowed from our eyes. None of us could speak.

After a while we all got on our knees in our Scorpion One tent and said a prayer.

The days that followed after that fireworks night still brought a fearful feeling. The fighting action slowed down a bit, but there was still a lot of odd rapid shooting at night. We would sleep during the day or early evening and be prepared for the fighting gunfiring at night.

At the beginning of December, the US Senate pressured the Cuba and Russia to terminate assistance to Angola. The radio news echoed through the camps that the Soviet Union was going to send more military weapons, hardware, and instructors to Luanda. What the hell was going on? First the Cuban and now the Russian instructors were training the MPLA soldiers. Who would be next?

Many of us could not grasp why the people of this land had to settle things in a military way. I guess black power in Africa was one leader's decision to rule and ruin a country and its people because of tribal differences. In Africa, almost all the leaders destroyed Africa. It is a continent of fear and instability

The constant sporadic gunfire during the day time became the norm, and many times we could hear them whack the trees. During these battles in Angola, it seemed as if the black leaders in the central part of Africa could not live together. They were killing the ethnic tribal people and taking what they wanted. There were just too many different tribes and black extremists wanting to control the land and its people. What I had witnessed and all the inhumane killing made me feel hollow inside.

From one day to the next, we heard that we would be relieved and that the next wave of SADF guys was on their way to relieve us. In a way, we were lucky to get the hell out of this mess. On December 3, just before 10:00 a.m., our Scorpion unit relief guys arrived. They were in Bedford troop carriers. Most looked older than us and seemed to be experienced at what was going on up here in the northern part of Angola.

We did the hand-over. Just after lunch, we were loaded on the Bedfords and made haste to get to Waku-Kunga Airfield to fly out to Namibia. Trevor made sure that we were all safe for our Hercules flight back to Grootfontein.

Our Scorpion unit was in the front Bedford. I was with all the guys from the Scorpion Panzer troops. I always liked to see where we were traveling; my seat position was at the back flap. I was smart and undid my sleeping bag to position it under my bum. The Bedford hard bunks would be uncomfortable on a 350-kilometer journey. The rest of the guys did the same move.

The road was dry and dusty, but in some ways it was better than traveling in the rain on muddy roads. The traveling would be faster to get us all the hell out of Angola.

On route back to Waku-Kunga, the Bedfords were going flat-out. At Quilenda we saw some African folk waving at us as we hustled through the village. The same cheerful singing and happy waving happened as we drove slowly through Gabela.

The Bedfords did not stop as we drove toward Quibala. The stretch of gravel road was in better condition than some others. It was just after 4:00 p.m. when we reached the town of Quibala. The last section to Waku-Kunga was tar road, and it was a blessing not to experience the dust from the gravel surface.

By late afternoon we were at a small airfield on the outskirts of Waku-Kunga. We had our dinner and boarded three twin-prop Hercules planes. It was now dark, and we were all relieved to be alive and going home.

The three Hercules planes revved up their propellers, and we took to the skies, flying low under the radar to Grootfontein. The flying time was around three hours, and half that time we were flying low. Then the Hercules did a scary, sudden upward lift. We climbed to a higher altitude fast, and that made our ears block up. It was raining; we felt the plane descend toward Grootfontein Air Base.

During the flight back, I thought of my awesome life. *God had spared all of us in our Scorpion unit.*

From the time I was a small boy, I had seen many parts of Africa. My travels took me through Angola, SWA—Namibia, Tanzania, Zambia, Zimbabwe, Swaziland, and awesome South Africa. My adventures were exhilarating. The majestic landscape and places in Africa made my heart explode from excitement.

Most of the black African people were friendly. Their happy white-toothed smiles, their harmonious singing, and their gratitude and shaking our hands made me proud that we had been there to protect them from the slayings in Africa.

I came from South Africa, an apartheid country, where the black and white people were segregated. I thought, *Why are we here in the neighboring countries? The SADF white army is fighting and dying in the neighboring countries for the black people living there.* It was a confusing time; Africa seemed to be so messed up.

The Hercules landed at just after 10:00 a.m. We all proceeded to the large hangar, where just three months ago, we'd been given our orders to proceed to the borders and into Angola.

On this occasion, only Major Briggs and General Botha spoke to us. They thanked us for our good defense and the speed at which we had driven the MPLA and its mercenaries back towards Luanda. General Botha mentioned that the United States had intervened. It was because of the Soviet Union's and Cuba's support in supplying the MPLA with arms and weapons and that Cuba was sending twenty thousand Cuban troops to support the MPLA—so far, eight thousand had arrived.

The war raged across Angola and talk did not achieve much. General Botha said, "The SADF will support UNITA until all this chaos has been resolved."

Then we heard the unhappy news. "Most of you will be returning here in early January, if the conflict gets worse."

We all received a badge and a handshake for our border-protection service. That was it; we were dismissed.

In the morning, the Southern Transvaal bunch was going to fly back to the Wonderboom base in Pretoria, South Africa. I had a funny feeling that I was coming back here in early January, but I was off duty for a Christmas break. The guys that relieved us in Angola were mostly Permanent Forse guys.

After the debriefing, Trevor rounded us up. It was after eleven at night, so we were all taken to our tent sleeping quarters. Trevor thanked us all for the good teamwork. He said, "Our Scorpion troop and section support guys was the only unit in the 2-SSB that had no deaths recorded."

He was a staunch Christian and said, "God has been with us in this weird Angolan war. We all know why we were sent here. God asked us to protect the UNITA and Southwest Africa Namibian people living in this awesome part of East Africa." Trevor was one of the best guys I had ever met. While he was talking to us, many tears ran down his cheeks.

He gave us each a brown envelope that we were to give to our company management. This was to inform them that our standby army border call-up duty was still in process. That night, Trevor organized some beers for us. None of us fell asleep. We talked all night about our army experiences. We drank beer until breakfast and talked about what we all did in our civilian lives.

It was the most interesting night. We were South African "bro's" and we had seen and done it all. We had grown to care for each other. During our talk, Trevor told us, "I have requested that the same Scorpion guys return as a unit." I felt comfortable with that—it was better to be with guys you can trust with your life.

After breakfast our Scorpion unit scattered to different locations after saying our good-byes and giving how-zit handshakes and shoulder bumps. Life had given my buddies and me a break—we were alive.

Just before our first group boarded the Hercules plane, I called my sister Elise and asked her to pick me at the Vereeniging train station. She was confused when I mentioned that I was in Grootfontein in Namibia.

We boarded the Hercules at 8:15 a.m. We were the first Hercules plane to fly to Pretoria Wonderboom Air Base. I was feeling sad and happy to leave. These extreme Angolan conditions and my experience at Katima Mulilo had changed my life forever.

Greg was with me, flying to Pretoria. We talked about Civvy Street and what we were going to do over Christmas time—it was just a month's break and then we'd be back here doing our SADF duty.

At Wonderboom, we handed in our weapons and then got haircuts. It was just before lunch when I received my dismissal papers and a train ticket to Vereeniging. Greg and I did the how-zit handshake and said, "See ya soon."

When I arrived at the Vereeniging train station that evening, Elise was waiting for me at the platform. Her first words were, "Wow, you look so different and more grown up." The three months I was away had gone by fast. I enjoyed driving my Ford Cortina, again. On the borders, I had handled only firearms for shooting the bad guys.

Elise and I had dinner. I then dropped her off at her flat and drove to my Iscor flat, feeling so alone. Yesterday morning, I was in the fighting zone next to the Longa River. Thirty hours later, I was in my flat all alone. I wondered why my life always went from one extreme to another. In my army life, there was never a dull moment. Some nice days were heavenly, and there were some extremely frightening days.

Africa is a continent full of exhilarating moments. In all my travels around this wonderful world, I have found Africa to be the most awesome experience. Katima is in the heart of majestic Africa. It was exhilarating to experience cold shivers at a river at sunrise; the majestic sunsets with the red rays streaking within the clouds; the billions of bright shining stars at night; the fresh scent just before it rains. At the river bend, when the moon glittered on the calm waters, sparkling as the fish make a splash, you feel alive. All these wonderful moments made me happy, and tears ran down my cheeks because I had seen and felt it all inside my heart.

My happiest feeling was when I experienced a low-flying helicopter maneuver down the Zambezi River toward Victoria Falls. The helicopter skimmed the water, and Cappie did a spring-lift just before the falls and then proceeded to fly high in the sky. The forceful wind blew on the side of my face. I saw the large falls in full flow, with a beautiful rainbow in the mist. The sun was setting, and I saw the sunrays flashing red against the scattered clouds. The view was out of this world. We did a helicopter roll and dove in free-fall toward the earth—I remember that I felt as if my heart almost stopped. We experienced the spray of the endless, fast-flowing rapids gushing over Victoria Falls. As we slowly hovered close to the falls, it felt as if I could touch the water with my hands. It was by far the most heartwarming feeling in my life, and as I remembered it now, tears flowed from my eyes. I had been on top of the world, looking at all its beauty from above.

When I was eleven years old and living in the worst reform joint in South Africa, the Govie, I was close to death's door. I was confused about my life and was hours away from slitting my wrists and ending my awful, sad life.

But then, someone in the heavens gave me a break. I went on to experience life to the fullest. I was happy to be alive.

Chapter Twelve

Closure

The Extreme Events in My Life

While I was growing up in harsh conditions, many extreme events happened to me. I experienced some near-death moments, but there were times when I was fortunate to experience heartwarming, happy feelings that made me realize life was worth living.

My Nightmares

From a young age, it was as if a light bulb was switched on in my brain. I could then remember everything clearly. I experienced extreme nightmares. When I was twelve and was locked up in the reform joint called the Govie, my nightmares intensified.

Night after night, I experienced spinning discs between my ears. They would accelerate until my body went into a shivering motion. The spinning disc sensation seemed to be compressing my brain until my head wanted to explode. I passed out from the jerking. I can't remember falling asleep.

I was in such a state that I wanted to end my life by slitting my wrists with a shaving blade. Just before I fell asleep or passed out from the spinning-disc brain-crushing event, I would experience ghostlike figures coming to rape me. My body would shake so much that I'd go into a shivering motion. This always happened when my eyes were wide open and staring like large shining saucers. I would count stuff or try to think of anything to overcome the sensation of the spinning discs crushing my brain. I always failed, and then the fear would take over my body, so much so that I'd get into a panic jerk fit stage. My body went berserk and my head wanted to explode from the crushing feeling.

In the mornings, my body felt drained, as if the devil had taken my soul. I always cried and I just wanted it to end or let it take over my body, so that I could die and sleep in peace.

My Extremely Sad Time

When I was six years old and living in Northern Rhodesia with my strange folks, my mother almost beat me to death. During that time in my life, we were living in a colonial house on the outskirts of Chingola. My folks were wealthy, and the house parties were plentiful.

My dad was away a lot on business. During his three- to four-day trips away from home, my mother had affairs. It was on this strange day when I was caught by one of the guys having sex with my drunken mother. He pulled me out from under the sofa and gave me a whack across my face. The four guys with my mother panicked and left in a hurry. I was in shock, not knowing what to do.

I stood there until my mother woke up. In her confused state of mind, she started to threaten me. The more I cried, the more my mother hit me. I eventually got loose of her grip and ran out the house to my safe haven, the little caravan under the tree. I entered the caravan and locked the door behind me. I lay there on the double bed, crying endlessly, not knowing what to do.

From the outside of the caravan, I could hear my mother whore banging with her fists against the door, shouting at me, "Open the fucking door." I closed my ears with my hands; I did not want to hear that banging noise. This went on and on for five to ten minutes. She eventually calmed down and the banging stopped. I guess her arms and fists were hurting.

I lay there on the bed for more than an hour, wondering what would happen to me next. I was just a little boy being adventurious, why were all these bad things happening to me? I was always curious to know what is happening in our home. I knew that I needed to confront my mother and the sooner the better.

When I eventually came out of that caravan, I slowly walked toward the back door of the house, where the kitchen was. As I entered the kitchen, my mother was sitting on a chair at the table. Her elbows were resting on the table, with her hands beside her head. I noticed she had the plank in front of her that she used for hitting us.

She was in a dismal, confused, drunken state. I guess her thoughts were exploding in her head as she thought, *what the hell has just happened?* With a wary, scared look, I stood there staring at her. My legs were shivering so bad, it felt like I was doing the tap dance. She lifted up her head, staring at me with her bloodshot drunken eyes, and she frowned weirdly. She was breathing heavily and making hoarse sounds, I heard her say loudly, "I fuckin' hate you."

I was confused and scared shitless. By now my legs were shaking so much that I was literally doing a fast tap dance. I knew that very soon, something bad would happen to me.

I saw her grab the plank, and I closed my eyes. I heard the wooden chair flying backwards to the floor. I felt my arm being yanked and grabbed with force. I felt that plank on my bum and back. The pain was awful. *Oh, God, why?* I felt some plank whacks hit me on my upper legs. *Oh God, help me, please.*

My brain was on fire, and my body was hurting; I was in burning hell. I started heaving and screaming from the extreme pain, my awful mother would not stop hitting me. The more I screamed, the more she hit me with more brute force. I could not escape; my mother was going to kill me. Luckily for me, her arm got tired. It was not my time to die yet.

I was in so much shock and pain that I could not breath. The whacking stopped. My awful mother shoved and threw me toward the floor. My drunken mother stormed out of the kitchen, going berserk, screaming at me at the top of her fuckin' lungs, ""I ... *fuckin'* ... hate ... *you!"*

I was heaving and sobbing, not knowing what to do or where to go. I thought, *why does she hate me so much?* I exploded in tears; they were like a waterfall. I lay there on the floor in extreme pain, jerking and having a shivering attack, choking and throwing up from the hurt pain that I was feeling. After a while, I found the strength to move. I gradually got up and made my way, crawling toward my bedroom. I locked the door behind me for fear that she would come in and give me more pain.

I lay on my bed, sobbing quietly and shaking from the extreme thrashing that I had received for no reason at all. I must have passed out or fell asleep because it was Sunday morning when I woke up. My body felt like a train had hit me. The pain and the burning sensation lasted for many days. My back, bum, and upper legs were black-and-blue from the thrashing. From that day forth, there was no more love for my awful mother. From that plank-thrashing day onward, everything changed in my life.

I was so young, but I had lost all respect for my mother. When my mother looked at me in my eyes, it was with hatred in hers.

I Was Saved

When I was five years old and living in Northern Rhodesia with my strange folks, I was almost swallowed by a huge python snake. My mother had put me to sleep inside the caravan that was parked on blocks next to our colonial house. The door was open for fresh air. I was sound asleep."

Inside the house, around mid-afternoon, she was lying shit-faced drunk in bed. My dad, Daniel, was always busy with his copper work, making bangles and such in the shed. He heard a loud scream from our black mama servant, shouting, "Snake! Big snake gonna eat little Mike in the car'van."

Luckily, Daniel heard the black mama's screams, and in a panic, my dad ran toward the caravan. The python was slithering at the door. The snake's head started to enter through the open doorway of the caravan. My dad had his peen-hammer in hand that he was using on the copper wall plaques. With force, Daniel started to whack the python on its body.

That python seemed as if it had no pain and continued to slither inside the caravan. That python was hungry like a beast and wanted me for a snack. The snake continued to move with more force through that open doorway. Daniel struggled to get a grip around the snake's slimy tail. He finally twisted the bottom tail portion of the python around his arm, looking like a coiled spring.

The snake was so powerful that Daniel had to wedge both his feet on the steps by the doorway. With all his weight leaning backward, Daniel pulled the snake out of the caravan. As he pulled the python from the entrance, the snake attacked Daniel. Its mouth was wide open with its fangs exposed, and it was swaying from side to side, lunging at Daniel. It was luck for somehow my brave daddy got away.

The black mama servant grabbed me and ran off.

Petrified, she took me in the house. Black mama woke up my mother, still lying shit-faced drunk on the bed. She was screaming that I'd almost been eaten by a big snake. Mary woke up in a daze, and in her drunken state, she said, "Take the child away and leave me alone."

I was saved, and I was later told, "It was a huge python snake. The snake could swallow a six-foot man easily, with room to spare." I guess I was just an appetizer for that python.

My mother, Mary, had no feelings and did not care for me. After that snake incident, things were not the same in our so-called "happy home." Daniel always blamed Mary for not taking proper care of me. They began to argue more and more.

I Was Spared

About a month before my ninth birthday, I was almost killed by a huge black African fella. We lived in Pretoria in a suburb called Valhalla. At the back of the block of flats, there was a public sports field. On most afternoons after school and on some weekends, we would play soccer. There were always a lot of kids playing on that sports field, and most of the boys were older than me. They were all the naughty kids who lived in the Valhalla neighborhood.

At the other side of the park, there was a large, steep hill, about a hundred meters high. A sandy trail led up the large hill. About two-thirds up the hill's face, there was a tar road that came from behind the hill. With a struggle, we sometimes had to use our hands while climbing up the path to the tar road above.

Below the hill was a wide sandy path at the back end of the park and the block of flats where we lived. Every day, there were always a lot of black African guys walking up and down the path.

One day, one of the boys said, "This soccer game is boring. Let's go do something different." Another guy suggested we make some ketties (slingshots). He said, "We can hit some cans set up on rocks."

Another boy said, "That is boring. We should try to slingshot the black guys while they are walking down the path."

Some of the boys went home and made three ketties. We continued having fun, playing soccer, until they returned. My brother, Steve, and I were a bit wary of what the naughty boys wanted to do. It seemed risky, and we knew that most black guys did not like the apartheid way of life. They had a lot of anger in them.

What happened on that nice, sunny day was lucky for me. The guys made the ketties from Y-shaped branches and attached some car tube rubber that was cut in thin strips. When they pulled back on the rubber strip, they could slingshot a stone through the Y.

The boys tested the ketties by trying to hit some cans placed on a rock. I don't know why, but I had a nervous feeling that bothered me all the time. We all went about halfway up that hill toward the tar road. We hid behind some large rocks that were near the path. I was stupid for I was hiding farther up, at some distance from the path.

The guys waited for the black guys to walk on the path below and then shot small stones at them, trying to hit the black guys. What the hell were those young boys thinking? It was some time before they hit the first black guy. When the stone hit him, we all hit the dirt for cover behind the large rocks. The first three black guys who were hit walked off and did not bother us. We were eight kids on the hill with three of the boys lower down.

Two large black guys walked by next—and one of the boys hit one guy on his head.

I saw that black guy fall down on the ground, holding his head in pain. As he fell, the other big black fella looked up toward that hill. We all forgot to hit the dirt.

With speed, the big fella ran up the hill toward us. We all panicked, and I heard Steve shout, "Mike! Run!" I was the smallest kid on that hill, and I was struggling to make my way to the path.

My mind went blank, and it felt as if I was carrying ten kilos of weight on my back. As I ran, some of the bigger kids and my brother passed me. I was in shock, and my legs felt like jelly. One boy passed me, and I felt him pull on my shoulder. I fell down to the ground. Steve shouted at me, "Mike! Run, for God's sake. Run! He is close to you." I looked up and saw Steve at the top of the path, waving his arms as he shouted at me. I got up and ran toward my brother without looking back. *God, help me, please!* I thought frantically. As I reached the top of the path, I slipped again.

This time my brother was there for me. He grabbed me by the arm and shouted, "Run up the road." When I looked back, the black guy was so close that I could smell his sweat stench. He was only a few meters behind me, struggling like a fat blob of sweaty-goo jelly.

When I looked at him, he had a look of hatred in his eyes. He was a huge black fella, struggling with extreme force to grab me with his hands and kill me.

I looked down the tar road and realized that the other kids had their bikes parked on the road, and they were all gone. It was only my brother, Steve, and me—and this huge black guy on my heels.

Steve grabbed my arm, and we ran up that road, like the wind of a tornado, without looking back. My heart was burning from fright, and I was totally out of breath.

I don't know how far we ran up that tar road, but it seemed to be forever. My legs felt like they had lead in them. Finally, my brother turned around to see if we were in the clear.

We had escaped death. We collapsed on that tar road, utterly exhausted. We stared at that black guy standing at the top end of the path. He was out of breath and bending over, holding his wobbly gut. He was staring at us, and we could see the sweat running down his face, like a full-on water tap flowing over his face and body. He was totally exhausted and heaving very loudly from being out of breath. For many minutes, we sat in the center of the road, looking back at the black guy.

For some time, that black guy was panting so badly that he could hardly talk. Then, like a spring coil, he came alive. He stood up and started to wave his hands in the air, giving us the fuck-you finger sign. We heard him scream very loudly, shouting at us at the top of his lungs in his hatred black language. With a hatred look on his face, he ran his thumb across his throat, showing us he would kill us. In a panic, we stood up, Steve and I waited for him to run toward us, but he disappeared back down that path. Steve and I stood there on the roadside for a long while. We were both panicked, and we could not move from exhaustion.

After about ten minutes, we were breathing normally, and it seemed as if the coast was clear. Steve walked slowly toward the path to see if the black guy was hiding somewhere, but he was nowhere to be seen. Steve showed me to come down the path. After a short while, we decided to take the long way back home.

My Near-Death Experience

My next near-death experience happened when I was nine years old, during our third school term holidays.

We were living in Pretoria in a suburb known as Valhalla, and we knew the area well. Sometimes we would play in a large storm drain that was not for from our flat. There was a path on the side of the bridge that led through a barbed-wire fence to the storm drain. Next to the bridge were steps leading to the bottom.

While walking in the storm drain, we look for scorpions that sometimes were under rocks. We would put the scorpions in a small cardboard box and watch them fight to the death.

On this day, we were playing with five other kids. Some of these boys were in Steve's class at his school. It was a bright sunny day, with some rain clouds in the distance. While we were playing in the storm drain, I felt a cool breeze hit me, making me shiver from fear. I was feeling a bit uneasy and looked around the drain. I knew that something was not right. Just like thunder, we suddenly heard a strange sound.

As the seconds passed by, the sound got louder. We were all puzzled, looking at each other. We could not figure out what it was. As the scraping sound got louder and louder, some of the boys panicked and started to run toward the bridge.

Steve figured out what it was. He grabbed me by the arm and forced me to run up the embankment. The problem was that the incline got steeper as we run up higher. While we were struggling up the embankment, I looked down the drain and saw all the other boys hauling it toward the bridge through the storm drain.

Steve and I had made it about halfway up that side embankment when I looked to where the strange noise was coming from. I saw a wall of dirty brown water with junk and branches coming toward us. In a flash, it gushed forcefully past us. We were lucky for the storm water was below our feet, but some of the branches scraped our legs and arms.

My heart was pounding so fast that I almost fainted.

Steve was there again to rescue me. While we were sitting there in shock, Steve looked frightened. He knew something was not right. Out of breath, he said, "The water will keep on rising fast until it catches up to us. We need to crawl out of here." My heart pounded even faster as I realized that our time might be up.

We removed our floppies, and Steve grabbed me and put me in front of him, saying, "For fock sake, crawl." To get some traction on that concrete embankment, we crawled barefoot, just like a bunch of crazy monkeys. We were gunning it toward that bridge.

We were about eighty meters from the bridge, and my feet were burning from the hot concrete slope.

Every now and then I heard Steve say, "Move faster. The fockin' water is coming up higher." I looked at the fast water gushing by us as we ran. I panicked, thinking, "Oh my God, my time is up."

We must have gone into fast auto-pilot mode. We increased our speed as we crawled toward the safety of the bridge. I guess if some bystanders were watching us, they would have wet themselves, watching the two of us hauling it toward that bridge. I don't know how we did it; we never slipped once.

When we finally reached the bridge, the water was gushing extremely fast by us. The storm water flow was just below our hands and feet, with only a few feet to spare.

While still frightened, we cheered and shouted loudly, "we have beaten fockin' Mother Nature," and we continued to shout, "We are kings!"

Then we laughed loudly.

And then ... one of the other boys who were playing with us asked, "Where's Kev?" We looked around the bridge and walked toward the tar road and the back again, but Kev was gone. We were all in a panic, shouting his name but getting no reply. One of the boys started to cry, saying, "He is gone! I saw him; he was right behind me when we were running, and I saw him."

Later that night, we heard the radio news: "A twelve-year-old boy has drowned in a storm drain near Valhalla." The area described was close to where we were living.

I Survived. I Was Hit by a Vesper Scooter

A lot of my near-death experiences all happened within one year, when I was nine years old.

The December school holidays were one of the most boring times in my young childhood. Below the flats was an open car park where we would play one-bounce touch ball. Steve and I were pretty good at it and would play for hours on end. One day just before Christmas, we were playing with a tennis ball at the main entrance of the flats—this was where the concrete driveway was wider than on the main road.

Sometimes the ball would bounce very close to the busy main road. I was reckless and lobbed the ball hard to Steve. It hit his head and went bouncing across four lanes of traffic.

Steve said, "Mike, it is your fault. Go fetch it." Without thinking of danger, I ran between the cars to the other side of that busy road. Some cars honked their horns at me. That was when I thought, *what did I just do?*

On the way back with the ball in my hand, I stopped on the double white line down the center of the road. I looked left; the sun was shining in my eyes.

I could see no cars, so I put my head down and just ran for it. As I was running, I felt something hit me hard.

Steve later described it as a "fat guy on a Vespa scooter," who hit me square on my left leg; I flew into the air and landed, sliding on my right leg. Steve told me, "As you landed on that concrete, with speed, you got up. Just like Flash Gordon. You ran—*whoosh*—past me toward the flat. I chased after you but could not catch up. You were running like that cartoon Road Runner."

When I entered our flat, I was totally out of breath. My left leg was swelling up fast, and it had a massive blue mark on it. My right leg was grazed really badly; from my bum the scrape marks were halfway down my leg toward my knee. My right leg was also slightly bruised and swollen.

I sat on the edge of the bathtub as Steve tried to clean me up. When the cold water touched my legs, I screamed in pain. After a few minutes, I stood in the bathtub, shivering and crying endlessly. Steve eventually washed off all the little stone pieces imbedded in my leg. After a while, I lay in the bathtub that was half full of lukewarm water.

The old folks were out drinking at the pub. When they came back home, my mother shouted at me, "What the hell has happened to you?" She put some mercurochrome on my graze, and it hurt like hell.

The next day, the Vespa accident was reported in the newspaper on the second page. The large fat guy who hit me was riding on the Vespa scooter. In the paper, it read, "A young boy was racing across the main road when a large man hit the boy with his Vespa scooter. This man then hit his scooter against a power pole, which resulted in a broken arm and leg. The boy is still at large. The police are investigating the matter."

The ol' man went ballistic and started shouting at me. That was it; no more playing outside for all of us kids. Well, I could hardly walk.

My Life Was in a Dismal State of Near Death

The next extreme event in my life happened when I was twelve years old and living in the Govie. The place was out of control. The official men looking after us were doing what they liked. I always thought that the Superintendant was covering up what the officials were doing to some of these disturbed boys. I had a heartaching thought: *Why am I here?*

My life was on the edge, and my mind was bending. On a Friday night of our first week's holiday in early December, I felt my mind was losing it.

I was lying in my bed, trying to sleep, when I heard something. It was around midnight and quiet in the dorm—most of the young boys were drugged up or asleep.

I saw the bad boy Junky Jake get out of his bed and go up the hall to a thirteen-year-old boy's room. I wondered what Jake was up to. After a few minutes, he returned to our room and came really slowly toward my bed. I lay there with my eyes half closed, but I was ready him. I had my veggie knife and scriber (sharp pin circular marking tool) in my hands, waiting for him to grab me. I always had my bed blanket and sheet loose on the sides, so that I could kick them off fast. My heart was exploding, from fear as I wondered what he was doing.

Jake leaned over me to see if I was awake. I thought, *well, he is by himself. What is he doing?* Just then I heard two boys come into our bedroom. I knew that they wanted to grab me and hurt me. Jake was just about to put his hand over my mouth when I let rip.

I kicked my sheet and blanket off me. With speed, I sat up in bed. I slashed at Jake with my knife and cut his arm open, and we both started to scream. I swiped at him with my scriber in my left hand. I stuck him in his shoulder blade. I quickly stood next to my bed. I don't know what happened to the two thirteen-year-old boys; they were gone.

From all the sorrows in my life, I had so much hatred in me, and my actions went ballistic. I slashed with the knife again and caught him across his gut. The scriber was still stuck in his shoulder blade. He stood there in front of me with a ghostlike stare. I slashed again with the veggie knife, cutting him with more force across his chest, from his collar bone across to his gut. This slash was deeper. I had lost it, and my mind went blank.

By now the commotion was loud, and many of the boys were awake, including Steve. Junky Jake was howling from the pain. I was tripping out, standing beside my bed with the veggie knife in my right hand, shaking like a leaf. There was blood everywhere. Luckily, Jake made a dash for it, running down the hall to the bathroom, screaming and shouting.

By this time I was hyperventilating so much that I was choking on my own breath, from fear of being raped. Steve and the guys were there in a flash, trying to control me. I lay on my bed, shaking uncontrollably from the shock and the fear in me.

Steve crouched over my body, holding my hands and sitting on me and trying to calm me down. I was having a fit attack; I was flaking out and jerking excessively. I was a total gone case, shaking my head with force from side to side.

I heard running down the hall, and then officials entered my room. The officials tried to calm me down, but I was tripping out. They tied me with rope to my bed. I was crying and screaming at the top of my lungs, "I want to die!" My life was over; I'd hit the bottom of the pit.

In all this commotion, Steve backed me up by saying to the official, "Jake tried to kill Mike with the knife." Steve had lied to protect me. He had also said, "Jake threatened to kill me, and that is why Mike had my scriber as a weapon."

After the officials cleaned up Jake's wounds, he was taken to the medical center in the mentally disturbed section.

After some time, I was taken to the med center for an injection to calm me down. When I returned to the dorm, all was very quiet. I got back in my bed, shivering from the event that had just taken place. After a short while, Tommy and some of the boys came over to my bed. Tommy said, "You're an animal—no, you're a 'knife-ster.'"

I lay there for a long while, staring into space and sobbing gently. I knew Jake would be back. I got my razor blade out and put it again against my veins. I was in a trance and totally exhausted. I just wanted to end this messed-up life of mine.

I pressed the corner of the blade into my arm next to my veins. I felt the pain. All I had to do was to pull the blade. That night, I tried to kill myself many times. I must have passed out from being scared and the lack of sleep. While I was in that state of mind, I experienced my most extreme nightmare, where a large ghost was going to rape me, and the spinning disk event was more severe. I was so close to ending my miserable life.

Fighting for a Girl

In the mid-year three weeks holiday of my last year at school, my teacher Loraine convinced our Hostel headmaster to have me go to her folks' farm for the holidays.

While staying at the farm, I met a few of Loraine's girlfriends. On Friday night, we were invited to go to a barn house party. It was not too far from where her folks lived.

I was with a rich girl and living it up with rich farm kids. At the barn party, we danced and had a fun time drinking bottles of beer and dancing in a group until around 10:00 p.m.

Loraine's mom's favorite farm boy turned up at the party with two of his friends. This boy was around the same age as Loraine, and I guessed they were together during her school days. I heard Loraine sigh, and she held me around my neck while dancing a slow dance. She said, "Oh shit, my mom's favorite blue-eyed boy is here with his stupid friends. I have a feeling that we are going to have trouble."

I was an ex-Govie boy. I felt a bit hyped up and knew that we were going to fight. Strangely, I felt brave, with no fear. All that I thought about was protecting Loraine, no matter what happened.

Loraine spoke in Afrikaans to her other dancing girlfriends, saying, "Johan is here. Mike and I are going to leave soon."

It was too late for Johan and his two buddies were walking toward us. The good thing was that he was around the same size as me. His two buddies were slightly bigger and stronger. He walked up to us and stood in front of Loraine, giving her the eye and looking at her up and down as if she was his tart. Loraine loudly said, "Leave us alone, Johan. It has been over between us for many years. I hate you." She glared at him with a wild-cat kind of stare. My awesome teacher was giving this Johan guy a serious talking to.

He looked angry and said, "You are mine, and no one-time piece of shit guy will take you away from me." He raised his voice in a brave, shouting manner. "You are mine. I am going to kill this guy. Who is he?"

I'd had enough of all this shit. I moved slowly in front Loraine and stood between her and Johan. I said loudly, "I am bad-boy Mike, and Loraine is my girl, and no shit-mouthing asshole boy will talk to her like that."

He moved in front of me while clenching his fists and saying, "I will box you", I calmly looked at him in his evil eyes and backed off two steps. I lifted my arms in a boxing position and said, "Okay, we will fight to see who will have Loraine, but only you and me."

By this time the party-goers were all gathering around us in a big ring. It was only Johan, Loraine, and me in the center. I kept my distance.

I glanced at Loraine and told her, "Go stand there with your friends. This will be over soon." She looked at me, worried and puzzled. One of her girlfriends pulled her away from us.

I was smart; I quickly removed my shirt and gave it to the nearest boy. This way this Johan the bad boy would have nothing to grab. While I was living in the-Govie joint, I had many boxing fights. I was smart with my footwork and keeping my distance from my opponent. I would always observe what my opponent's moves were before giving punches.

I was very fit because of all my after-school activities. When my shirt came off, I was not the skinny boy from yesteryear. My upper body was firmly built. This Johan boy was looking at me strangely as I got into a blocking boxing stance.

All these farm boys shouted, "Come on, Johan, you can take him down." He was a cheat for as he lunged forward, he had some sand in his right hand, and threw it toward my face. I blocked my face, but some of the sand blew in my eyes. I felt the first few punches whacking my arms and one in my gut. I tried to move away, but I felt him kick me. I fell to the ground.

He made a mistake for he stood there shouting, "Yeah, down and out." He waved his arms in the air. Those few seconds gave me a chance to wipe the sand out of my eyes.

I slowly got up and could now see this asshole farm boy standing in front of me. He was waving his hands as if the fight was over. During the loud commotion, I heard Loraine screaming, "Stop the fight!" Some farm guys were shouting, "Fight! Come on and fight." I regained my stance and shouted at him, "You fuckin' cheat."

I stood there for a few seconds, regaining my view; I knew that he was going to make the move first. As he lunged forward with his fists, I sidestepped and hit him with my left hand on the side of his head. Then I hit him square on the nose with my right hand. He staggered back in a daze.

As he turned, I was ready, but he swung around and went ballistic with his fists. He caught me a few times on my face as I was trying to block the many fists swinging at me. I side-stepped again, regaining my stance. We were separated. I regained my boxing stance, while glaring with hate at him. We stood there for a few seconds, sizing each other up. I could see that his nose was bleeding and the blood was running into his teeth. I had some blood trickling a bit from the side of my mouth, and I licked it with my tongue; the blood tasted bitter. My hands were up; I was ready for more action.

During all this commotion I could hear Loraine screaming and crying to stop fighting. The crowd around us was all hyped up and someone said, "Mike, take Johan down. He is an asshole." Energy entered my body, flowing like red-high-octane fuel through my veins. I felt strong, like a bull.

This Afrikaner kid was tough, and I knew that I needed to end this fight fast. He was not going to stop fighting me until one of us was down and out. I had luck on my side for as we boxed forcefully, I moved back and forward in a box move. He swung with many fist movements, missing me as I side-stepped. I had a lucky punch and hit him square on his forehead.

He staggered back but regained his boxing stance. I changed my tactic's I side-stepped and launched forward toward him. I whacked him again with my left hand against the side of his head. He was close to me, and I hit him on his chest with my elbow. The elbow landed good and hard. His arms opened up from the pain on the side of his head and on his chest.

I lunged forward and hit him with my right hand forcefully on his jaw. I connected solid and so hard that he flew backwards and landed on his back. He flopped to the ground—lights-out for him.

The crowd went completely silent for few seconds. In disbelief, I heard someone say, "What happened?" I was glowing and stared at Johan lying on his back on the ground in front of me. It was the best fighting experience ever. I looked up and saw Loraine running toward me. She jumped into my arms and kissed me on my lips. We had a long, mouth-locking kiss.

During all the commotion, I heard the barn explode from all the cheering escalating around Loraine and me. I felt many hands patting me on my back. I saw asshole Johan's two buddies lift him up. He was unconscious when they carried him away by his arms and legs. He looked like a weasel, as if he was crying.

The boy came up to me and gave me my shirt. He grabbed my hand and shook it forcefully. He was a big guy and asked me, "Where you from? Wow, you took down Johan. That is great."

I told the boy loudly, "I come from a bad place known as the Govie. It is here in Pretoria. Look it up."

Loraine was standing next to me with a huge smile on her face. She said to everyone around us, "When Johan wakes up, tell him to leave me alone. I hate him, and he is done being the bad boy in our valley." Loraine was on cloud nine, knowing that I had beaten the crap out of her ex-boyfriend. She put my shirt on me and tucked my shirt in my jeans.

While gazing in my green eyes, she lovingly said (so that all her girlfriends could hear), "I am yours for tonight." She kissed me again on my lips. This made all her girlfriends go, "Ooohhh, aaahhh," while laughing loudly. It was a good night, and all seemed to be in my favor here in this farm community. Loraine and I were ready to go home. We made our way to her mini-car. During the happy noise, I heard many people shouting, "Yeah, awesome night."

When we approached her car, Loraine asked me, "Can you drive?" I took her keys from her hand and said, "Like the wind of a tornado. My dad taught me to drive when I was five years old. No problem."

In a gentlemanly way, I opened the passenger door for her to get in and gave her a fast kiss before she sat down in the seat. I adjusted the driver's seat for my leg position. I was glowing like a 1000-watt bulb. I started the car and spun the tires as we left the barn house.

Loraine put her hand high up on my leg and said, "How come you know so much? You amaze me." I smiled and answered, "I told you my life is the extreme."

While driving away down the sandy road, I slowed down to a relaxing speed. I looked over at Loraine's amazing smile. She told me, "I can't believe that you are only seventeen years old and behave like a twenty-five-year-old."

Closure

In this book, the events in my life, until my flight back to Civvy Street after the Angola War made me realize that life is special. My life had many heartaching moments and some extreme events that almost killed me. There was always someone up there, looking after me.

I still bear the scars on my right hand vein. When I look at the scar, my sad memories flood through my thoughts of that evil place, the Govie. The scar on my right hand vein is a mark and a reminder of my extremely sad childhood. Just like waking up after a bad dream, we were taken away from the Govie, never to return to my hell of a life.

I was saved.

When I look at the scar, it also makes me strong to carry on and to know that I have experienced life in this wonderful world. Katima and the majestic, magical African moments that I experienced, make me always treasure them.

Life is worth living. Have faith. Trust me. All is good."

"Hey, ma Bro's …
Stay happy now."

Printed in the United States
By Bookmasters